She fascinated him

That's why he was following Briar. For too long he'd had no diversions in his life. Sure, his career absorbed him almost totally, but there was another part of him that needed something else...someone else.

He hefted the bag of groceries from one hand to the other and moved closer to her, sidling along to the next table in the marketplace. If he needed someone else, Briar Lee certainly wouldn't be the right candidate. He almost laughed aloud. She wouldn't want to be.

The ribbon was gone from her hair; probably fell out. Now she was talking to another friend. Dominic sidestepped several more feet so she wouldn't see him. He studied her straight back, her nicely rounded hips—and the way her wavy hair swished back and forth over her shoulders.

Dominic leaned against a wall and raked his fingers through his hair. Why, in the name of all that was natural, was he obsessing over a woman who would never be important in his life?

Dear Reader,

Spring is in the air! It's Easter—that special time of year bursting with bright sunshine and colorful flowers. Stella Cameron celebrates all the new beginnings of the season in this month's Calendar of Romance title, *A Man for Easter*.

In A Calendar of Romance, you can experience all the passion and excitement of falling in love during each month's special holiday. Join us next month for Anne Henry's *Cinderella Mom*—a celebration of motherhood.

We hope you enjoy 1992's Calendar of Romance titles, coming to you one each month, only in American Romance.

Happy Easter!

Debra Matteucci
Senior Editor & Editorial Coordinator
Harlequin Books
300 East 42nd St., 6th floor
New York, NY 10017

STELLA CAMERON

A MAN FOR EASTER

Harlequin Books

TORONTO • NEW YORK • LONDON
AMSTERDAM • PARIS • SYDNEY • HAMBURG
STOCKHOLM • ATHENS • TOKYO • MILAN
MADRID • WARSAW • BUDAPEST • AUCKLAND

For my dear friend, Suzanne Simmons Guntrum,
a true connoisseur of the ways of the desert!

Published April 1992

ISBN 0-373-16433-5

A MAN FOR EASTER

Chapter One

"There ain't no God!"

Briar looked from August Hill's pale but glittering eyes to his wife's patient face and back. "Then why am I here, Mr. Hill? *Again?*" This wasn't the first time the old man had sent an urgent request for her to come to his room in Seattle's Ocean Medical Center.

He winced and arched his neck on the pillow. For a moment the only sounds were intermittent blips from the monitors behind the hospital bed.

"We'll talk again later, but I'm going now," Briar said softly, and to Mrs. Hill, "Don't hesitate to have me paged if you need me. If I have to leave the building they'll track me down."

"Thank you." Mrs. Hill rarely spoke. She nodded to her husband and said, "I'm sorry. I do think he likes you to come." When she smiled, her creased face looked younger.

August Hill muttered, "Don't ramble on, Lottie. And don't talk like I'm not here."

"Thank you," Mrs. Hill told Briar once more.

"Not at all. Please, if you need me, just send a message."

"I'm the one who needs you," August snapped. "Supposed to minister to the poor and needy, ain't you?" His voice rose with each word.

"You should rest now," Briar said, backing away.

"I'll rest when you tell me this holy stuff is all a hoax. Live a good life, do good to others and God'll take care of you. Garbage! Just say it. There ain't no God!"

Briar shook her head, turned, and hurriedly sidestepped a tall man in a blue surgical scrub suit. He'd entered the room silently behind her. Dr. Dominic Kiser, renowned heart surgeon, needed no introduction, certainly not to Briar. In her two years at the medical center their paths had crossed regularly.

"Good morning." Now, as on previous occasions, Kiser nodded politely, curved up the corners of his mouth and immediately shifted his dark gaze away. Dismissed, she thought and noticed, not for the first time, that his indifference troubled her.

"Now here's a witness for the prosecution," August Hill announced with gusto. "Morning to you, doc. Just the man for the moment. You're the one to make this missy tell it like it is, bucko."

When he looked at his patient, Kiser's smile changed, softened. His almost black eyes became warm and interested. He took a chart from beneath his arm and flipped it open. "How're you doing, August?"

"Fine!" August's bony, blue-veined hands jerked restlessly at the sheet covering his frail body. He drew a noisy breath. "I'm always fine till this do-gooder comes talkin' about her God!"

"I didn't—"

"Reckons if I believe I won't mind that I'm dying." Thick white hair bristled like a long crew cut and a bushy mustache added to the pugnacious set of hawkish features. "Well, I do mind. Be a damned fool not to, wouldn't I?"

"Mr. Hill—" Briar avoided Dr. Kiser's handsome, but suddenly cooler face "—Mr. Hill, you sent for me, remember? Please relax. I'm leaving now."

"The hell you are! Not till you say it!"

"Mr.—"

She got no further.

"Let's step outside." Dr. Kiser rested a firm hand on Briar's back and the next second she stood in the hall. This time there was no choice but to meet those intent eyes.

Briar smiled.

Kiser managed the upward tilt of his mouth again. He wasn't really smiling and definitely not at her, not really at her. And the effort didn't camouflage the change in his expression: speculative, with a hint of impatience.

"He's a nice man at heart," she said, lifting her chin. "Just angry because he's still got a lot of unanswered questions and he's not sure whether or not he's ready for the answers."

"It's kind of you to defend August, but I already know how good he is underneath the crusty exterior." Kiser bowed his head and Briar heard his short, sharp intake of breath. "Do you think you have all the answers he wants, Miss, er... ?"

"Lee. Briar Lee." If he thought she could be intimidated by that kind of baiting, even if mildly couched, he was mistaken. "Whether or not I have the answers isn't the issue, Dr. Kiser. I have a job to do—trying to help people—just like you do."

"Hardly. But that isn't the point. Maybe you should just tell the man the truth. He'll let you know if it's what he wants to hear."

Now Briar did feel color rise in her cheeks. "And what would this truth be?"

Kiser shrugged. Dark hair curled from beneath the surgical cap. His square jaw showed the stubble of a long night's growth of beard. Shadows underscored his eyes. He was tired, Briar realized, probably fresh from many grueling hours in the operating room where undoubtedly *he* was God. She instantly hated herself for the spiteful thought. The man was tired, exhausted, but still attending to business, dealing with his duties before he took obviously much-needed time for himself.

"I'd better get out of your way." She nodded pleasantly and made to go around him. "I'm sure you're anxious to get on with your morning rounds."

He stepped to block her way. "I don't want to sound aggressive, but I do have responsibilities. Please remember that in an intensive care unit, particularly a cardiac intensive care unit, patients shouldn't be excited."

Her face throbbed this time, and her limbs tingled. "I'm aware of that, Dr. Kiser."

"August Hill is a special case. He expects more than ordinary consideration."

"And he gets it because he's rich, and..." Briar caught her bottom lip in her teeth, mortified at her own outburst.

Kiser shrugged. "August is rich. That's why he can afford to make the choice to finish out what time he's got left in that bed. He's also an extraordinary man. If you knew his history, I wouldn't have to tell you that."

"I do know his history. Rags to riches. Rough diamond philanthropist. I know it all, doctor. That isn't what we're discussing. The point to be made is that I don't insinuate myself on people who don't ask to see me."

"Mmm." He raised his face, stared down at her, intensifying a sensation that he was empowered and she a nuisance—also that she was a short, no-more-than pleasant-looking woman in the presence of a big, apparently spectacularly fit and overwhelmingly attractive man. Yes, Dr. Dominic Kiser of the vaguely saturnine countenance was one charismatic man.

Briar blinked but didn't let herself look away. She supposed that Kiser was the epitome of what they called "sexy." And she must be tired, too. After all, she hadn't left the hospital until eleven the night before and August's call had brought her back before six this morning.

She realized Kiser had spoken. "Excuse me?"

"I said, this isn't the time or place for a discussion of any kind," he said without apparent irritation. "But I do think we might want to talk over just what your function is here. Possibly some changes need to be made."

"Meaning what?" She planted her fists on her hips, her usual control wobbling dangerously. "I don't answer to you, Dr. Kiser."

"Of course not." His voice dropped and its gentleness held danger rather than reassurance. "We won't go into who you think you answer to. My only concern is that Mr. Hill is a man with a terminal cardiac condition and he doesn't need to be upset—by you or anyone else."

She couldn't look away. Behind the controlled facade was something else, some need, she'd swear to it. "Of course not. I do assure you again that I don't come unless he sends a very insistent message asking me to—which he has done several times." She paused, deciding whether or not to say what was on her mind. Caution had never been her strong point. "Do you disbelieve, Dr. Kiser?"

He still held the open file. Now he clapped it shut. The last traces of neutrality dropped away. "Disbelieve? In what?" He made a rapid inspection over her baggy grey sweat suit and all the way to her worn tennis shoes.

Briar experienced an unfamiliar regret that she couldn't be counted among the world's beautiful people. "Do you disbelieve in, er... In a higher being?" She'd always been told she was fearless, so why did this man make her feel so nervous?

His short laugh startled her. "What I do or don't believe isn't your affair. Thanks for the concern anyway. I'll let you know if I ever feel in need of spiritual counseling. In the meantime, I think I'd prefer it if you didn't agitate my patients anymore."

That was one decision that wasn't entirely his to make. "Why would you make a statement like that?"

"Because agitation is bad news, particularly for terminal patients like Mr. Hill."

"If he's terminal..." she shot back. "I mean—"

"I know what you mean." A muscle twitched in his jaw. "For me, the ball game isn't over until the umpire calls time. And, unlike you, I try not to make decisions for the umpire."

The genteel Dr. Kiser knew how to goad her. "I'm sorry," she said evenly. The term "umpire" was vague, but it did suggest that he thought someone other than himself called the final shots.

"Forget it. Maybe I'm being too cautious. I usually encourage the use of any psychological boost that might help my patients through their inevitable depression. And I'm sure your efforts are relatively harmless most of the time."

Harmless efforts? She gaped, at a loss for words.

He moved out of her path. "Have a good day. Looks as if we're going to get some sun for a change."

Briar found her voice. "I would like to talk to you, Dr. Kiser. When you have time. I know you're a member of the finance committee. The chapel hasn't been refurbished in years. With Easter coming up in a few weeks I thought it might be nice if—"

"Miss Lee—" his change in tone almost froze her "—this is not an appropriate—"

"Under normal circumstances I would agree with you." Sometimes minor aggression was justified. "Unfortunately, *appropriate* channels haven't done me any good. The finance committee ignores me. And, since we're on the subject of Easter, I'm hoping to arrange a little party for the pediatric unit this year—the day before—Saturday afternoon."

"I'm sure the children will enjoy it."

Briar smiled. "They will if I can get the money to pay for it. I was hoping—"

"That the finance committee would foot the bill?" Dr. Kiser's voice had an unsettling way of growing softer and softer. His gaze never wavered. "This kind of thing is hardly what I can be expected to spend valuable time on. But I will tell you that any extra money we have is needed for the unit—for training, research, equipment—concrete areas that can actually do some good."

"But surely you believe—"

"I've already told you that what I believe is no business of yours. But, for the record, if I did believe in your 'higher being' I'd have a lot of questions of my own for him. I've got a hunch that he—or she—would answer with the same deafening silence that seems to greet most of the questions asked by the people in beds around here."

"Oh, no." Briar touched his arm impulsively and immediately braced for his rejection. "We should talk."

Dominic Kiser looked down at her hand but didn't shrug away. "Talking to you might be enjoyable...but not for the reasons you have in mind, Miss Lee. Or should I call you Reverend?"

BRIAR JUMPED from the bus on the corner of Denny and Broad and jogged the two blocks to her apartment building. Beyond the work sites that separated Western Avenue from the waterfront, the sun Dr. Kiser had touted scintillated off the blue surface of Elliott Bay, but that sun certainly did nothing to warm a clear but chilly early March day. The same grit-filled wind that bustled discarded hamburger wrappers and stray pieces of newspaper along sidewalk and gutter threw Briar's hair across her face and stung her eyes.

"Mornin', smiley," a rumpled man called from his post on a grimy blanket beneath the dusty windows of a defunct graphics outfit. "Got any spare change?"

"You know the answer to that, Fred," Briar said, laughing. "Seattle's got a free bus service within—"

"Yeah, yeah. Within the downtown zones. I know. And I can get a hot meal at one of the shelters."

As Briar passed, she patted the head of the very healthy and satisfied-looking golden retriever who was Fred's partner in life. "You've got it. Isn't March the month Tinkerbel gets her shots?"

"Already done," Fred said good-naturedly. "Some memory you've got."

Some memory, indeed, Briar thought, racing up steps to wrought iron gates that led to a courtyard on the ground floor of the building where she'd lived for three years. She unlocked the gates and passed inside. An elephantine memory seemed Briar's main claim to fame, her most notable attribute. That and the unshakable faith that sent her rushing headlong through a life that held few other distinctions.

Feeling sorry for herself? Hah, that would be the day. Even the unsettling brush off from Dr. Kiser was beginning to pale slightly. Very slightly.

A long, hard winter had reduced the courtyard plantings to scraggly, brown-leafed specimens. But here and there the brave, brilliantly colored blossoms of primroses showed, and clumps of daffodils bobbled their bright heads. She might not be as elegantly or dramatically endowed as the flowers, but she was just as determined.

Two flights of stairs took Briar to her apartment on the third floor. Praying that her current boarder would be at home, she unlocked the front door and went in. "Yarrow! Hello! It's me."

The front door opened directly into an airy living room. Painted white, stark walls bore no artwork or decoration. Slightly faded and admittedly ugly green carpet covered the floor. A brown corduroy daybed—a hand-me-down from Briar's brother, John, and his wife, Sandy—two mismatched armchairs and a big triangular coffee table of some bleached wood were the only furnishings. The one excess the room sported was Briar's vast collection of books that crammed makeshift bookshelves made of boards supported by concrete blocks.

"Yarrow are you here?" Briar's throat had begun to tighten with apprehension when slapping footsteps sounded on the tiled floor of the hallway leading to the rest of the apartment. "Yo, Yarrow," she said, smiling at the sight of the mussed-looking blond woman who appeared.

"Yo, Briar." Yarrow Stalk mimicked Briar's cheery tone. "God, I hate people who get up in the morning grinning the way you do."

"Sorry about that," Briar said, not at all sorry. "I've been up for hours. I was already at the hospital."

Yarrow turned round blue eyes on Briar. "You've already been to that place and back? Geez, I don't know how you do it. What time is it?"

"Eight-thirty. And I like what I do."

Yarrow stretched her tall, voluptuous body, arching her back to thrust large breasts against the filmy nylon of a leopard-print nightie that barely covered matching panties. "How could anyone like spending their time with dying old people?" She gathered a lustrous tangle of white-gold hair into a tail atop her head and bound it with a rubber band. Curls fell around her face and ears.

"Not everyone I talk to is dying. In fact, most of them aren't." But August Hill, whom despite his best efforts she couldn't help liking, was dying.

"How's the old Hill guy?" Yarrow said as if reading Briar's thoughts. "Any less of a pain?"

"August is August," Briar said. "He's a man who had very humble beginnings and managed to achieve a great deal with no help. Apparently he pulled off everything he attempted. He came to believe he could control anything he touched. Now he's dying and the realization that this is one thing he can't control is hard for him to take."

"Seems to me death's hard for anyone to take." Yarrow sashayed across the room to the window, waved left and right to imaginary watchers in other apartments and moved into a wiggling, unaccompanied dance. "You afraid of death, Briar?"

"Yes," Briar said simply. "But I don't obsess on the subject. And I hope I'll manage to make some sort of peace with the idea eventually. Let's get some coffee."

"Aha!" Yarrow swung around and minced back to the hall with Briar close behind. "Lady chaplain admits doubts. Thank God. People who aren't human scare the hell out of me."

The kitchen window afforded a view that could be most kindly described as having character: Flat, tar-papered roofs, jumbled antennae, exhaust pipes, and the occasional rusted deck chair abandoned by the desperate sunseekers of forgotten summers. Farther away, the brazen skyward thrust of the Space Needle with its flying saucer crown, and the graceful white arches of the Pacific Science Center toyed with the eye.

"Sandra called," Yarrow said, scuffling in furry backless slippers to pour water into the coffeemaker. "Said she'd track you down later."

"Thanks." Briar's sister-in-law had become her closest confidante. "I've got to go back to the hospital for a while, but I'll meet you for lunch the way we planned."

Yarrow scooped coffee into the filter and turned on the machine. "You really like this old August guy, don't you?"

Briar looked sharply at the younger woman. At twenty-five, Yarrow was still drifting, still paying the price for a childhood and youth devoid of anchors. And she was changing the subject. "August Hill would try the patience of a saint. And I'm no saint. But, yes, I like him. I wish I could help him."

"You can't help everyone," Yarrow said, more snappishly than should have been necessary. "Sometimes you have to know when to give up and let people make their own mistakes."

"True," Briar agreed. "We decided to meet near the magazine stand at the market, didn't we?"

"Magazine stand?"

Briar hissed out a breath, irritated at the signs of avoidance that had become easily recognized in the six months since Yarrow had showed up at a center for battered women where Briar occasionally counseled.

"Lunch, Yarrow. We're having lunch today and we'd agreed to meet at the magazine stand."

"Today?" Yarrow, a mug in each hand, turned from the counter. "Was that today?"

Sometimes Briar felt a great deal more than five years older than Yarrow. She must remember that this woman had learned to lie to pacify the wandering would-be-musician father, a leftover flower child, who had dragged her around the country while he followed his dubious star.

"We had a date for lunch today, Yarrow. If you hadn't been so late getting in last night, we could have confirmed then."

Yarrow hitched her elbows on her hips and flapped the mugs back and forth. "Oh, wow—" she puffed up her cheeks "—and I completely forgot. I can't make it today, Briar. I really am sorry."

"Why?" Briar had quickly learned not to tiptoe around Yarrow. The direct approach worked best.

"Well . . . I, er . . . I've got an appointment."

Briar narrowed her eyes. She dropped to sit in one of the three canvas chairs at the brown Formica-topped table. "Appointment with whom?" The probable answer turned her stomach.

"Look, I know you're being kind letting me live here for almost nothing, but I do have to have my own life."

"True." But Briar didn't even flinch at the intentional put-off. "I still want to know who you have an appointment with."

"It's great of you to give me a safe place to be. I never knew anyone as generous as you are."

"I only do what feels right, Yarrow. I'm no do-gooder." Despite what August Hill said—and what Dr. Dominic Kiser undoubtedly thought. Briar saw Kiser's heart-stopping face all too clearly. She wished she didn't. "Yarrow, has Dave contacted you?"

"No." But Yarrow's ivory skin flushed bright red.

When Yarrow showed up at the shelter, her fair skin had been marred, not by a blush but by bruises. Her entire body showed signs of a beating, one of many beatings she'd received from the man she'd lived with for more than a year.

"Why don't I believe you?" Briar asked.

"You never would try to see Dave's point of view," Yarrow muttered.

"What?" Briar stood up and went to stand close to Yarrow. "What point of view would that be? Is there something I've missed? Did you deserve to have him punch and humiliate you whenever he needed someone weaker to take his frustrations out on? Yarrow, answer me. Has he made contact?"

"I said no." She set down the mugs.

"Who are you meeting today?"

"Dave never had any breaks. His mother left his dad flat when Dave was a baby and his dad was an alcoholic. Not much of a life for a kid."

Briar sighed. Sometimes it was hard to feel more than businesslike distaste for a scenario she heard repeated a dozen times a week. "Sounds a lot like your childhood, doesn't it? Mom took off. Dad drank and did drugs and trailed poor affection-hungry little kid all over the country. Poor little kid spent her days and nights trying to please daddy. Partly because she loved him and wanted him to love her back, and partly because when dad was happy he didn't use her as something to punch his frustrations out on. Really similar, I'd say."

"That's not the point," Yarrow said, but her pretty eyes grew bright and her mouth trembled. "I was stronger than Dave. I didn't end up hating my mother and wishing my father was dead. I'm okay, Briar. Or I will be when I really get my feet under me."

Briar softened. "Sure you will be. How's the job at the espresso bar?"

"Fine. Good." Yarrow liked working at the stand on Fifth Avenue where she could interact with dozens of people during her evening shifts.

"You do know that Dave did end up hating his mother, don't you?" Briar asked.

"You can't be sure of that."

"Maybe. But I can guess. Until he gets really good help he's not a safe bet for any woman. But you're not seeing him, right?"

Yarrow hesitated. "Right."

"Yarrow?" Briar waited, then added, "You're here with me because you need somewhere safe where Dave can't reach you. If he can find you here, I need to know and take precautions."

"He doesn't know where I live."

"But you've talked to him."

"Yes!" Yarrow flounced and dropped into a chair. "Okay, okay, yes, I've talked to him."

"What does he want?"

"Nothing."

"Money?"

Yarrow scrubbed at her face. "He doesn't get any breaks."

"So you've said. Did you lend him money?"

"No."

"But you're going to. That's where you're going to-day."

"Please let it drop. You and I can have lunch tomorrow." Raising her face, Yarrow smiled imploringly at Briar. "Would that be okay? If we met tomorrow—same place we'd planned..."

"Same place we'd planned for today? Today when you didn't intend to turn up. I suppose you'd have told me later that it completely slipped your mind."

"I'm sorry," Yarrow said quietly.

"Please work at not lying," Briar said. "It always trips you up in the end and no one respects a liar."

"No one respects me, anyway," Yarrow muttered.

"I do. When you're yourself and you're honest."

"You don't understand." A defiant light glittered in Yarrow's eyes. "How could you? You've never loved a man."

Briar's teeth came together and she swallowed. Her skin tightened. "That's not relevant."

"Isn't it? If you'd ever felt like you'd die if you didn't see someone you cared about, you wouldn't be so quick to tell me not to care about Dave."

"Dave abused you."

"But he loved me, too. And I loved him."

Briar's heart made a nasty leap. "We've been through this. His love wasn't healthy and you'll learn to love someone else."

"You don't know that. You don't want to be in love."

Briar looked at her tennis shoes. Why did she always have to swallow her feelings? And why did everyone she came in contact with feel so free to make pronouncements about what she did or didn't want, did or didn't feel?

She wanted romance...just once...just to find out how it would be.

Smoothing the worn gray fabric of her sleeve, Briar stared through the window at the arches of the Science Center. What was with her today, anyway? She didn't need romance. Romance was for women without a real mission in life. Romance was for moonstruck females whose feet never quite reached the ground.

"I don't mean to be rude, Briar."

Shaking her head slightly, she went to pour the coffee that had finished perking.

"What I said is true, though. You found a way not to need people—except when you need to help someone because it's part of your job."

Briar closed her eyes. She felt a little sick.

"You're lucky, Briar. You don't *need* anyone. You're completely happy on your own."

She mustn't say, *"No, I'm not. I want to be loved, too. If I knew how, I'd look for a man to share my life with. I'd like a home and children and all those other things I once thought would never mean a thing to me."*

"Briar? Are you mad at me?"

"No. We'll meet for lunch tomorrow. Same place, same time."

"Good. Don't worry about me, please. I'm not a freak. Really I'm not. You don't understand what it's like to have a man look at you and want you, is all. You don't know how it feels to see love in a man's eyes and know it's for you."

With one hand, Briar clung to the edge of the sink. With the other she sent water gushing pointlessly down the drain. How right Yarrow was about her "adviser's" practical experience in the area of love.

Briar cut off the water but didn't turn around. She found her vision had blurred. Biological time clocks had always been something she'd thought of as belonging to other women. But she was thirty now. There did come a point when it was too late for some things—like having children—if she wanted them. That was another of her problems, she wasn't sure how she felt about things that could be dangerous . . . like marriage and parenthood.

"You okay?"

"I'm great," Briar lied. She took a sponge and wiped an already spotless counter. "I'd better get back to the hospital."

She better get back to the safe anonymity of losing herself in other people's problems.

Who did Dominic Kiser of the marvelous dark eyes and firm, sensual mouth love? How did those eyes look when they warmed and heated with wanting a woman he cared about deeply?

Briar dropped the sponge. She felt hot all over. How would it feel to be the woman Dominic Kiser loved? Her insides fell away. Embarrassment rushed hot blood to her neck and face. How the cool, confident doctor would laugh at the thought of dowdy little Briar Lee daydreaming about him looking at her with anything other than amused curiosity.

"I'm leaving." Half running, she made sure her keys and change purse were still in her pocket and hurried to the front door.

"Briar, wait!" Yarrow followed, her skimpy nightie flattening to a body that would tempt any man. "You're mad at me, aren't you?"

"No, I'm not."

Briar didn't stop running until she reached the bus stop. Her reactions came from the sensation that Dr. Kiser might, by some mysterious means, be peering inside her head and seeing her ridiculous daydreams.

She had nothing to fear. Dominic Kiser barely knew she was alive. And he wasn't interested enough to care what she did or didn't think about—he never would be.

Chapter Two

Dominic stepped from the elevator and paused while the doors slid shut behind him.

Night's hush blanketed the ICU. Lights had been lowered. At a central station three nurses kept vigil over banks of continuously winking monitors. Beyond the glass walls of patient cubicles, more screens glowed about the beds.

Peace settled on Dominic. He understood that to patients and their families, this could be a frightening place. Often he'd wished it were possible to imbue these people with the sense of hope and optimism he felt here. Here things happened, boundaries were pushed—and breached—daily. Here, more than anywhere else, he felt in control and powerful. Not powerful because he was the senior heart surgeon, but because he could make a difference, he could fashion the delicate renewed designs and sew the fine seams that gave back lives.

Slipping his hands into the pockets of his scrub pants, he strolled past the nurses' station, met raised eyes with a nod, and approached August's cubicle.

Old buzzard.

Dominic grinned at the spectacle of August Hill wielding a lengthy stick made of wedged-together drinking straws. Concentrating ferociously, he batted at brightly colored paper butterflies dangling from a homemade looking mobile.

"Evening, August." Dominic leaned a shoulder against the doorjamb.

"Evening, doc," August said in his customary raspy voice. "What're you doing in these parts? Don't you know it's the middle of the night?"

Dominic shrugged upright and went to stand beside the bed to watch the jerkily swinging mobile. "I know what time it is. And I'm here because you used your sneaky little system for getting me here. You missed your true vocation. You should have been a criminal of some sort."

"You sure I'm not . . . or wasn't?"

"No." Dominic laughed. "Those nurses out there didn't have anything to do with calling me here, did they?"

August sniffed and zeroed in on a purple and green butterfly of large enough proportions to cause a permanent list in the overhead contraption. He didn't answer.

"You've got a telephone somewhere in this room. That's against regulations."

"Never had much use for regulations."

"In the drawer, is it? Cellular, I suppose?"

"Man gets bored lyin' here. Never been used to loafing about."

Sobered, Dominic regarded this knobby, felled war-horse of a man. "No, I don't suppose you were ever very good at doing nothing, were you?"

"Nope."

"So, you got bored, talked poor Lottie into smuggling in a cellular phone and started placing nuisance calls to busy people."

August brought the tip of his plastic weapon to within an inch of Dominic's nose. "I pay my way around here. More than pay my way. The man with the bucks is never a nuisance." He drew his jutting brows together. "How'd you know I was the one who made the call?"

"'*Dr. Kiser. Get your ass to August Hill's room.*' No member of the medical staff in this hospital would send a message like that. And urgent calls go directly over the intercom system, not via the switchboard. What do you want?"

August resumed his attack on the butterflies. "Ever see such a dumb blamed thing?"

"Lots of times in one form or another. Who made it for you?"

"Kids. Sent it for Easter, they said. Early. So I can enjoy it extra long." He sent the mobile whirling. "Because they know I won't make it to Easter, more likely."

August was at his obstreperous best tonight. Dominic thought of Briar Lee, facing off with him in the corridor, for God's sake. Apparently everyone was getting into Easter this year. "Your kids sent it, August? Your grandkids?"

"Never had any kids." He screwed up his eyes. "Probably just as well if they'd have turned out like me."

Dominic wasn't about to argue.

"Seventh grade class at one of the central schools sent it over."

"They just *sent* it?" Dominic hauled up a chair, spun it around and sat astride the seat. "Why would they do a thing like that? How did they know about you?"

"Their teacher worked for me summers when he was a teenager. In the Ballard canning plant through Junior Achievement. Smart little devil he was—still is. He started on the packing line and moved on to doing computer credit searches within a week."

"And he had his class make that. Nice."

"They came to the house to see my collection." He waved the stick distractedly back and forth. "Butterflies. Been collecting them all my life. A lot of rare stuff. Worth a fortune now. The whole class came first. Then the interested ones came back every week."

"You never mentioned the butterflies before."

"No reason to. Wouldn't interest you."

"Try me."

"I've got what's probably the largest private butterfly collection in the country. End of story." End of story, but the tough features had softened, the flinty eyes turned reflective—wistful even.

"Will you show me some time?"

August's eyes regained their pale, steely quality and he focused on Dominic. "I'd like that. But I won't, will I, doc?" He waved a hand. "Don't argue with me. We both know what the real answer is. This glass box is where my corpse is being viewed—"

"August—"

"A little early, is all. I never did like to do things the way other people did 'em. Fancied sticking around for my own lying in state. Gonna be a closed coffin, y'know? If anyone wants to look at me, they'd better get it over with. When I'm wheeled out of here, I'm history. Lottie knows what I want. She'll see to it."

Dominic dragged off his cap, layered his arms along the back of the chair and rested his chin. "I wish there was something else to be done," he said finally, breaking his own rule and voicing the frustration that was never far away at these moments.

"Sure you do. I know that. When you gotta go, you gotta go."

"Doesn't make it easy."

August rested his head back on the pillow and rolled his face toward Dominic. "I like you. Tough as tacks o'course. The whole world knows what a tough number Dr. Dominic Kiser is. But good. And I know you aren't hard all the way through, bucko, even if nobody else does."

Dominic cleared his throat. "Did you have a specific reason for wanting to see me at almost midnight?"

"Maybe."

"I just spent six hours in surgery. I've got to be back there at seven in the morning and if that patient's going to have a fair chance at the best I can offer I'd better get some sleep."

"How old are you?"

"Thirty-six. You didn't get me up here to ask that."

"Yes, I did. That and a few other things."

"The rest will have to wait. I'm going to arrange for you to have something to help you sleep."

August hauled himself up on his elbows, then settled more comfortably. "You married?"

Dominic closed his eyes and pinched the bridge of his nose. "Why do you want to know?"

"You know a fair bit about me. Why shouldn't I know something about you?"

"I'm not married."

"Kids?"

"Not that I know of."

August gave a gusty chuckle. "Nobody would have you, huh?"

"What does that mean?" Dominic blinked and yawned.

"You wouldn't want the type of woman who'd be happy to share you with a mistress."

Dominic frowned. "What the hell are you talking about now?"

"This is what matters most to you." The old man poked at his chest. "Playing God with other people's bodies makes you tick, doesn't it? It comes first. When's the last time you had a woman?"

"What?" For a moment Dominic thought he might have misheard.

"You're not a blushing schoolgirl. You know what I'm asking you."

"And it's none of your business." Dominic stood up, but he grinned. "Next time you get bored in the middle of the night, pester the nurses."

"What time is it now?"

Dominic looked at his watch. "A few minutes before midnight."

"It's time then." August peered through the window into the corridor.

"Time for what?" Dominic asked indulgently.

"Here she comes now."

Dominic turned in time to see Briar Lee walking briskly toward him. She hesitated in the doorway, glanced briefly at him, then smiled at August. "I got your message, Mr. Hill. I'd have come earlier but—"

"But you were do-gooding at some blamed dump for down-and-outers and you didn't get home till eleven."

"I wasn't..." She shook her head and slowly un-
snapped and unzipped the yellow oilskin jacket she wore
over the same gray sweats of that morning. Droplets of rain
glittered in wavy, red-brown hair that reached her shoulders, and ran in thin rivulets on the jacket. "Yes. That's a
pretty good description of what I was doing, I guess."

Interesting woman. Small but not fragile-looking. Good
body from what Dominic could see of it. Unaffected. He
liked the way she met his eyes. Nice face. Healthy. Heart-
shaped hairline and pointed chin. Brows that feathered
slightly upward above her best feature—great big green
eyes. No makeup. He liked that, too, which surprised him
since the women he occasionally spent time with wouldn't
be caught dead in public without spending hours before the
mirror.

A small noise from the bed made him transfer his attention to the bed. August pressed his lips together in a smug
smile. "Good-looking woman, ain't she?"

Dominic realized his mouth was open and closed it
firmly.

"Enough said." August pointed at Briar Lee with his
straw stick. "What do you do for the bums?"

"I talk to them," she said without hesitation. "And listen. Mostly listen, in fact. Just because you've had a lot of
bad luck, it doesn't mean you don't need to talk to someone about ordinary things sometimes."

"Like your God who'll give 'em mansions and limou-
sines and fat bank accounts if they'll just sign up for his
program?" The straw jiggled. "Maybe you should tell 'em
to write a letter to the Easter Bunny—or arrange for him to
visit. Right time of year for that. You could make it kinda
like Santa Claus. *And what do you want for Easter, old
man? A Playboy bunny? Well, I just happen to have a few
of those in my mansion. I'll send one right over.* Whatever
it takes to sign 'em up for the program, right?"

The smile that twitched at the corners of the good chaplain's nice, full mouth made Dominic want to laugh with
her. "Whatever you say, Mr. Hill," she said. "We bright

people know how all this works, and we've got to be as helpful as possible to one another, don't we?''

"Don't be smart with me, miss." But humor buffed the rough edges of August's voice. "Where is this place you go?"

"I go to a number of places. Tonight I was at the 2nd Avenue shelter."

"Until this time of night? A little bit of a woman like you down in one of the worst parts of Seattle on her own? Tell her what you think of that, doc."

Dominic shifted his weight. "I don't think anything about it." He ought to go. He would...soon.

"How old are you, missy?"

"Um..."

"How old, I asked? Don't be coy."

"I'm thirty, Mr. Hill. And coy is something I've never been. You sent a message to my home. My friend said it was important for me to come here as soon as possible. What can I do for you?"

"Maybe it's what I can do for you. Friend, you said. Are you married?"

The lady chaplain's soft-looking creamy skin flushed an interesting shade of pink. "No." She glanced at Dominic and he smiled brightly.

Miss Lee didn't smile back.

"Any kids?" August persisted.

"I beg your—" She raised her brows and turned even pinker. "No, I don't have any children."

"Never been married I should think, hmm?"

"No. Was there something personal you wanted to talk about? Personal about yourself, that is?"

"Ah, that explains everything then," August said, with what resembled a triumphant lift of his white stubbled chin. "No wonder you're such a righteous little cuss."

"Mr. Hill—"

"Dried-up spinster is what you are."

Horrified, Dominic took a step toward August. "That'll do for tonight. Time you got your beauty sleep."

Briar Lee stood as if incapable of moving, and stared at the irascible man in the bed.

"A woman needs a man," August said, clearly on a roll. "A flesh-and-blood man to take your mind off all the holy stuff. Live a little, missy. You're dead a long time. With or without your God."

"August's been having a bad night," Dominic said, unable to look at her face.

"The doc here's thirty-six. He's saving himself up, too. At least, he's not married. Doubt if he saves himself much—good-looking stud like him. Admitted he didn't know how many children he's got scattered around."

"What the hell are you saying, August? I never said—"

"Don't be modest. You're among friends here. I'm just letting the lady preacher know you're well-qualified."

"Well-qualified for what?" Even as he asked, he knew he should have kept his mouth shut.

"To show the preacher what life's really about. You're a red-blooded American boy, doc. Sacrifice yourself."

He risked looking at Briar Lee. The flush had drained away, leaving her pale. Her remarkable eyes glistened.

Shooting a glare at August, Dominic took a deep breath while he decided what brilliant comment would slide them all gracefully out of this.

Briar ducked her head. "Good night, Mr. Hill. Good night, Dr. Kiser." She left the room, not exactly running, but not walking either.

"You are impossible," Dominic said in a low voice. "What the hell are you thinking of?"

"I'm a sick man, doc. Sick men have to be humored."

"You look better than I've seen you look in months," Dominic retorted. "Making other people miserable agrees with you."

"Poor little thing did look a bit stunned. I shouldn't have made her unhappy like that. Put it down to the sleeping pills. They've probably started to work. Dulled the brain, I shouldn't wonder."

"You haven't *had* any sleeping pills yet." Dominic strode to the door and added, "But you will," before making a dash for the small figure getting into the elevator.

The door closed him out and he punched the button too late to open it again.

Running, pinning his hopes on the elevator car having to stop at several floors before it reached the lobby, he took the flights of downward steps several at a time. Tough he might be, hard as tacks even, but he wasn't cruel. No one deserved to be embarrassed as that woman had just been.

He skidded into the lobby. The elevator Briar had used stood open. A flash of yellow caught his eye—she was heading through the revolving front doors.

"Hold up!"

She didn't hold up, or even pause, but he reached the bottom of the steps to the forecourt even with her.

"Look, I'm sorry about... Well, I'm just sorry."

Her head was bowed. Hesitantly, Dominic put a hand on her shoulder...and felt her shake. The poor little thing was crying. Damn August. What the hell had gotten into him.

Very carefully, Dominic turned her toward him. "That was unbelievable."

She nodded. Her body still jerked. A lamp made red lights in her hair. He felt inadequate. He also felt like gathering her into his arms and hugging her until the embarrassment went away.

"This morning you told me August was a nice man under the crusty exterior. Now it's my turn to excuse him."

Briar said nothing.

Slowly, he rubbed her shoulder. "Are you okay?"

She nodded again and Dominic put a forefinger beneath her chin to raise her face...and looked down into her laughing eyes.

"He is absolutely awful." She grinned.

He dropped his hands. She'd been *laughing,* not crying!

"Dreadful," she sputtered. "Beyond redemption... I— I mean, there's probably never going to be any changing him."

"So why are you laughing?" Now he was the one who felt foolish.

"Because that had to be one of the funniest dialogues in history. Funny, awful. Absolutely awful, really. And I'd rather laugh over it than cry. Good night—again."

"Good night," he said faintly. There was nothing else to say.

She spun away and ran out of sight.

An extraordinary woman. Not like any other woman he ever remembered meeting. He glanced up into the light and saw fine rain slanting through the beam. Better get home and catch some sleep.

Thirty. Never married. She hadn't said whether the friend at home was male or female. Did lady chaplains have live-in male friends? Dominic wiped a film of dampness from his face and went back into the hospital.

He'd like to know whether or not the friend was a man . . . purely to satisfy his curiosity, nothing more.

Chapter Three

"Come on, come on," Briar muttered. "Where are you, bus?"

At least the rain of last night had given way to another beautiful day. She anxiously checked her watch. In fifteen minutes she was due to meet Yarrow for lunch and didn't want to be late. Yarrow was likely to use the excuse of Briar not turning up exactly on time to skip out again.

With her heels on the curb and her toes in the gutter, Briar leaned toward the street, peering in the direction from which the bus would come. She'd left the hospital with minutes to spare so she couldn't have missed the 11:40. Usually she told herself that owning a car in the city would be nothing but a liability and was glad she didn't have one. Today she wished she didn't have to rely on public transportation.

She was tired. Again. Too often lately she'd spent late-night hours at the hospital. Usually she at least felt the effort worthwhile, but last night she hadn't really been needed.

Briar smiled and held her bottom lip between her teeth. August Hill was a disgrace, but she couldn't help liking the old reprobate.

And Dr. Dominic Kiser... She stopped smiling. He'd been kind, concerned about her feelings. But he'd have done as much for anyone in the same situation, wouldn't he?

Without the scrub cap, with his dark curly hair mussed, and the shadow of a beard, he'd looked... He'd looked *sexy* for goodness sake.

She raised her suddenly heated face to the cooling breeze. What had happened to her? No man had ever made her think along these lines.

A sleek gray car turned out of the main hospital gates, swung across traffic and slowed down a few yards from Briar. The leaping feline ornament on its hood told Briar the car was a Jaguar. At least, she thought it was. What she knew about cars would fit on an abbreviated postage stamp.

Didn't the driver know he couldn't stop in a bus zone? *Where* was the bus?

The Jaguar crawled closer. Surely she was mistaken in thinking—or rather feeling—that the driver was peering at her. How could she know through a tinted windshield with sun shining on it?

Closer. Inch by inch, closer.

Instinctively, Briar moved back from the curb. She was anything but overly cautious. However, one did read of women being dragged into cars.

She heard the smooth shush of a window electronically lowered. Her heart had begun to beat harder. Clenching her hands into fists, she turned away and started to walk with determined strides. Why was there never anyone else around when you really needed them?

The car drew up alongside. "Miss Lee?"

Now her heart gave a gigantic leap. "Yes." That slightly gravelly, very masculine voice was one she'd recognize anywhere. She looked down into the almost black eyes of Dr. Kiser. He leaned across the passenger seat, his right hand on the window rim.

"Were you waiting for a bus?"

"Yes."

"Missed it, huh?"

No. She'd still been waiting. What did he think she'd been doing standing there? "I guess I must have." No way would she tell him she'd taken him for a maniac with designs on her body!

"Where are you going?"

"Into town." Her skin turned cold, then hot. Good grief. He was going to offer her a lift.

"Hop in. I'm going through town myself."

Muscles in her legs locked. Goosebumps shot out on her arms. "That's okay. Thanks, anyway. I'm used to walking." Not all the way downtown, but he didn't have to know that.

"It's no trouble. Get in." He pushed open the door.

Either she got in or was rude to him. The latter would make her look a fool. Anyway, she wanted to accept. "Thank you," she said, climbing in. At least the sweatsuit she wore today was a pretty shade of coral—and it was almost new. She closed the door and glanced down. The tennis shoes weren't any newer today than they'd been yesterday.

"Seat belt."

Briar looked at him. "Oh, yes. Sorry." She buckled in. This man had an infinite capacity for making her feel silly.

He maneuvered into traffic. "Are you as tired as I am today?"

"Probably," Briar said, concentrating on cherry trees in full bloom. He would have to bring up last night's fiasco with August.

"I guess we worn-out old bachelors and spinsters should try to get more rest, mmm? Give our aging bones the respect they deserve."

Briar laughed. "Dried-up spinsters—and bachelors—trying to save themselves, you mean?"

"You've got it."

She liked him—could like him. For a long moment, Briar studied his profile. When he smiled, his upper lip bowed away from strong, slightly uneven but very white teeth and lines scoured from the corner of his eye. He had a dimple beside his mouth.

"Did your car break down?"

His question took an instant to make sense. "No. I don't have a car."

He frowned and glanced at her. "How did you get home last night?"

"Taxi."

"You had one waiting all that time?"

"No. I walked down to Jackson and hailed one."

The car, swerving abruptly to the curb and halting, threw Briar against the door.

"You walked all the way to Jackson and hailed a cab? At midnight?" His voice rose. "Why in God's name would you do such a dumb thing?"

The urge to ask why he chose now to acknowledge God was quickly squelched. "I didn't have any alternatives. The buses had stopped and I had to get home sooner or later."

"Or not at all if some psychopath decided to hit on you."

She laughed nervously. "I'm not the sort of woman psychopaths go for." Awkwardly, she scanned back and forth, checking to see if they were holding up traffic. They weren't.

"Really? And exactly what kind of women *do* psychopaths go for? Taller ones than you? Shorter ones? What kind, Miss Lee?"

Intensely uncomfortable, Briar hunched her shoulders and tried to decide if she should leap from the car. "I really don't think this interrogation of my actions is appropriate, Dr. Kiser. Not by you."

"Is that a fact? Who would it be appropriate from?"

"No one." This was ridiculous.

"I suppose it would be okay if your friend raised an objection?"

"Friend?" If he didn't start driving again—now—she'd be very late.

"The friend you live with. What does he think about you running around at night—at shelters for drunks and through dangerous streets?"

"Oh. Yarrow isn't a man."

"Who's Yarrow?"

"Yarrow Stalk. She lives at my apartment. Look, it's very nice of you to give me a lift, but I'm getting really late for an appointment."

She could swear he relaxed. His broad, long-fingered hands loosened on the steering wheel. And he did drive on.

"You should have asked me to drive you home."

"You?" He must be joking. "I wouldn't have dreamed of such an imposition." And she could hardly believe they were having this conversation.

"Well, the situation is unlikely to arise again, but if it does I'll make damn sure you don't walk out into the night on your own."

There was no point in arguing. "Thank you." Somehow she would never have expected the cool Dr. Kiser to care what happened outside his domain. She should feel badly about making such a judgment about someone she hardly knew.

"Where exactly are you going?"

"First Avenue. The magazine stall at the entrance to the market. Anywhere close would be great." And the closer, the greater since she only had five minutes left to get there. "Yarrow's expecting me at twelve."

"What kind of name is Yarrow Stalk?"

The man didn't miss a thing. "The kind of name left-over hippies gave their defenseless children. There's a weed or grass of some kind called Yarrow."

"I know."

Naturally. No doubt there was very little he didn't know. "I guess her father thought it went with Stalk. Weed. Stalk. If you get it."

"I get it. Poor kid."

A light turned red and they stopped. Downtown workers surged across Fourth Avenue. Women in suits and wearing tennis shoes marched purposefully alongside their male counterparts. All looked overheated in the unexpectedly warm sunshine.

"That color suits you. Pinky orange. Nice with your hair."

Briar sat perfectly still, her hands folded rigidly in her lap. "Thank you." He was only being kind again.

"I think I prefer your hair down, though."

She'd tied it back with a black ribbon.

"Look at me."

With a stomach intent on doing a full somersault, she slowly turned her face toward him.

"Hah!" He grinned and the effect knocked the bottom out of her stomach entirely. "You'd think I just punched you. Don't look so scared."

"I'm not scared." Just completely unnerved.

"Okay. If you say so." The lights must have changed because he slid the car forward again and worked his way to the left lane. "Whatever you're feeling at the moment is very appealing on you anyway. I suppose people are always telling you how green your eyes are."

Briar threaded her fingers together and held on tight. Why on earth would he say such things to her?

"Don't they?"

She felt him glance at her and shook her head.

"I find that hard to believe. I think you've got the biggest, greenest eyes I've ever seen."

"Oh."

"Oh." He laughed again. "You're really rather lovely, Miss Lee. Very unspoiled unless it's all an act. Is it an act?"

Playing sparring games with gorgeous men wasn't something she'd had any practice doing. "What you see is what you get," she said and gritted her teeth. Sophistication had never been one of her goals but she hated feeling so inadequate. "I don't pretend. We'll have to turn down Pine."

"And cut back along 1st. Yes, I know."

"You don't have to do all that. Drop me anywhere now."

"Wouldn't dream of it." He turned left at Pine Street, stopped for a meandering jaywalker with a suspicious-looking bottle-shaped brown sack, and swept on again. "Where do you live?"

Questions, questions. "Western Avenue."

"Hmm."

In other words, he didn't think much of that, either.
"Where do you live?" Matching information was only fair.

"Mercer Island."

"Hmm." Predictable enough.

"You do know I would have liked to tell August off last
night, don't you?"

Did she? "I suppose so."

"I didn't because I have to avoid agitating him. We both
want to keep him around as long as possible, I think. Difficult as he is. Don't we?"

"Absolutely," Briar said fervently. "I'm very fond of
him really."

A left turn on 1st Avenue plunged them into dense,
sluggish traffic.

"I believe you," Dr. Kiser said. "Would it be okay if I
called you Briar? Miss Lee makes you sound like . . ."

Briar chuckled. "Like a dried-up old spinster? By all
means call me Briar." Though she couldn't imagine why
he'd want to bother.

"Good. My name's Dominic."

"I know," she said and blushed.

"Mmm." Those black eyes were slanted in her direction. He regarded her steadily for an instant, then returned
to watching the road. "Call me Dominic, okay?"

With an uncomfortable sensation that she was being
manipulated for some reason that was a complete mystery,
Briar said, "Yes, of course," and pointed. "Could you let
me out there?"

"If you're sure you want me to. I'm going to have lunch
if you'd like to come."

Amazement scrambled her reaction. "Er, no thank you.
Like I told you, I'm meeting someone."

"Not a good place for a woman to meet anyone."

"It's the middle of the day and there are hundreds of
people around. Thanks so much for the ride." Where was
Yarrow? "This is the perfect spot."

Dominic Kiser stopped the car and Briar got out. She
slammed the door and bent to smile at him through the
open window. "Really. Thank you so much."

"You're very welcome, Briar."

She backed away, searching for Yarrow. If she'd begged off again there would be more than a few pointed questions asked.

The Jaguar stayed where it was.

Briar's smile began to wobble. She waved at Dominic.

"It's after twelve," he called. "Maybe she isn't coming."

"She'll come."

Still he didn't drive away. And she could see the deep dimples beside his mouth as he ducked to watch her.

Fireworks. They talked about mythical fireworks exploding when a man and a woman felt attracted to each other. Or rather, in this case, when a woman felt attracted to a man. Briar seemed incapable of taking a full breath. Dominic Kiser couldn't possibly be experiencing anything but a mannerly urge to do the right thing by not leaving until he was sure she was okay. He'd probably laugh himself sick if he knew that for Briar, a display of Roman candles seemed imminent.

"Yo, Briar. Here I am."

Opening her mouth to suck in needed air, Briar spun around. Yarrow, in black leather mini-mini skirt, fringed black leather jacket, which left her midriff bare and thigh-high black leather boots, approached with long-legged, hip-swinging strides. Huge dark glasses obscured most of her face and her blond hair sprang from a tail on top of her head.

"Yo, Yarrow," Briar said weakly. From the corner of her eye and with sinking insides, she saw that Dominic Kiser hadn't moved an inch. She squeezed her eyes shut for a second and reminded herself that God didn't care what people looked like and neither should Dr. Kiser.

"I'm starving," Yarrow said when she reached Briar. "Let's go to that Indonesian place in the market."

"Okay." Why should she care about Kiser's opinion of her friends? Briar thought crossly. And why didn't he just drive on?

"Let's go then."

"Right." Briar couldn't "go" quickly enough. "Watch out!"

Too late. A gangly teenager on a skateboard whipped by and clipped Yarrow. She flinched, and jerked away—and lost her sunglasses.

Briar stooped to pick them up. "Dangerous. You aren't supposed to skateboard on the sidewalk—for obvious reasons." She held out the glasses . . . and winced. "Yarrow! Oh, Yarrow."

One of the younger woman's eyes was swollen shut and purple.

"YEAH, YEAH." Dominic waved distractedly to the driver of a white car he'd just cut off at an intersection. "Okay! I'm sorry."

He'd made a circle around Westlake Mall and the central downtown area—for the second time. What did he think he was doing? What did he think he *could* do—about a lady chaplain evidently bent on throwing herself in danger's way. She wasn't a kid. At thirty she'd probably been charging into hazardous situations for years. And he'd promised himself a couple of hours with his mother who didn't see nearly as much of him as she had a right to expect when they both lived in the same area.

Yarrow—he knew that's who the woman had been because Briar called her name—was either a hooker or doing a more than passable imitation of one. And she'd had a mangled face! That innocent little idiot who thought she was invincible was living with a woman who was quite possibly a prostitute. And someone, probably her pimp, was into beating women.

Not your problem, boyo.

He reached 4th again and headed north. Driving in circles wouldn't do a thing to help the chaplain anyway.

What if the pimp was hanging about somewhere in the warren of alleys around Pike Place Market? What if Yarrow owed him money? That could be why he beat her up—for holding out on him. He could have talked Yarrow into luring Briar someplace where he could terrorize her into giving him money...or he could do something much worse.

Hell. Yesterday morning she'd been a face he vaguely recognized. And she'd been a nuisance with big green eyes. Now she was a different kind of nuisance with big green eyes and she was Briar, not Miss Lee. Briar of the smiling green eyes who was a sitting duck in a vicious world she thought was a friendly place. And it was his duty to make sure she was all right.

Ignoring honking horns, he cut across traffic and retraced his route. He'd also heard the blond woman say something about eating at the market. Driving fast enough to expect a siren at any moment, he zigzagged toward Elliott Bay and parked under the Alaskan Way Viaduct that bordered the market. Stairs led up to the lines of stalls beneath their glassed-in roofs.

Scents assailed him: fruit and vegetables, flowers, fish, spices, aromatic candles, oiled wood, incense. Scents and sounds and myriad colors and a crush of wandering humanity.

He'd lost his mind. Finding someone in this chaos would be impossible.

Giving up—on anything—was against his religion. Despite mounting annoyance, Dominic smiled. Dedication to accomplishing whatever you set out to do was a fine religion, but Briar was unlikely to be impressed.

"Mount St. Helens ash," a voice said very nearby. "I've got toothbrush holders and soap dishes as well."

Dominic looked at the woman who had spoken and realized he'd stopped in front of a stall covered with rough, putty-colored pottery. She must mean volcanic ash was used in the clay. He turned up the corners of his mouth. "Very—" *Briar.* She and the blonde were standing not more than a few yards from him. Briar was holding the other woman's arm and talking earnestly.

"This is a really good piece, sir. The dark glaze makes the textures show up nicely."

Letting out a silent whistle, Dominic concentrated on the stall keeper. "Yes. Wonderful. I'll take it." She wrapped whatever "it" was up in newspaper and he paid the price she asked, keeping his face turned away from Briar and her companion.

Nonchalantly replacing his wallet in the inside breast pocket of his jacket, he looked sideways. They were walking on.

Keeping an expanse of jostling shoppers between himself and the two women, he followed. They stopped. So did he—not quite quickly enough. He turned toward the closest stall and picked up an eggplant.

"You've got to." Briar's voice reached him clearly.

"Will one eggplant do you, sir?"

Dominic started and stared into the eyes of the fruit and vegetable seller. "Um, yes."

"If I do, he'll kill me." This was Yarrow talking.

A brown paper sack was deposited in front of Dominic. "Is that it, then? How about some white peppers. Very different, they are."

Very different. "Yes, all right. I'll have some of those." What was really very different was Yarrow Stalk from Briar Lee. Worlds different. They didn't even appear to come from the same planet.

"Could you use some ginger root, sir? Very good this week."

"Yes."

"How much?"

"Oh," Dominic waved a hand. "More, I should think. Probably a lot."

"And what if you don't make a report, Yarrow? What then?"

The other woman laughed, a forced, mirthless sound. "I suppose you're saying I'm dead if I do and I'm dead if I don't. Is that right?"

Dominic realized he'd made a fist and deliberately opened his hand. There were nail marks in the palm. He strained to hear Briar's response. The sudden nasal wail of a harmonica drowned out everything. Looking up, he could no longer see Yarrow's fountain of bleached hair—or the bright orangy color of Briar's sweats. The harmonica player had quickly gathered a screening crowd.

"Is that it now, then?"

Smiling distractedly, Dominic pulled out his wallet. "Yes. How much, please?"

"Forty-three even."

Dominic eyed the heap of bulging brown sacks before him. What the hell had he bought for that much money? He paid, anxiously searching for a patch of orange, and murmured gratitude when the man stuffed his purchases into an oversized carrier bag. He tucked in the pottery himself.

Cooking was his mother's main passion and hobby. She'd be thrilled with the eggplant and peppers.

And now he should leave the market and go to see her. She wasn't expecting him, but he knew she'd be at home.

Ahead, at the back of a ring of people watching a clown make balloon creations, he caught sight of the two women again. Briar was talking to a disheveled man who, even at a distance, bore the stamp of the practiced vagrant. She moved her hands, animated, and the man shrugged. From her pocket she pulled a card, which she handed over. From the other pocket what was clearly money was produced and pressed into a grimy hand. In return she received a flower the man plucked from the collar of a dog at his side—and an amiable salute.

She fascinated Dominic. That's what all this was about. For too long he'd had no really interesting diversions in his life. Sure, his career absorbed him almost totally, but there was another part of him that needed something else . . . someone else.

He hefted the bag from one hand to the other and moved a few careful steps closer, sidling along next to the stalls. If he needed someone else—presumably a woman—Briar Lee certainly wouldn't be the right candidate. He almost laughed aloud. She wouldn't want to be. No one could call her dried up, but she was very definitely a confirmed spinster—at least from what he could see.

The ribbon was gone from her hair.

Probably fell out.

Now she was handing out a card to another character who looked straight out of Oliver Twist. Dominic side-stepped several more feet.

"Give them this," she was saying. "See, that's my name. Briar Lee. Tell them I said you need a shower and a place to sleep for the night. They'll feed you."

"I'll go. Honest I will. You got any change, lady?"

"No. But I'll come along later and talk if you like. There are alternatives to this. Believe me. I'll introduce you to people who made the transition. They've got jobs now, and places of their own to live."

"Nobody's gonna give me a job."

"If you really want one, you'll get one—in time. All you have to do is be willing to share responsibility for yourself. Give up thinking you're on your own with this. The world's too hard to cope with alone. Take some help."

Muttering, the man shambled away and Briar returned to watching the balloon clown.

She was peddling her God. Even here where people were either too busy or already too far gone to care, she pushed her faith.

Briar Lee was brave. Dominic screwed up his eyes to watch her straight back, her nicely rounded hips—and the way her wavy hair swished back and forth over her shoulders. She should be someone's wife, someone's mother, a driver of car pools and baker of cookies.

And why, in the name of all that was natural to him, was he obsessing over a woman who would never be important in his life?

She looked over her shoulder.

Dominic swiveled on his heel and said, "I'll take one of those," to the nearest merchant. Dyed lengths of ropes tortured into grotesque shapes coiled all over the stall.

Another brown-paper package was fashioned.

Her fearlessness appealed to him. That was another thing that was different about her. And her unwavering assurance that what she did was all important intrigued him. Oh, it didn't usually intrigue him that anyone should be comfortable and self-confident with their chosen vocation, but when your business was persuading other people they ought to be better and they ought to believe what you believe—now that was intriguing, even if only because it seemed incredibly audacious.

"Thirty-five," the vendor of tortured rope announced. "Dollars. Nice day, isn't it?"

"Yes," Dominic agreed faintly, handing over more bills. Enough was enough.

A second carrier bag was added and he surveyed the crowd. Briar and Yarrow had disappeared once more. And so should he—while he could still carry all this junk he'd already bought.

There she was again. He stood very still. A young man, muscular, wearing a T-shirt with the sleeves cut out to show off his tattooed biceps to best advantage, held Yarrow's arm. Her head was bowed.

Dominic searched in all directions, looking for the local bicycle cops in their helmets and dark Bermuda shorts. None was in sight. He'd just have to be ready to act if necessary.

The man, his thick black crew cut greased to shiny points, talked intently to Yarrow. Briar crossed her arms and planted her feet apart.

Yet again Dominic had the urge to laugh. She really was fearless—a pint-size gladiator. And someone needed to keep an eye on her.

Hell, she'd obviously done a fine job of taking care of herself to date. But this guy could be the pimp. If there was a pimp at all. He couldn't just walk away and leave Briar at the mercy of such people.

No one had asked him to play protector.

She'd be furious if she knew he was following her like some deranged amateur sleuth.

Of course, she might just like it if she knew . . .

And he was nuts.

And she was looking this way.

"They're all handmade," said the keeper of the current display he fastened his attention on. "Rosewood, cedar, oak and pine, that one."

"Nice."

"Little kids really like them. The pieces are easy to handle."

"Nice."

"This is special, too. Invisible seams. And this—" the woman held up a game board "—makes a great display piece. Lots of men go for the wooden-backed brushes. Women like the hand mirrors."

"Great." What would he say if Briar marched up and asked him what he was doing following her when he'd said he was going to lunch somewhere.

"You'll never find them at better prices."

"Fair enough." He could say he'd changed his mind and stare her down. He'd noticed a few cracks in the fearless veneer earlier when he'd mentioned her eyes.

"Will they fit in one of your bags, sir?"

"What?" He eyed the ominous new pile of packages, these in newspaper. "I guess so," he said and submitted to having his paper panniers crammed to bursting point.

He paid up, wincing at the astronomical amount he'd absentmindedly spent this time.

Well, Briar and Yarrow were nowhere to be seen now. With relief, he saw that Mr. Biceps was walking toward him. Fine. Evidently Briar hadn't been abducted. Now he'd go surprise May with his haul.

"Sorry," he murmured to a man whose shins he whacked with a bag. Scooting, turning this way and that, he made his way toward the closest flight of stairs leading back down to Alaskan Way.

Orange. Black leather and a bleached topknot. And he was on a collision course with them. A speedy check showed that any hope of escaping unnoticed was impossible.

They were bearing down on him, Yarrow gnawing chunks of food from a skewer while Briar frowned and gestured broadly. She was angry. Well, she'd probably be angrier when she saw him and realized he must have been following her.

The direct approach always worked best. And who was he fooling with the humble bit. She'd be flattered by his interest. He hadn't failed to notice that she was very aware of him in the car.

This was it.

He halted in her path, smiling broadly. "Surprise, surprise," he said heartily. "We meet again—and so soon."

Those terrific green eyes came to rest on his. "Oh," she said...very distantly. "Hi."

"Hi."

Her attention sliding away, Briar took Yarrow's elbow and skirted around him. "You're sure he doesn't have your address?" she asked Yarrow.

"I told you he didn't. You worry too much."

Dominic watched them go. She'd turn back, frown, smile, wave—*something.*

In seconds the tall figure in black with her shorter sidekick were swallowed by the mass of bodies.

"Hi," Dominic muttered. "Just like that. Hi. Like I was no more important than the bums. Hell, they're more important to her."

He started down the steps. "*Hi.* Not, hi, Dominic. Or, what are you doing here?" The string bag handles dug into his fingers. "She didn't even look at me, not really look at me. And she walked on without looking back. Like I was part of the scenery."

Reaching his car, he shoved the bags into the back seat and pointed the Jag's nose in the direction of his mother's Queen Anne Hill house.

"That's it, Reverend. End of my white-knight efforts."

Chapter Four

Yellow afternoon sun slanted through the mostly glass wall of May Kiser's cathedral-ceilinged kitchen. The buttery-colored glow washed over thick wooden counters and scintillated on copper pans hanging in rows above the range. Sheaves of onions, bunches of herbs and tiered wire baskets of fruit hung from exposed beams.

Dominic entered the room as quietly as his rattling paper burdens allowed.

May, her pretty silver hair curling up from the bent nape of her neck, worked diligently at a chopping block by the sink. The smell of garlic was heavy in the air.

Rising to his toes, Dominic approached.

"You'd think a heart surgeon would know better than to try sneaking up on people and shocking them out of their wits."

He almost dropped the bags. "How'd you know it was me?"

"I can feel you, that's how."

"Feel me?"

"Yes, Dominic. I can feel you. I know when you're in the room." She turned around, wiping her hands on the calico apron she wore and smiling broadly. Her eyes, as dark as her son's, sparkled happily. A little plumper than she had been while he was growing up, she looked healthy and attractive in a dark green sweater and matching pleated skirt.

Dominic did put down the bags now. He gathered her into his arms and kissed her cheek. "You can't *feel* me, May. That's hogwash."

"If you say so," she said, completely unruffled. "One of these days you're going to have to look into feelings, my boy. You can't take them out and look at them like you can a heart." She shuddered, and turned her generous mouth down. "Thank goodness for that. But feelings are in there when you're mature enough to deal with them."

"Hah." He set her from him. "I'm not in the mood for one of your discussions about my stunted emotional growth."

"Someone called Bunnie tried to reach you here. She said she's a dear friend who needs to get in touch with you quickly."

Mild annoyance made him straighten his shoulders. "She must have looked up the name in the telephone book. My dear friends—if I had any—wouldn't have to find me in the telephone book." The fact that he'd ignored the woman's many messages on his answering machine wasn't important.

"Sounded like a bit of a bimbo."

"Geez, May, your lingo gets worse."

"You have to keep up with the times." She sliced a bundle of herbs from a sheaf near the sink. "Maybe she isn't a bimbo. Maybe she's someone you should get back to and consider persuing a meaningful relationship with."

Dominic had a swift, partly erotic, partly irritating mental picture of red-haired, voluptuous Bunnie "surprising" him at his apartment. She'd been waiting, dressed in rows of black silk fringe—and nothing else. Evidently the fringe had been sewn to some sort of body stocking and the fabric had run out in the area of her breasts. Stretched on her back on his couch, her fringe had parted to reveal perfectly circular holes filled with nothing but naked Bunnie... On second thoughts, the vision had definitely been more erotic than irritating.

"Dominic? What do you think?"

"About what?"

"About the future of your relationship with Bunnie?"

"If she calls back, tell her she's got the wrong Kiser."

"Run your own interference."

"Gee, thanks, May."

"You're welcome. It's time you got a life."

He stared at her, askance. "Who've you been hanging out with—the neighborhood juvenile delinquents? *Get a life?* My mother is tossing teenager parlance around?"

"What's all that?" May said, passing on to another subject with her usual facility. "In the bags?"

Sheepishly, Dominic plunked the bags on the round oak table in the middle of the room. "I had to stop at the market to buy myself a few things." Reverend Briar wouldn't approve of that invention. Not that he cared what she would or wouldn't approve of.

"Do you want to keep them in the refrigerator while you're here." May peered into a bag. "It's a good job I got too busy to eat lunch early. You'll join me, of course. I'm experimenting with a new sauce. Thought I'd have it with green tea noodles."

May had a somewhat singular taste in food. "Sounds...interesting. My stuff's still in the car. I bought these for you."

She looked up, clearly surprised.

He shrugged. "Well, I don't think to get you something nearly often enough. Today I decided to choose some things you could use." And for that, the Reverend Briar would consider him consigned to hell.

"How sweet, Dominic." One by one, May removed and unwrapped the lumpy packages, murmuring "Oh, my," and "Well, look at this," from time to time.

The single, if huge eggplant was the least of his excesses. The vegetable man had taken him at his word. Seven very large white peppers soon glistened milkily on the table. And two heads of radicchio, several ginger roots and a pile of other stuff he didn't even recognize.

"This is—" May glanced up, her brows drawn together "—this is so nice. Like, er, Christmas."

"Glad you like it."

"Oh, yes. Belgian endive. Wow!" What May held up looked more like Romaine lettuce to Dominic. "And kumquats."

The slimy son-of-a-gun vegetable seller had taken full advantage of Dominic's fractured concentration. "I thought the kumquats looked particularly good."

"They do. They do. And fava beans. And jicama. Oh, I've never ever used jicama." With the vegetable balanced in one hand, she turned her mouth up in a cheerful smile. Her eyes flashed messages that suggested she wondered if he'd lost his mind. "Last but not least, lemongrass! Ah, useful stuff, lemongrass. Maybe I'd better invite the neighborhood over to share."

"Sounds like a good idea." He refused to be ruffled. "You need to meet more people."

"Mmm." She eyed him briefly and unwrapped the pottery. "Dominic! What a pretty thing."

"I'm glad you like it."

"Oh, I do...I do." She turned the piece over and over. "What exactly is it?"

"It's, er, a bowl. Yes, it's a bowl for fruit."

Slowly, May studied the bottom of the piece. "For fruit? Why does it have holes in the bottom?"

Dominic scratched his head. "Did I say a bowl. How stupid of me. I meant a colander. It's one of those fashionable new pottery colanders."

"But the holes are so tiny. No bigger than pin pricks."

"Exactly. It's a tapioca strainer. The holes are tiny so that when you strain it the little tapioca blobs don't go through."

May looked up at him without raising her head. "I see. Interesting. When's the last time you had a real day off?"

"I'm going to take one off soon—next week probably."

"My, my." Another brown sack was taken from the second bag. "What have we here? You did mean that all these wonderful things are for me?"

"Oh, yes."

He should have dropped them in the bay. No one would have missed any of them.

One by one May removed the rest of his purchases and spread them on the table and along a counter. He was forced to survey the carved wooden box he'd bought, the one with no seams, and the man's hairbrush, the lady's wooden-backed mirror, a jigsaw puzzle in the shape of a whale and made out of many different types of wood.

Finally, May removed the dyed rope creation and held it aloft.

Dominic turned aside, opened the refrigerator and found a bottle of white wine. "Seems like a white-wine afternoon. Will you join me in a glass on the deck?"

A small, strangled noise made him close his eyes. He should have known better than to try to pretend he'd been transformed into a man who made impetuous purchases. And if he'd known what a pile of junk he'd bought he wouldn't have brought it in.

"Oh, Dominic, you shouldn't have."

Sarcasm was heavy in May's voice.

With the bottle in hand, he faced her and shoved the refrigerator door shut behind him. "If I didn't know you're too kind a woman for such behavior, I might think you didn't like what I brought you."

"But you do know I'm too kind." Turning the Medusa creation this way and that, she clucked and sighed, a beatific smile in place. "Lovely. I'm going to call it Stranded Bouquet. Do you like it?"

He hooked a corkscrew out of a drawer and bent to open the bottle. The corners of his mouth began to twitch. "Is that what they're supposed to be—flowers?"

"Don't pull my leg, son. You knew you were buying me a rope flower sculpture. I hear they're all the rage."

"They are?"

"Oh, yes. I just can't remember *where* it is that they're all the rage."

Dominic began to chuckle. His attempts to stifle the noise were useless.

"Okay, okay, spill it."

He stared at her, his mouth open. "*Spill* it? May— Mother dear, what has happened to your vocabulary?"

She flapped her hands. "I've been watching a lot of movies. All those teenage things. You know the ones."

"No, I don't, but I'll take your word for it."

"Okay. Now, back to the subject we were discussing. There's a story behind this, er, eclectic *gift* collection and I want to know what it is."

When May was tracking the key to a puzzle her nose wrinkled and she took on a vaguely puckish air.

Dominic considered whether he should tell the truth. Maybe an abbreviated form, a tiny chip off the whole, would be appropriate. "I was... well, I went to the market to... There's someone I met recently who's really... She's delightful, May. In an offbeat, straight-laced, kind of irritating way."

"Offbeat, *straight-laced* kind of way? And you find her *delightful?* Glory hallelujah. Maybe my prayers are finally going to be answered."

Dominic caught the bottle an instant before it would have crashed to the floor. Righting it carefully, he discovered his famously steady hands shook slightly. *Glory, hallelujah? Her prayers answered?* Coincidence, just coincidence.

But May didn't talk like that.

"Do you know a chaplain called—" Of course she didn't.

"Called what?" May's eyes glinted with interest.

"Nothing. Forget it." And he was going to do likewise. "I was concerned about a woman who works at the hospital—part of her time, anyway." When she wasn't hanging out with riffraff. "She has a way of getting herself into potentially tight corners and I decided to stand by while she was meeting some unsavory characters at the market. I didn't think she'd take kindly to discovering I was following her around so I had to... I kind of hid every time she turned around. I kept accumulating this stuff as a sort of cover. You know what I mean?"

May's lips had parted. She shook her head slowly—then nodded. "Of course. You've fallen for a woman at last. She's a member of the underworld and you're worried about her. What is she, a drug pusher?"

Horrified, Dominic gave his mother a piercing look—and found her barely suppressing giggles. "You're impossible. How can a man feel secure when his mother's a chronic practical joker. I'm not discussing this anymore. I was trying to do a good turn. It caused me to buy you a lot of useless stuff that you're welcome to throw away. End of discussion."

"Of course." May managed a serious expression. "Only you're not throwing away my goodies. I love them. That box is going on the coffee table in the sitting room. I'll keep the whale for my first grandchild."

Dominic glowered at her innocent face and poured the wine. He was her only child—only remaining child—and she always managed to hint that she longed for grandchildren.

"Who is she?"

He handed her a glass and raised his own. "Here's to mutual respect, respect for privacy—and many more sunny afternoons, white wine and wonderful company."

"Here, here. Does she live near you?"

"I'm not sure where exactly she lives and probably never will be. Will you leave it alone now, please?"

"Yes," she agreed demurely. "Has she been married before?"

"*No!* And that's *all* I'm saying. You are absolutely impossible."

The phone rang. May, smiling impishly, went to pick it up. "Good afternoon. I do hope you're not selling anything. I never buy things over the phone and I donate through my church."

Dominic looked at the ceiling. Some things never changed but it was his mother's indomitable spirit and unfailing good humor that had brought her through times that would have crushed most people.

"You want to speak to Dominic?"

He spun toward her, shaking his head ferociously.

"Why, you must be the woman he's been talking about. Bunnie, right?" She avoided his scowl. "Yes, yes. You're in luck. Dominic's here with me, but he's all yours. Here he is.''

The receiver was thrust into his hand and May sailed through the open back door onto a deck overlooking the city and Elliott Bay.

Slowly, he raised the phone to his ear. "Hello, Bunnie."

"Dominic, you naughty boy, why haven't you called me?"

"I've been busy."

Bunnie tutted. "You know what they say about all work and no play? And I like you just the way you are—exciting, Dominic. We certainly wouldn't want you turning into a dull boy."

"Look—"

May trailed back in, passed him and opened the oven door.

"Are you busy tonight, Dominic?"

"Yes. Very."

"Well, I think I might be able to persuade you not to be."

The smell of baking bread burst into the kitchen. May adjusted the heat setting and closed the oven door again.

"Dominic? Are you listening? I think I can convince you that you'd like to be busy with me."

"I doubt it."

"Here," May mouthed, handing him his wine. She returned to the chopping block and began sweeping ingredients into a bowl.

"Didn't you enjoy our last time together?" Bunnie whispered in husky tones.

He cleared his throat. "It was fine." She sounded slightly drunk. If he hung up she'd probably call back. Best get this over with.

"Did you like the things I did for you?"

Dominic turned his back to May and hunched over. "You didn't *do* anything for me, Bunnie. Remember? You'd already finished the bottle of champagne you brought by the time I got there."

"So I was a little tipsy." He could almost hear her pout, see her full mouth pushed out. "It wasn't my fault you were so late. I went to a lot of trouble—and it was just for you. You could have woken me up."

"I didn't want to wake you up." He didn't *want* casual sex, period.

"I'm awake now." Her tone wheedled. "And I'm all alone, Dominic."

"It's the middle of the afternoon, for heaven's sake."

"Mmm. Hot sex on a warm afternoon. Lovely."

"Not with me, babe. Not today." He closed his eyes and prayed May was engrossed in chopping herbs. "I have to get back to the hospital."

"Arrange for someone to cover for you. Come by for an hour. We could use the hot tub, then go up to the roof garden and see if the sun's warm enough to tan us . . . all over. Or is that hard rump of yours already tanned, Dominic?"

"Goodbye, Bunnie. See you around." He hoped he wouldn't.

"Don't, hang up."

His temper was sliding out of control.

She sniffed. "Come over, Dominic. You can just name the place. How about—"

"Goodbye, Bunnie." She wouldn't hang up.

"Dominic."

"What?" He looked over his shoulder. May, knife in one hand, bowl in the other, stood watching him with rounded eyes.

"What are you wearing today?"

"What? I . . . Suit, white shirt and tie. So what?"

In slow motion, May set down the bowl and knife. Wiping her hands on her apron, she tiptoed across the kitchen to check the bread again.

"I'd like to take off your jacket. Then I think I'd take off your tie and unbutton your shirt. Button by button." In other circumstances, he'd laugh. "Then your shoes? Yes, definitely your shoes and socks come off next. Bare feet are sexy."

"Bunnie, to you anything is probably sexy." His eyes slid past May's. She was doing a poor job of appearing oblivious.

"How right you are, darlin'. Your shirt would go next . . . and mine."

He was starting to react, dammit. "Goodbye Bunnie." Even Kiser, otherwise known as Mr. Cool, was only human.

"If you were cold without your shirt I could keep your chest warm with my chest."

Not an unappealing idea. "My chest doesn't get cold." He'd probably be up for sainthood after this.

A crash snapped his attention back to his mother. Her dark brows were fiercely knitted together. She'd put a portable chopping board on the table and was reducing onions to juicy mush. The table was so close Dominic could reach out and touch it . . . and May's ears had turned red.

"What does get cold for you, Dominic?"

"My mood, Bunnie. It get's icy cold. That's right before it blows."

"Would your mood blow while I was—"

"Thank you for calling, Bunnie." He smiled sweetly at May. "If I ever do feel like hot sex on a warm afternoon— in the hot tub and in the roof garden where the sun can burn your pretty tush, I'll let you know, kid. Bye." He hung up.

"My, my," May said. "The world has certainly changed."

"Has it, Mother?"

"Certainly. In my days young women weren't nearly as forward." Without as much as cracking a smile, she handed him his glass. "Drink your wine before it gets . . . warm."

They both laughed then.

"I'm sorry you had to listen to that."

"Don't be. I really rather enjoyed it. You can't imagine how dull it gets around here sometimes."

Dominic shook his head. "You amaze me. Doesn't anything ruffle you?"

"Not too much. Why weren't you at all interested in that girl?"

"I think you know the answer. Pushy women turn me off. Bunnie's not only pushy, she's a nymphomaniac and she's not subtle."

May waggled her head. "Don't some men enjoy women with a healthy appreciation of sex?"

"You always did feel free to discuss anything. Yes, of course they do. I do. But not with just anyone, particularly in the times we're living in."

"I told myself a long time ago that I'd never ask you this."

He took a deep swallow of wine. "But now you're going back on that decision?"

"Yes. Dominic, haven't you ever met a woman you felt like... Well, *have* you? You know? Someone you could make a life with?" Her hope was in her eyes.

For a brief, stunning instant he visualized other eyes. Green, not guileless, yet devoid of worldliness—or more, devoid of cynicism. Beautiful eyes that echoed the heart of an optimist. Carefully, he set down his glass. Briar had grabbed hold of his unwilling attention.

Sun caught in the gently swaying, golden wine in his glass. He reached to tap the rim. *Uncomfortable.* Yeah, he was uncomfortable because the question in his mind roamed straight to a picture and a sensation: a natural, feminine little woman in his arms, raising her lips to his, running her capable fingers around his neck and into his hair. She'd feel soft. And her hands would tremble—he knew they would.

"Dominic?"

"Yes?" For the first time in his adult life normal fantasy felt—

"*Is* there someone now? There is, isn't there? I can see it in your face. It's this straight-laced, offbeat person."

The fantasy felt... sacrilegious!

"Drop it, May, okay? Let's have lunch."

Without another word, she busied herself taking the bread from the oven.

A breathlessness expanded Dominic's lungs. Spreading his fingers, he picked the wine glass up by the rim. "Damn!" Breathing hard, confused by what he felt and shouldn't feel, he rammed a hand into his hair. "Damn it!"

"What is it? What's the matter." May dropped the pan on the range with a clatter. "Dominic?"

"Nothing. Everything?" He shrugged. "May, this is crazy. Some woman I'll never ever get close to... I wouldn't even if I could because she'd drive me nuts..."

"Yes? You want to get close to her, do you?" Her upraised palms urged him on.

Dominic downed the rest of the wine. "No. I'd kind of like to know her is all...as a friend. Nothing more."

"Oh, I see." More clattering followed.

"What are you smiling about."

"Smiling?" May turned her beaming face up to his. "Yes, I suppose I am. It's the bread. There's something about newly baked bread that always makes me smile."

Chapter Five

"They told me five hours."

"It's only just five hours now, isn't it?" Briar asked the thin elderly woman who paced from corner to corner in the cardiac intensive care unit waiting lounge. "Those time frames are always pretty loose."

"Why?" The five harrowing hours she'd spent in this irritatingly orange and lime green room showed on the woman's lined face.

"Because there's no way to be sure of exactly what they'll get into once...during surgery." Heart bypass was undoubtedly a miracle that saved thousands of worthwhile lives, but the stress on the patient's family, as well as the patient, was overwhelming.

Dorothy Svaboda returned to an orange vinyl chair and perched on the edge of its seat. "They said it wouldn't be longer than five hours." She clung to the seat, her knuckles white.

"Are you sure they didn't say it *shouldn't* take longer than five hours."

"No. Maybe they did." A shaky breath moved lace that edged the square neck of a homemade print dress. "Wouldn't they be likely to tell you it might be longer than they expected it to be, though?"

Briar moved to the chair beside Dorothy's and offered a hand. Dorothy hesitated, then slipped cold fingers around Briar's palm and held tightly.

"Five hours was probably a long estimate, wasn't it?"

With a sigh, Briar smiled. "It could have been." There was no point in pretending when Dorothy's logic was so obviously good.

"So they must have... When they opened Arthur's chest they must have found everything was much worse than they thought it would be."

"No! No, Dorothy. That doesn't have to be what happened at all. I'm not going to make light of what you're going through—or what Mr. Svaboda's going through, of course. But I've been in this room many times with many people. Take it from me—more often than not bypass surgery takes longer than expected."

Dorothy frowned. "You're just trying to make me feel better."

"Yes, I am. But I'm not lying."

"No, of course you're not," Dorothy said in a flurry. "I'd never suggest you were. But—"

"Don't waste time worrying about my feelings," Briar said gently. The old inhibitions that crept in for so many lay people dealing with religious never failed to annoy her. "I've often wondered if the surgical team actually expects the operation to take longer than they say but that they're afraid the family will be overwhelmed if they mention some astronomical number of hours."

"You really think so?" The desperate blue eyes were red-rimmed from crying and lack of sleep.

"Yes, I do. Would you like some tea?"

Dorothy shook her head. "I've drunk too much already."

"You told me earlier that your son would be coming."

Immediately Briar wished she hadn't made the comment. Dorothy's eyes filled with tears again and she blinked rapidly. "He will when he can. Leonard's got a very important job and it's hard for him to get away."

"I'm sure it is." Sometimes Briar had a tough time not saying what she really thought. "Tell me about Mr. Svaboda—Arthur. How long have you been married?"

"Forty-one years."

Briar smiled and chafed the dry hand. "That's wonderful. And you've obviously really loved each other for all those years."

"Yes, we have."

"Being a hospital chaplain, I haven't performed many marriages. But it's daunting to say the words that are supposed to join people for life and then wonder if the marriage will last."

"Things have changed," Dorothy said. She glanced shyly at Briar. "Not just with so many people getting divorced. Years ago you never would have seen a woman minister."

"I know." The topic was too deep for the moment. "Does it bother you—dealing with a female chaplain, I mean?"

Dorothy considered, then smiled a little. "It's nice. You're easy to be with. You make me feel that I can say anything and you won't think I'm just a silly woman prattling on."

"I certainly won't." Intense pleasure brought a rush of warmth to Briar.

Dorothy Svaboda tipped up her chin and swallowed. "Sometimes you kind of take someone for granted. Arthur, I mean. Oh, you know you love them and they love you, but you don't really think about it. We've had so many good times together. Some hard ones, too. We lost three babies before Leonard was born. That was hard. But we didn't pull apart like some couples do. Arthur was always gentle with me. He never got impatient because I cried so much."

She stopped talking. Her grip on Briar's hand tightened again.

"I blamed God for the babies dying." A harsh choking noise came from her throat. "I thought if he was good he'd have saved them. But I wasn't myself then. I know God doesn't make bad things happen to people."

"No, he doesn't," Briar said with a feeling of bright peace.

"And—" tears overflowed "—if Arthur dies... If he does, it won't be because God's being spiteful."

Briar wanted to say she was certain Arthur wouldn't die, but the power to make everything all right for Dorothy wasn't hers.

The door opened and a blue-clad figure came in.

"Doctor!" Dorothy scrambled to her feet. As quickly, she sank down again. She appeared suddenly much smaller and more frail. All color drained from her face.

Briar looked into Dominic Kiser's dark eyes and frowned. He stared straight back at her and she'd swear she saw anger in him. She hadn't known it was Dominic's team that was operating on Arthur Svaboda. Reaching out, she found Dorothy's fingers again. "Dr. Kiser was pretty accurate with his time estimate," she said with forced cheeriness. To Dominic she added, "Dorothy said you'd predicted about five hours. How did it go?"

From the puzzlingly thunderous glare he sent her, Briar almost expected him to tell her she had no right to ask about a patient's condition.

He drew in a short, audible breath and sat at Dorothy's opposite side. "Mr. Svaboda's doing quite well."

"Oh!" Dorothy turned to Dominic and grasped his right hand in both of hers. "Do you mean it? He's still alive?"

"Of course he is," Dominic said with such gentleness that Briar's heart warmed to him. "I promised you we'd look after him."

"But you didn't say he couldn't die."

"No one can say that, Mrs. Svaboda—about anyone. Can they?"

"I suppose not."

He smiled, crinkling the corners of his eyes. His mask trailed beneath his chin and his cap was sweat-stained over his brow. "There weren't any surprises. Your husband has the incision in his leg we talked about where we used sections of the saphenous vein to repair the points where the blockages were. I explained that his chest will be sore for quite a while. But very soon he'll be up and walking."

"Oh, thank you." More tears coursed down Dorothy's face. She continued to hold on to Dominic. "We'll never be able to thank you enough."

His grin became broad. "You already have. There'll be more hurdles to jump, but they're positive ones. No more of those wonderful cream cakes Mr. Svaboda loves you to bake, though."

Dorothy shook her head emphatically.

"A dietician will talk to you about all that. And it will be best if you accept advice on dealing with any depression."

"I'm not depressed," Dorothy sang out.

"Your husband's depression. It's very common in cases like his. He's faced a lot and he'll probably need to talk to someone who can help with his misgivings about the future."

"You'll talk to Arthur, won't you Briar?" Dorothy said. "I know you'd say the things he needs to hear."

"I'll be glad to."

"That's fine," Dominic said, his smile gone. "But I meant we'd like you to use a counsellor who's trained in this sort of thing."

Again he was putting her in her place; Dominic Kiser considered her a meddling amateur around here.

"Whatever you say," Dorothy said happily. "Can I see him now?"

"He should be back on the unit shortly. If you like you can go and wait in his cubicle."

"Thank you," she said again, and to Briar, "I told you God isn't spiteful. He's good, isn't he?"

"Yes," Briar agreed. "He's very good."

She watched Dorothy leave and expected Dominic to follow. Instead, he lingered and she saw yet again the shadows on his face that testified to the intense effort he expended beneath great lights in cold, shiny rooms where miracles happened.

"You look tired, doctor."

He stood up and stretched. "I am."

"Would you . . . Could I get you some coffee or tea."

His dark, speculative appraisal unnerved her. "I don't know."

The man was an enigma.

"Might give you a little boost," she said, hearing how lame the words sounded.

"It might." He pulled off his cap and wiped the back of a hand over his forehead.

"It must feel wonderful to be able to bring people such good news."

"Beats the other thing."

Would he always find a negative to offset a positive? "Of course. That must be very hard."

"You can't win them all."

"No." He must be drained, that was why he couldn't be as exhilarated as she was. "Come on down to the cafeteria. I'll buy you espresso, or something."

Surprise replaced speculation.

"If you want to, that is," she added. Why did she always wade in without counting the possible cost? "I've got to thank you, too, for what you did. I'm so grateful for the gentle mercy Mr. and Mrs. Svaboda received today."

His lips parted. He stirred and began to slowly untie the remaining strings on his mask.

Without warning, he turned away and opened the door. "Mercy?" He balled the mask with the cap. "That's an interesting term for advanced medical technology and skill. I'll pass on the espresso."

IF MAY HAD HEARD how he'd treated Briar this morning she'd croak. Or, more likely, she'd give him her opinion of his totally uncalled-for rudeness in terms guaranteed to sting.

The descending elevator bumped to a halt on the second floor. The door slid open and a stocky blond man, also wearing blue scrubs, got in.

"Nice job this morning, Dominic."

He nodded, acknowledging Norris Simpson, anaesthetist and enthusiastic playboy—possibly not in that order. Norris moved into a corner of the elevator and punched a button.

"Thanks for the vote of confidence," Dominic said.

"Had lunch yet?"

"No. Just got through on the unit."

"Care to join me downstairs at Chez Offle?"

Dominic smiled and shrugged away from the wall. "Thanks again but I think I'll pass. That cafeteria has a way of depressing me. I'm going to skip lunch and run instead."

"Sans lunch?" Making clucking noises, Norris followed Dominic into the lobby. "Not healthy, old man. Did anyone mention the party this weekend?"

Parties, any parties, were Norris's lifeblood. Fortyish, divorced and perpetually skirt-chasing, he was notorious among the nursing staff, most of whom treated him with caution. They also did their best to stay slightly beyond his reach.

"I've got something on this weekend," Dominic lied.

"Aha." Norris leaned close and winked. "Anything good? Anything you should share with a good friend?"

"No." Dominic laughed. "This is strictly one-on-one stuff."

"*One-on-one*, huh?" Norris leered. "Anyone I know?"

"No one you know. Better get going if I'm going to get a run in. See you around."

"You bet. Running to get in shape for a little *one-on-one*." He snickered. "Give it your all, buddy. Don't let the side down."

Dominic turned blindly down the first corridor he came to and didn't stop walking until he reached a fire exit at the other end.

Damn, but the Norris Simpsons of this world made him want to puke. He slowly retraced his steps. Why? He was no saint himself.

Maybe he was getting old.

"*I'll pass on the espresso.*" What had gotten into him? He'd never be labeled Mr. Charm, but point-blank and completely unnecessary rudeness wasn't his style either. He hadn't even said: "I'll pass on the espresso—*thank you*"!

He went to the front desk. "Can you find out for me if Briar Lee's in the building," he asked a receptionist. "In the log. I don't want her paged."

"That's the chaplain, isn't it, doctor?"

Dominic nodded at the young man.

"I thought I saw her come in." He flipped pages.

"She was here this morning. Did she leave?"

"Nope. Here she is. She hasn't signed out so she should be in the building." He looked at the clock on the wall. "Try the chapel. There's a noon service. It'll be over by now, but she might still be there."

Murmuring thanks, Dominic headed back to the elevators. He'd never actually been inside the chapel but he knew it was on the third floor.

He found it tucked into a corner beyond an obscure little library. Panels of orange pebble glass ran the length of double doors.

With his fingers on a handle, Dominic halted. What was he going to say? He'd been rude more than once—although they had seemed fairly comfortable with each other when he'd driven her downtown. But that was days ago. And when she'd seen him in the market she'd hardly seemed to notice his existence.

Oh, no, he'd best just leave things alone.

He was bigger than that. What would it cost him to offer her a cup of coffee—bring up her idea for an Easter party in pediatrics, perhaps—and apologize for this morning?

Mortification if she gave him the brush-off.

Briar Lee was into mercy. She wouldn't give him the brush-off and if he showed her he could be contrite for bad behavior she'd think better of him.

He wanted Briar to think better of him.

Dominic stepped back. When a man didn't care one way or another about a woman, he also didn't care how good— or bad—an opinion she had of him.

He cared.

Music blared, suddenly and loudly enough to send his hands to his ears before the volume was modified. He looked along the corridor. His ego was big enough not to dent if someone saw him hovering outside the chapel like a kid deciding if something scary was on the other side of the door; but he'd just as soon no one saw him there.

Rock and roll music. Intrigued, he carefully pulled a swinging door open—just enough to give him a peek inside. Rows of wooden pews and a standing floral display before a stained glass window in varying ugly shades of orange and brown were all he could see.

He could hear even more clearly. The Beatles, or one of The Beatles—Dominic wasn't sure which—was singing his ode to Eleanor Rigby.

Dominic pushed the door a little wider—and held absolutely still.

Dressed in the gray slacks and white cotton blouse of the morning, Briar was barefoot. Her tennis shoes lay on one of the two steps leading up to a simple altar. Beside her stood a man, a good-looking, dark-haired man who appeared to be about the same age as Briar. He also appeared to be completely entranced by his companion. Briar, her hair curling about her shoulders, smiled up into the man's face. Dominic could see her lips moving. He couldn't hear a word.

The man shook his head, no.

Briar tilted her head…and slipped her hands around his neck.

Dominic narrowed his eyes.

She was trying to persuade the man of something.

Eleanor Rigby continued on her way to the graveyard. Dominic had the fleeting thought that he supposed one might make some sort of religious connection although he wasn't sure what.

He saw Briar's lips move again. "Yes," she must have said, and again, "Yes," when the man shook his head—less emphatically this time.

The song finished to be quickly followed by another.

They began to dance. At first Briar made all the moves, laughing, holding her reluctant partner's hand and swinging away, then rolling herself back in until she thumped into his body.

They both laughed then. Dominic heard the unselfconscious sound of Briar's laughter join the deeper sound of the man's as she drew him into the dance. Soon the two were moving as only a couple who had danced before—many times before—would move. And Briar smiled as Dominic had never seen her smile. This man made her very happy.

The music squealed, then stopped.

"Ah!" Briar shouted. "I ran out of tape there. Darn it."

"Just as well for my sake, my girl. I'm not as young as I used to be."

The guy looked pretty damn good to Dominic.

"You're wonderful," Briar said. "I do love you, John."

She was drawn into an embrace, swung slowly around in the man's arms before he released her and they held hands to walk toward the door... and Dominic.

He turned away, but not before his eyes met Briar's.

Latent gentlemanly instincts were for the birds, and that had been all that sent him looking for her. So much for feeling uncomfortable about treating a woman of the cloth like a human being. The lady was no different from any other woman.

DOMINIC had looked... angry?

"Who was that, Briar?" John asked.

Yes. Angry. Again. Who could figure the guy? He had been rude and belittling that morning. Briar had been left feeling as if she'd committed some sin simply because she'd treated him like an equal. And now he turned up at the chapel apparently just to glare at her again. Well—

"Briar? Who was that man?"

"No one you want to know, John. Certainly no one I want to know. Forget him." She smiled at her brother, and realized her feet were still bare. "Whoops. Got to get my shoes. You came to ask me something. What was it?"

"He looked angry." John had never been easily diverted. Briar's few memories of the father who had died shortly before her eighth birthday were of a happy but determined man. John was like their father. "Sis, he looked angry with *you.*"

She retrieved her tennis shoes and sat on the end of a peeling pew to pull them on.

"Okay," John said when she didn't answer. "We'll come back to the tall, dark stranger in a minute. Sandra tried to reach you on the phone. No answer."

Briar grimaced. "Yarrow doesn't like the answering machine. She probably turned it off." The previous afternoon Dave had left a threatening message that Yarrow had heard with Briar present. Embarrassed, Yarrow had avoided the real issue and railed against the evils of "those damned machines."

"We were hoping we could get you to take an evening off—maybe a Saturday—and come to Jazz Alley with us. Not for a couple of weeks, but we figure we have to get our request in early."

"Arrogant," Briar muttered.

"Briar, you're talking about the man you said didn't matter, aren't you?"

"Am I?" Obviously Kiser had stumbled on the chapel by accident. His reaction to seeing her was simply the same as it always was. He didn't like her. "He's arrogant and overbearing. And he thinks he's God. I swear to you, John, I've never met a more infuriating man and I've met a lot of men who made me angry."

She finished tying her shoelaces and stood up.

John studied her, his head tipped to the side.

"I can't promise a definite night for Jazz Alley. I'd love to come though. Can we try to work something out at the last minute?"

"Uh-huh." John chewed his bottom lip. If Briar could think of a good reason for such a thing she'd say he looked smug. "Why did he take one look at you and stalk off like that?"

Briar bobbed to her feet. "Who knows why Dr. Kiser does a lot of the things he does. Tell Sandy I'll drop by sometime over the weekend for a chat at least. Things are really hopping here at the moment. I'm going to have to work up another formal proposal to present to the finance committee. This chapel gets plenty of use and it needs renovation. People shouldn't have to come and pray in a depressing room with faded carpet and peeling walls."

"If you say so."

John never understood her vocation, but he supported her and that was what mattered. "It's just so hard to get any money out of the committee for anything that isn't directly related to patient care—physical care." And she'd discovered that Dominic Kiser, golden boy, meteor on a direct course to stardom in his field, was the strongest voice on the finance committee. "Oh, men! Kiser's on the committee. And he wouldn't even commit to prying loose some funds to put on an Easter party for the children's unit."

Chuckling, John took her elbow and walked her into the corridor outside the chapel. "I do believe you like that guy."

"What guy?" Her face heated.

"We both know what guy. Dr. Kiser. Big, handsome Dr. Kiser. He didn't wander here by mistake. He was looking for you."

"No he wasn't." She marched ahead and opened the door to the stairs. Standing in the elevator with John staring at her wasn't an appealing thought at the moment. "He lost his way somehow."

John clattered down concrete steps behind Briar. "Oh, yes he was looking for you." Laughter laced his echoing voice. "What haven't you told me?"

"Nothing!"

"You can't fool me. He's got you rattled. That means you like him."

"I try to like everyone." She opened the door to the floor where a sky-bridge crossed to the parking garage where John had left his car. "Tell Sandy I'll call," she told him, angling away toward the elevators.

"Okay. Can I tell her you've fallen for someone, too?"

Exasperated, Briar halted. "That's the silliest thing I've ever heard. You know I don't have room in my life for that sort of thing."

"Are you sure?"

"Yes, I'm sure. Even if I did, I can't *stand* that man. And don't you forget I told you so."

Rather than summon an elevator, Briar waited until John walked from view and went to stand near the windows. Below lay a side courtyard surrounded by trees that stretched over several acres of hospital property.

Should she try to find Dominic? John was right, there was no way anyone would go to the chapel other than by design.

Clouds drifted in grayish clumps over a paling sun. Shadows ebbed and flowed on the flagstones and central grassy area in the courtyard.

Briar rested her forehead on cool glass. Later she must go and see August again. He hadn't been his usual obstreperous self this morning. She sighed and watched her breath spread on the window. Knowing that he was failing didn't make it easier to accept.

A single figure appeared immediately beneath the windows. Briar looked down on a thick head of curly black hair and pressed even closer to the glass. Dressed in running tights and a tank top, the man had come from the hospital.

Dominic Kiser.

Briar straightened and almost stepped back. Then she reminded herself he was unlikely to look up, and if he did he wouldn't be able to see her through the tinted windows.

He walked briskly to the wall surrounding the grassy area. Bending, he tightened first one shoe, then the other.

Briar let out a slow, whistling breath. Even at a distance, it would be hard not to notice that Dr. Kiser had . . . This was a big man and there was no fat on him.

Propping a foot on the low wall, he began to stretch. He leaned into the raised thigh, bounced out the back foot and sank slowly, repeatedly, flexing legs no woman was likely to ignore.

Except for women with no interest in such things. Briar rolled in her lips and frowned. Admiring an excellent physical specimen was no sin. It was right to appreciate God's efforts.

"Quite something, isn't he?"

She jumped so hard her pulse slammed in her throat. A nurse had approached without Briar hearing her. "Dr. Kiser?" Pretending not to know what the woman was talking about would be pointless.

"Yes. Some man."

"He certainly is . . . um, nicely built." She was blushing again, drat it.

The nurse stood beside Briar and watched while Dominic pulled alternate knees to his chest. "Too bad he's such an arrogant man."

Taken aback, Briar glanced sideways.

"Whoops." The nurse, pretty and blond, pulled her shoulders up to her ears. "You're the chaplain, aren't you? Sorry about that."

"You don't have to be." Briar was grateful the woman had been too absorbed in her own reactions to Dominic to note that "the chaplain" was also watching the man below with more than casual interest.

"Do you know him?" the nurse asked.

"Not well." That shouldn't feel almost like stretching the truth.

"Probably just as well from what I've heard. He's difficult to get along with. I know that much from personal experience. He's an SOB. . . Oh, dear." The blonde giggled. "I mean, he's very demanding in surgery."

"I can imagine."

"But he is also very good. I guess his reputation is international."

"That doesn't surprise me either." He was almost like a being from another race, a powerful, not-quite-human race.

"He runs out there every day. Sometimes more than once. You'd think he'd have run off some of the hostility by now."

"*Is* he hostile?" Surely the impression he gave could be no more than the result of a very unusual manner.

"I don't know what else you'd call a man who reduces medical students to tears on a regular basis. He can't—or won't—tolerate the smallest mistake."

"Perfectionist probably." The running tights were black with a single red stripe coiling from the waist around one hip and leg. Now he was grasping his calves and pulling his chin to his knees. Fit. Beautiful if a man could be called beautiful.... He *was* beautiful.

"He's a perfectionist all right. And he's not human—unfortunately. Easy on the eyes though, isn't he?"

Briar smiled. "I suppose so. Any idea what makes him so demanding?"

"Nope. That question's been asked plenty. No one knows anything about him, not really." She hesitated. "Sometimes I think he's sad or disappointed. But I'm probably imagining excuses I'd like to believe. No woman likes to see a hunk like that on the loose because he's too much of a... It's a pity to see him go to waste because no one wants to get too close to him."

"A pity," Briar agreed.

The nurse looked at the watch pinned to her pocket. "Better get on. Nice to talk to you."

"'Bye," Briar said, returning her attention to the window. Dominic began to jog in the direction of a path leading through the trees.

He had come looking for her.

The slacks she wore weren't intended for running, but they'd do. At least she had on tennis shoes. And she could go right home and shower afterward.

He'd come because he wanted to talk to her about something.

Disappointed and sad. Maybe that wasn't so far from the truth. Professional success didn't guarantee personal peace of mind.

If she followed him, he might think she was being forward.

He'd come after her first.

She hovered several more seconds.

"So he tells you to get lost," she said loudly. "You can tell him what he needs to be told. 'You can be a pain in the ass, Kiser. Shape up.'"

Chapter Six

The day had definitely cooled. Brisk air struck through Briar's thin shirt. On the one day when she really needed her sweats, she'd decided to go for a more professional image. And she'd done so, if she were honest with herself, just in case she happened to run into Dominic.

That was funny. Almost.

She sprinted from the side exit that led to the courtyard and the path through the woods. Briar Lee hadn't been one of the stars on Roosevelt High School's track team for nothing.

Entering the trees, she smiled grimly and opened her stride. The worst that could happen would be that he'd inform her—imperious as only Dominic Kiser could be—that she should run somewhere else—or words to that effect.

When she caught sight of him she wasn't surprised. He was jogging, briskly, but still only jogging and Briar was running flat out.

Dominic's style was easy—long, loping strides and relaxed arm swings. Briar could almost see tension evaporating from his broad, muscular shoulders, his straight back and narrow waist...his solid, perfectly delineated rear...his long strong legs.

Sleek and powerful.

Her breath became a little shorter. The red stripe flexed with every stride—so did his buns.

Good grief. *Concentrate on the man.* This was the time to look at the man—the internal man beneath the apparently impenetrable facade he'd accomplished. He could certainly hold his own with the horniest crustacean.

Oh, dear. Briar pounded on. Perhaps it was time for a retreat, for some quiet reflection with her spiritual adviser.

He broke into a more rapid stride. Every muscle took the impact of his weight on the ground. That red stripe . . .

Oh dear, oh dear. Was one supposed to consider the merit of an eminent surgeon's buns?

"Hey!" she called with as much strength as her constricted lungs allowed. "Dr. Kiser! Dominic!"

He slowed, turned around and ran backward. Surprise showed clearly on his tanned face. Dominic *was* tanned. She hadn't noticed before. He really must run a lot.

Struggling a little now, Briar dashed to catch up. "I saw you from the hospital," she said honestly. "You inspired me. I thought I'd get out for a while."

With no apparent effort, he continued to clip along backward. "Aren't you hot?"

"Yes," she admitted, unable not to be honest again. "But it looked so appealing out here. One of the reasons I wear sweats most of the time is so I can run if I feel like it." She managed a small smile. "And because they're easy and cheap. I don't like spending money on clothes. And I don't like dressing up." As if he cared about her petty hangups.

"I haven't seen you out here before."

"No. I usually go to a track by a high school on the way home."

"Very wise." Finally he returned to running forward again and Briar was aware that he slackened his pace. "I'm glad to know you occasionally consider your own safety."

"Are you an unhappy man, Dominic?" Anticipating his reaction, she almost grimaced.

"Why the hell would you ask me a question like that?"

Not exactly the response she'd expected. "You seem angry most of the time."

"Then maybe I am angry."

"Is that because you're sad?" The pace was heating up, and so was Briar.

"I've told you before, Briar, my state of mind isn't something you need to concern yourself with." He wasn't even puffing and there was a definite hard edge to his voice.

"I'm sorry. Habit, I guess."

"Habit, definitely. You should work on that."

And he was one difficult man, but giving up on people was something she refused to consider. "Why were you looking for me?"

He pulled ahead slightly, glanced back and slowed down. He didn't answer.

Overhead, tree limbs swayed, jostling tender leaves. The afternoon smelled of new things: clumps of lily-of-the-valley, forget-me-nots and fresh breezes through wild spring grass.

Briar could hear the quickened beat of her heart. "You came to the chapel. If you'd rather not discuss the reason we don't have to."

"Why wouldn't I want to discuss it?"

Ohh, so thorny. "I don't know."

"Well, I do want to."

She waited. His bronzed arms glistened now, and his chest where dark hair showed at the neck of the tank top. The breeze that shifted the grass ruffled his hair.

Help him, she told herself. For some reason he found it very difficult to deal with feelings—his own feelings anyway. Briar was certain there must be something he wanted very much to talk to her about. She glanced at him again with sudden trepidation. Chances were she was running with a man who was looking for another opportunity to dress her down.

"Aren't you roasting?" he asked.

"Um—" he did seem to have a penchant for changing the subject "—yes, as a matter of fact I'm quite hot."

"Get rid of the long-sleeved shirt, for God's sake."

Briar checked her stride, swallowed and ran on. Obviously he had an odd sense of humor.

"Take off—" Dominic didn't turn his head, but she saw him grin. "Sorry. Not thinking. Roll up your sleeves, anyway."

Obediently, she wrestled with her cuffs and shoved the sleeves above her elbows. "I'm really not dressed for this." Now he'd tell her he agreed and suggest she leave him alone.

"Do you like to dance?"

The question startled her. "Yes. Why?"

"I wondered. That's all."

He wondered? "That's not true."

"I beg your pardon?" There was a trace of uncertainty in the iciness. Briar was an expert on tone of voice.

"You don't wonder if I like dancing. You probably saw me dancing in the chapel."

The pace speeded yet again. "Yes, I did. That doesn't mean I know whether or not you like it."

"Yes, it does. You're a perceptive man. Anyone watching me would know I love it."

Faster. "You're probably right. I didn't really notice."

"Why are you angry?"

He laughed...unconvincingly. "Yet again, I am not angry. I've got no reason to be angry."

"Well you certainly sound it—and look it."

"Of course I don't."

"Even my brother said you did and he doesn't usually comment on those things." She wiped a forearm over her brow. "He doesn't even notice if people are upset most of the time."

"Your brother?"

Each breath seared her throat now. "John. He saw you at the chapel, too. I can't keep up this pace." And now he'd definitely tell her he hadn't invited her to join him anyway.

His look, a slight smile, might suggest he was thinking just that but he said, "Okay. Let's cool down a bit."

Dominic jogged and Briar fell gratefully in beside him.

"I'm really not angry."

"Good."

"I'm uncomfortable. That's all."

"Why?"

"That's what I came to the chapel to talk about."

She wasn't much cooler. "I'm sorry, Dominic. I should have known you wouldn't have been there if something wasn't troubling you." How could she have failed to guess that he'd been seeking counsel?

"Do you ever take off the collar?"

Briar frowned. "I'm sorry?"

"The collar. Do you ever stop being a professional do-gooder?"

"That's not nice."

For moments their breathing, his even, hers a series of gasps, were the only sounds.

"No," Dominic said. "It wasn't nice, as you put it. But I have told you over and over again that I don't want you poking around in my mind. I wasn't troubled. Not the way you mean."

There were times when silence was the best course. Briar waited for him to continue.

"This has gotten way out of proportion. I was pretty brusque this morning—in the waiting room. That was un-called for."

She couldn't stop her smile. "You were tired."

"I was rude."

There were birds in the trees. Briar could hear them singing. "Hours of surgery must leave you very tense."

"They do. You saw that and you said so. You were kind and I should have appreciated it."

The air felt fresh and cool again. It filled her lungs the way happiness filled her soul. "You're a nice man, Dominic Kiser."

"No, I'm not. Not very often."

"Yes, you are. Love yourself. You're worth loving."

He skidded to a halt. "You say the strangest things."

Briar stopped and bent forward from the waist. "I know. People have been telling me that as long as I can remember. So that's why you wanted to see me? Because you felt badly?"

"That and to offer you that cup of coffee we almost had."

Straightening, hands on hips, she smiled at him. "But you went away without offering it to me."

"You were busy."

"My brother was leaving. You could have waited."

"I'm that way." He waved a hand. "Changeable. Difficult. But you already knew that."

"No you're not." She grinned, brushing back her hair. "I know more about you than you realize."

He swung his torso from side to side before relaxing his weight on one leg and regarding her, smiling his own distinctive half smile. "I doubt that."

Briar unbuttoned her collar, and the next button on her blouse.

Dominic's eyes moved fractionally lower. She fiddled with that second button. Her imagination must be working overtime. It was doubtful he'd even noticed her as a woman and if he had, he was unlikely to be interested in her breasts. A sudden flaming heat in her neck and face made her blink. These really were the most unexpected sensations.

"You're generally considered to be hostile. Did you know that?"

He appeared to consider. "At some level, yes."

"But you aren't really?"

"Aren't I?" He raised a well-defined brow.

"I happen to know that you waive fees for people who are in financial difficulty."

His relaxed stance stiffened perceptibly.

"You're kind to patients. I've seen that. They adore you."

"No one adores me." His laugh was more a snort. "With the possible exception of my mother, but I'm her only relative, which probably explains it."

The lines of his face had set. There was a definite freeze-out in process once more. But his attention wandered—from her eyes, to her mouth. Briar drew in a breath and held her bottom lip in her teeth.

"Hostile men don't concern themselves with other people's troubles. August Hill thinks the sun rises and sets on your head. And August doesn't like anyone much."

"He likes you."

"He likes baiting me. The challenge perks him up. Don't change the subject. You are a good man who's not happy for some reason."

"Don't you have enough business already?"

"I don't regard what I do as business."

"We've sparred enough for one day. I'm perfectly happy. Blissfully happy. Why wouldn't I be? I'm a very successful man."

"You're troubled. If you don't want to talk about that directly, we could come at it from another angle. You don't want to admit that sometimes at least—for some people— there's more to healing than what medical science achieves."

"It's time I got back."

"Don't sidestep this. You're too mature to duck issues."

"Briar, *don't* tell me what I should and shouldn't do and what I am or am not. End of discussion."

"You really put up a tough front, Dominic." Cautiously, she stepped closer, reached up and pulled a leaf from his hair. More softly, she added, "I don't think you're nearly as tough as you'd like everyone to believe. And I'd like to help you feel comfortable about letting others get closer to you."

He caught her hand as she would have dropped it to her side. Turning up her palm, he removed the leaf she still held. For an instant, his fingers rested on hers. "Has anyone ever told you what a pushy woman you are?"

The next breath didn't want to go in or out. "Lots of people." She watched as he flipped the leaf aside and, with one long finger, traced a line from her wrist to her elbow. "Let go, Dominic. Stop being ashamed of being a very good man."

He withdrew his hand and looked away.

Briar felt him struggle. "Would you like to go back to the chapel now." Maybe there he'd feel safe enough to talk.

When he looked at her again her hand went to her throat. The barrier had descended. "You just don't get it, do you? I'm *not* pining to bare my soul to you, Reverend. I'm fine, absolutely fine. I came to say I regretted being rude to you this morning—not to make a confession."

"I didn't think you—"

"I'm not sure you do think—unless it's about fluffy clouds and angels strumming harps. Get your feet on the ground." Without warning, he started running again.

Feeling more exhausted than she ever remembered, Briar followed suit. "I didn't mean to—"

"Make me angry? I'm not angry. I'm rarely angry."

So he said—too frequently. She made no comment and they retraced their steps all the way to the courtyard beside the hospital.

He was a nice man. He wanted to be liked. She felt that. "Whew!" Reaching the door, she pushed it open ahead of him. "We've earned that coffee." Sitting with him, just in companionable silence even, would make her happy. She averted her face.

An elevator stood open. Briar stepped inside and waited for Dominic to join her.

"Which floor?" he asked, poised to press the button.

"Basement, I guess. Unless we want to use a machine, the cafeteria's our only choice."

Dominic frowned, and bowed his head. "I guess you misunderstood me."

Her jaw tightened. "You wanted to go somewhere else for coffee?"

"I wanted to go for coffee when I went to the chapel. I'm afraid I don't have time now." His face, when he looked at her again, was inscrutable. "Thank you, though."

The doors began to close. "You're welcome." Stinging with embarrassment, Briar jammed a wrist on a rubber door edge and walked out . . . and walked unseeingly away.

"Thank you," she muttered. Unfamiliar fury brought a pounding in her temples. "*Thank me? You* asked *me* this time, you jerk. I didn't ask you."

He'd done it to her again. But for the last time.

Chapter Seven

"A man ought to have a hobby," August said.

"Yes," Briar agreed, trying to sound more patient than she felt. "Isn't it time you got some sleep."

"Can't see why. All I do is sleep."

"That's not true." She pulled her chair closer to the bed. "You're always awake when I come." Which was getting to be more and more often.

"That's because I want to be awake when you come. At least you don't back away from a bit of...a discussion."

"An argument, you mean." She smiled at the offhand compliment. "You like to bait me, Mr. Hill."

"You could call me August, y'know. When you're sitting in on something as personal as a dyin' you ought to be able to use the victim's first name."

She bent forward, hiding her face. "It's nighttime, August." He didn't expect or want her to argue about his condition. "Nine o'clock. People in hospitals start thinking about sleep by this time."

"I'm not just people. I'm here because I want to be y'know."

"Yes. Dominic...Dr. Kiser told me."

"I know there's nothing else they can do for me. That's okay, too. Lived long enough anyhows. But it's for Lottie. Easier this way. She knows I'm getting the best care here." He shifted to see her better. "Good woman, Lottie. Had to be to put up with me. I'm not easy."

Briar smiled. "No, you're not."

"Nice of you to argue. Open that drawer."

She did as he asked, sliding open a drawer in the bedside table.

"Take out the envelope and give it to me."

Into his work-worn old hands he took a large, padded envelope. From inside he drew a brown-framed tray covered with glass. Briar could see butterflies beneath the glass.

"Lepidopterology. Butterfly collecting says it better. This has been my hobby for fifty years," he said. "There's some who say looking ought to be enough. Butterfly gardening's the thing with them. I suppose I might have gone for that if I'd started later, but I'm from another generation. I can't even say I set out wanting to know very much about them, or to make sure others got to see them. To me they were just interesting. Colorful, too, a lot of them. Then I wanted to have one of every species in the world. And I came pretty damn close."

Briar didn't feel like looking at them. "I'm sure it's an interesting hobby."

"But you don't like it, do you? You don't agree with it?"

"I didn't say that."

"You don't have to. You've got a soft heart, girl, and it's on your sleeve."

She rested back in the chair.

"Hearts on view are in a mighty vulnerable place." He laughed and the laugh turned to a cough. "Mine never was on view and look at the trouble it managed to get into anyway."

Footsteps brought Briar slowly upright again. A prickly sensation, climbing her spine vertebra by vertebra, soon proved warranted. Dominic Kiser sauntered through the doorway, stretched his mouth at Briar and—to her surprise—pulled up a chair and sat on the opposite side of August's bed.

He wore a dark suit, a white shirt that did great things for his tan, and a tie in shades of jade green and fuschia. Briar didn't know a thing about men's fashions, but Dominic looked terrific.

"We'll have to stop meeting like this, Reverend," he said while he worked a folded sheet of paper from his inside jacket pocket. His tone suggested it couldn't possibly have been almost a week since their disastrous last encounter.

Caught off guard, Briar mumbled agreement.

"You look like hell, doc," August said, hiking himself higher in the bed.

"August!" Briar sent him a furious frown. "What a nasty thing to say. I think Dr. Kiser looks wonderful, and..." She stopped, her mouth open.

August chuckled.

"Thanks for the defense," Dominic said. "But I *feel* like hell. It's been a long day."

"So why don't you go home?" August asked, sounding satisfied.

"Nice way to thank a man for stopping by to check on you."

"Thanks for checking on me. Go home." He hooked a thumb in Briar's direction. "Take her with you...to your home I mean."

She studied the ceiling and heard Dominic's explosive laugh.

"Briar's welcome to come to my home any time she pleases."

Slowly, Briar met his eyes.

His smile was purely wicked—and it turned her legs to jelly. She tried to frown but found herself smiling back.

Dominic's expression became serious, but he continued to stare at her. Briar couldn't look away. What was in his eyes? Some question? Some sort of uncertainty? When he smiled again, she did, too, and felt as if he'd touched her. How would it feel to have Dominic touch her the way men touched women when they felt that special possessive attraction she'd seen between couples.

"Easy on the eyes, ain't she?"

Briar jumped and gave August an exasperated glare.

"She certainly is," Dominic said quietly. "I'm sure every man she meets thinks so."

This was another amazing conversation. "Well, August, if we're through with this discussion—"

"We haven't had a discussion."

"No. But if there isn't anything else you want to say to me, I'd like to think about getting home."

"Got someone waiting for you there, have you?"

She hesitated. "I do have someone who shares my apartment, but she won't be waiting for me."

"So what's the hurry? I've got things I want to say. Man with limited time like me has to use it all up. Can't wait for two younguns to decide if you can spare a poor old man a minute or two."

"Somehow the poor old man bit doesn't touch me too deeply," Dominic said. He tossed the piece of paper on the bed. "You said you'd be interested in this so I brought it along."

August coughed and unfolded the paper. "Interesting," he said at last. "I expect you lie awake nights prayin' the reverend's God will send you the money." His expression bordered on malicious glee.

"I can't say I do, August. I do hope we'll raise the funds to expand the unit. We could certainly do a lot of good with the results."

"No shortage of good causes these days," August commented. He let his head fall to the pillow and stared upward. "Never a day goes by when I don't hear about some good way to invest money in charity. Not much return on that, y'know."

There was a silence.

"I was showing Briar some of my butterflies," August said abruptly. "Don't think she approves."

"I didn't say that."

"Didn't have to. I've got eyes." To Dominic he said, "My collection's worth a fair bit. Don't suppose it bothers you, does it, doc—butterflies under glass?"

"No."

"Butterflies mean something else to Briar. Resurrection!" He grinned gleefully. "Hah! Surprised you, didn't I? Bit of Easter symbolism there—for those who believe.

Anyway, I've been thinking of what I should do with 'em. Quite a collection, I can tell you. Could be I'll decide to give 'em to you, doc—to sell. It'd give you a fair-sized chunk toward this fancy research unit of yours.'' He jabbed the wrinkled paper.

"That would be very generous."

Briar moved restlessly. She tried to quell the thought that Dominic Kiser was more attentive to this man than he had to be. Dominic wasn't the type to woo anyone for money...was he?

"I haven't made my mind up yet, though," August said. "Better be quick about that, hadn't I?" He gave a gusty laugh.

Briar met Dominic's eyes again, but quickly looked away.

"I could give 'em to the research center to be sold." August sounded thoughtful. "They'd end up in a bunch of private collections, I should think. But then, it could be I'll do what I always planned. Give 'em to some fool museum. They'd put my name on a plaque: 'Kind donation from Mr. August Hill.' Always thought I'd like that. With Lottie and me not having any kids to carry on the name I might as well buy a bit of posterity any way I can get it. You can buy anything, y'know."

"Can you?" Briar said. She was no longer tired. She *was* uncomfortably aware of Dominic's large presence.

"Aha." August wagged a bony finger. "You need to learn to keep your fool notions to yourself, girlie. You can't buy your way into heaven—isn't that what you were thinking?"

"August, I don't think—"

"Don't interrupt, doc. I know you're getting sweet on the reverend, but you don't have to defend her. She can do a fine job of that for herself."

Briar stood up. "I'll say good night." There was only so much humiliation she could take.

"That was what you were thinking. That I can't buy my way into heaven. Admit it."

"Perhaps it was."

"Hah!" August slapped the sheets. "She doesn't even have the sense to lie when it'd make things easier for her. I haven't made up my mind what I'm doing with that butterfly collection, missy. You remember that. Maybe if you can persuade me over on to your side, I'll leave it to you for that new chapel the wife says you want so badly."

Briar stood very still and swallowed. She shouldn't wish he'd change his mind about the research unit and give the proceeds from the sale of the collection to the chapel fund, but she did. It wouldn't even take all of the money, she was sure of that.

"Thinking about it, aren't you?" August snickered. "I can see it in those big eyes of yours. Got the biggest green eyes I ever saw. How about you, doc?"

"Definitely."

That was definitely the signal to ring down the curtain. "I'll hope to see you tomorrow," she told August.

"You do that. Meantime, don't you forget I'm making a decision about a certain matter. Don't either of you forget. Maybe you'd better both be thinking of ways to persuade me."

"Are you declaring a competition, August?" Dominic asked quietly. There was no amusement in his voice.

"Could be."

Dominic rose. "I avoid competitions."

"So do I," Briar said abruptly.

"Of course you do." August settled down, a cherubic smile on his face. "You might want to keep an eye on each other, though. Make sure the other fella's not making more points with me."

"You are outrageous," Briar said. She didn't understand his motives, but couldn't be angry with him. "Good night."

She felt as much as heard Dominic follow her from August's room. "Are you heading home now, Briar?"

"Yes." She had no reason to be angry with him—not for tonight, anyway. "He's truly a challenge sometimes. August, I mean."

"Isn't he just. I do believe he's decided to declare a contest between us."

"Seems that way, although I can't imagine why."

They traveled together to the lobby and Dominic was at Briar's shoulder when she went to the desk to log out.

Immediately, she knew her mistake. The buses would have stopped running past the hospital by now. She intended to walk down to Jackson again. "Um, have a nice evening. What's left of it." Backing away, she waved and turned toward a darkened corridor that led to the administrative offices.

"Aren't you going home?" Dominic asked.

To her dismay, he came right along behind her.

"Ah, yes. Yes. Very soon."

A large firm hand descended upon her shoulder. Dominic forced her to stand still, then he urged her around to face him. "Briar, how are you getting home?"

"Bus," she said brightly.

"Do you have a schedule?"

"Oh, yes."

"May I see it."

He had no right to ask to see her bus schedule or to question her on whatever she chose to do...but she liked it that he did.

"Dominic, the buses don't run past the hospital after eight-thirty. It's almost ten now. I'm going down to Jackson. I can get a bus there that'll take me a couple of blocks from my apartment."

"No you can't."

"Yes, I can."

"Not anymore."

"Don't be ridiculous. I've been doing this for two years."

He closed his eyes and his fingers tightened on her shoulder. "*Don't* tell me that. Briar, that is very foolish behavior."

"I'm not a child."

"Then don't behave like one. I'm taking you home."

Her skin felt suddenly too small. "I really do appreciate your concern, but what difference does one more night make? You can hardly be around to drive me home *every* time I'm here late—which is often." Instantly she wished she could suck back the words.

Dominic appeared to consider. He took his hand from her shoulder and sank it into his pocket. "Tonight I am around. Would you please allow me to drive you home?"

She said, "yes," as she'd known she would, as she'd wanted to.

"Good." Dominic let out a sigh. He held her elbow and ushered her through the lobby and outside to a parking lot reserved for medical staff.

Once inside the comfortable leather confines of his car, Briar tried to shrug off the knots of tension between her shoulder blades. Dominic climbed in beside her. He didn't immediately start the engine.

Briar stared out into total blackness. She could smell his clean scent, like freshly laundered linen and freshly showered skin . . .

"Do you think you're invincible because you're a minister?" Dominic asked evenly.

"No."

"Then why do you think it's okay for you to run around the streets at night—alone?"

Telling him she didn't really think about it wouldn't be likely to buy her any peace on the subject. "To put it as simply as I know how: I believe God will look after me. And I also sincerely think that women like me are less at risk than some."

"That's roughly what you said before. Now will you explain why?"

"I'd have thought it was obvious. I'm . . . well, I'm ordinary. To look at, that is." She wasn't about to suggest she had a poor opinion of herself otherwise. "I don't dress in a way that makes anyone want to take a second look at me."

He started the car and swung from the parking lot, down the driveway and onto the street. "You are not ordinary. You're a very attractive woman and if you think no one notices, you're deluding yourself. In your case, with your stupid habits, that could be extremely dangerous."

Briar studied the road ahead with intense concentration. Goosebumps shot out on her arms and legs. She was stupid. The desire to put him in his place on that score came and swiftly left. He'd said she was attractive—very attractive—noticeably so. What he meant was that he thought she was attractive and he had noticed. This was going to lead nowhere but into embarrassment and possibly pain. He was just being nice, but she was evidently pining for him to really mean what he said. She wanted him to *want* her.

"Are you all right?"

She jerked around to look at him. "Yes!"

"You made a noise."

"Did I?" She hadn't realized. "I'm fine, thank you."

"Great."

Her legs felt funny. Could she be having some sort of emotional crisis? One read about single women of a particular age having crises when they realized they would never have a man in their lives.

She didn't want one.

Yet she didn't want to have to get out of the car in a few minutes and walk away from him. "I have heard that sometimes when we get to know people better—even plain people—they start to seem quite appealing." Panic rose in her throat. There had to be a way to get rid of the danger she felt in this moment. "In my case it could be that all that holy stuff August makes fun of is finally making me look good to people." She laughed. Inside she cringed.

"It could also be that you need to work on your ego. The other day you were quick enough to advise me of my lovable qualities. Why don't you try loving yourself—outside as well as inside."

There was no answer to that.

The powerful car swept over a rise and headed toward the heart of downtown Seattle.

Dominic stopped for a traffic signal. "Where exactly on Western?" He turned toward Briar and his eyes glittered in the light from the dashboard.

"You could drop me..." Any suggestion that he not take her all the way home would be pointless. "I live close to Broad Street."

The minutes it took to reach her building were either too short or too long. Briar didn't remember ever feeling so confused—or so vulnerable.

"In there?" Dominic asked, peering up to the court-yard.

"Yes. I'll be fine now."

She leaped from the car and slammed the door...seconds before Dominic slammed his. Briar closed her eyes.

"I'll see you in. There isn't a light anywhere."

"There rarely... It's just that you can't see any from out here. You don't need to come any farther. I'll be fine now." She was fine every time she did this, wasn't she?

Dominic's heels thudded on the street as he walked around to join her on the sidewalk. "Do the people you work for know you do this?"

"The people I work for?" He made it sound as if she were employed in an office or a bank. "The people I work for, as you call them, were persuaded to give me my assignment on the grounds that I had already proved my aptitude and commitment. How I do my job is up to me."

"I didn't mean to annoy you."

"You haven't. Thank you for bringing me home."

"I'll just make sure you get to your door safely."

"You are so—" Stubborn. He was a typically stubborn male.

"Stubborn?" he suggested.

Briar almost laughed. "Yes."

She backed up and stumbled against something lumpy. A collection of old blankets she knew were her indigent friend Fred, made a shadowy heap close to the wall. To-night, of all nights, he'd chosen to sleep closer to the gates than usual. Tinkerbel, curled at his feet, growled softly.

"What the hell is that?" Dominic thrust her behind him and bent over Fred.

The smell of alcohol made even Briar's hardened nose wrinkle. "Shush," she whispered. "It's Fred. He's sleeping."

Tinkerbel growled louder. "It's all right, Tinkerbel," Briar said in an urgently soft voice. "Settle down, girl."

"Tinkerbel?" Dominic almost shouted.

"Fred's dog. She's a love. They sleep here every night. It's not a problem."

Before Dominic could investigate further or make even louder comments, she rushed up the front steps, fumbled to open the gates and went into the courtyard.

Footsteps coming right along in time with hers made certain she knew her self-appointed protector was still on duty.

At the bottom of the staircase to the apartment she halted. "Home at last," she said. "You'll be exhausted by the time you get to your place. I'm sorry for that."

"You live on the ground floor?"

"No. Third floor."

"I'll just walk you up." His smile was visible in the dim glow from a gap in nearby drapes. "I've come this far. It would be a bit galling to read in the paper that you got stabbed on your doorstep."

Briar couldn't help shuddering. "You do put some horrible ideas in my mind."

"Someone has to. Lead the way."

There seemed no choice but to start climbing.

"This is a bad arrangement," Dominic said. "These stairs ought to be better lighted."

"You're probably right," Briar agreed. How could he be expected to understand that not everyone could afford the kind of rent that went with the level of security he probably took for granted.

At the top of the final flight she faced him. He stood several steps below and looked up at her.

"You are a very kind man, Dominic Kiser."

"I just like to do what's right."

Exactly. He'd take what he considered appropriate care of anyone thrown in his path.

Dominic joined her on the balcony outside her door. Briar made a miserable attempt at a smile and fished in her pocket for her keys.

He came closer.

Briar backed up.

"I tend to be pretty... abrasive?" Dominic said. "I regret that. Particularly with you."

The squeezing in her chest felt like an invisible fist closing. She took another step backward and felt the wall behind her. "I think I understand you. You're a perfectionist. You want to put things right—have them work correctly. When they don't you get... irritated."

"That's no excuse for treating a gentle woman with anything but gentleness."

All the air went out of the night. "You... are gentle." He was a strong, sleek, marvelous male and she felt justice and goodness in his soul—no matter how deeply he tried to keep it buried.

"I seem to find myself thinking about you, Briar."

"You do?"

He put a hand on the wall behind her. Only inches separated them. "This isn't easy." His breath moved her hair. "There's something intimidating about... I joke about what you do but it isn't funny to you and since I take you seriously it isn't funny to me. It's just... intimidating."

She could feel him, smell him. "I'm ordinary. An ordinary person doing the job I was meant to do."

"Come on, Briar. You've got to know there's nothing ordinary about what you do." Dominic touched her cheek lightly.

A funny heaviness pooled low inside Briar. She pushed her hands inside the sleeves of her sweater, wound her arms together.

"I'm not sure what I am thinking exactly," Dominic said, his voice low. "Would you rather I didn't... Am I bothering you?"

"No." She bowed her head—and bumped her forehead on his shoulder. "Sorry." Her giggle sounded like a hiccup.

Dominic didn't laugh. He settled a big, broad hand softly on her crown and stroked slowly, oh so slowly and carefully to her nape. He shifted, very slightly, and rested his mouth at her temple.

A roaring sprang in her ears. She closed her eyes. "Do you have any hobbies?" Oh, please, did she have to feel so inadequate—and so desperately wanting?

His mouth was firm, his lips a little parted. He sighed and slipped his fingers over her ear, through her hair.

"August was saying how important he thinks it is for a man to have hobbies."

"Briar."

"Yes." She would surely choke for want of a breath.

"I don't want to talk about August right now."

"I like baseball."

The kiss, and it *was* a kiss, made agonizingly delicate progress to her cheekbone.

"I'm a Seattle Mariner fan. Avid. Have you ever been to a game at the Kingdome?"

"Baseball, hmm?" He used a knuckle to draw up her chin. "You are really something. I've never met another woman like you, thank God."

She did giggle now and clutch at him for support. Knees that wobbled dangerously threatened to collapse. Her fingers slipped over his smooth shirtfront, over the warmth of his hard flesh beneath until she held the lapels of his jacket.

"What's funny, Briar?"

"Nothing." No way would she say she was nervous, or that she found it funny—and appropriate—that he thanked God he hadn't met other women like her.

"Look at me."

If she didn't hold on tightly she'd fall. "Yes." She raised her gaze to his face.

He was going to kiss her... on the mouth. Briar drew in short gasps. The night seethed. There were small sounds and sensations and the sensations were all from Dominic.

He would kiss her.

It began like the brush of lashes, like the stroke of a butterfly's wing at the corner of her mouth. "Briar," Dominic murmured, slanting his lips over the bow of hers. "Briar."

She squeezed her eyes tightly shut and let him ease her face up with the pressure of his mouth. His touch, was delicate, exquisitely careful, and whilst his lips tested and teased hers, his fingers played over her cheeks, her ears, the sides of her neck. Then he ringed her neck with his hands and the kiss became more deliberate.

Leaning against him a little more, Briar made her own small, tentative exploration of Dominic's jaw. It was slightly rough—and totally male. His clean scent, with its mysterious quality seeming unique to him, made her nerves feel singed open.

"You are something, Briar," Dominic said, his voice very low. "Really something." His lips, parted now, came down on hers once more and she felt the tip on his tongue flicker inside.

She couldn't do this.

Convulsively, Briar jerked her face to his shoulder, buried her forehead in his neck. "I'm sorry." There was no way he would hear what she said.

"Hey. What is it?"

Without intending to, she thrust her arms around his waist and gripped him hard against her. "Thank you," she said. "Thank you for bringing me home."

She let him go and spun around. Sending up a prayer of thanks when she found her key at the first pass, she opened her door.

"Briar, what's wrong? Tell me."

"Not a thing." With horror, she realized she'd begun to cry. "Thank you. Good night."

As she closed him outside she saw his puzzled shake of the head. With trembling fingers, she slid on the chain and started down the hall—and stopped at the sight of a sleepy Yarrow scuffing toward her.

"Yo, Briar. What's all the noise?" She yawned and rubbed her eyes, peering more closely. "What's wrong with you?"

Briar clapped her hands over her ears. "Don't ask me that. I don't ever want *anyone* to ask me that again."

"Okay, okay. Forgive me for living."

"Ooh, you don't understand." She stomped toward her room.

"So explain," Yarrow called after her. "Make me understand why you're crying."

"I'm crying because I'm confused," Briar wailed. "Is that okay with you? For me to be confused once in a while? I just...I just did something I haven't done for a long time. And for the *first* time it meant something. I loved it. It was wonderful. *He's* wonderful. But I blew it. And I want to try again but I'm not ever going to get another chance with him."

Chapter Eight

Lambert Barron, Dominic decided, could very well have been present at the ground-breaking ceremony for the medical center. The center had opened—admittedly in a very small way—in 1910. Lambert might even have been a vigorous young man then. Yep, quite possible. He sure as hell was a boring old codger now.

"...trouble on the horizon. Mark my words, gentlemen, the rot had better be hacked out now or the Ocean Medical Center will pay the price and we'll all pay right with it." Lambert droned on, his narrow, white-haired head nodding in rhythm with the words. They were words that might be dynamic, riveting even, if he didn't always—in his position as Chairman of the Finance Committee—use the same ones, in the same order and in the same ponderous tone at every meeting.

Dominic felt a collective shift of position in the men and women ranged around the glistening rosewood table in the similarly paneled boardroom.

"There's always a price to be paid, of course. We all know that. And we're all willing to make personal sacrifices to ensure the forward progression of this fine institution..."

Barney Friest, Chief Administrative Officer of the center, leaned closer to Dominic and murmured: "But not if our sacrifice only provides less responsible parties with an opportunity to feed off our bones..." He grinned behind his hand.

"...less responsible parties with an opportunity to feed off our bones," Lambert finished...several moments after Barney.

Dominic stifled a chuckle.

Lambert fixed his watery-blue gaze on one member of the committee after another. "We are here today, gentlemen—" the presence of women in these meetings had never penetrated Lambert's sensibilities "—to reaffirm our hold-firm position on any issue not absolutely essential to maintaining our position as a vanguard in health care."

"And so begins this day's battle," muttered Barney. "I hope things will undergo a change with the installation of our illustrious incumbent chairman."

Dominic only smiled.

The next two hours were spent, as they had been at every meeting for the past six months, in heated discussion over the proposed expansion of the cardiac unit. No one disputed the positive aspects of the venture. Everyone had grave doubts about where the funds would be found—at least in the near future.

"We'll address this issue again next month then, gentlemen," Lambert finally announced. "And I'm sure we'll all look forward to progress reports. You might let us know of any rich and failing uncles looking for a worthy recipient of their fortunes." His little joke brought a polite ripple of laughter.

Dominic thought of August Hill and as quickly battened down his mind on that possible source of capital infusion.

"Unfortunately we are forced to address the next issue today although I have managed to put it off for some months. Refurbishing the chapel." Lambert nodded sympathetically at several members who grumbled aloud. "I couldn't agree more. We've better things to do, but this chaplain person is persistent. I decided to give him a hearing just to, er, keep him quiet, shall we say?"

"Her," Dominic said loudly before he could stop himself.

All eyes turned in his direction.

Wiggling his pen between finger and thumb, he smiled around at his colleagues. "Reverend Lee is a woman. She's very active on the cardiac unit."

Lambert sniffed and told the recording secretary to show Briar in.

Wearing her hair drawn up into a curly topknot thing and looking very small, she entered and stood squarely in the middle of the threshold, a black folder clasped before her. Her face was pale, Dominic noted uncomfortably, and her knuckles showed white where she held the folder in a death grip.

"Good morning, er—" Lambert consulted his notes "—Reverend Linn."

"Lee," Briar corrected clearly, raising her pointed chin.

"Quite. Have a seat."

Dressed in a bright yellow linen suit with black polka dots and black piping around a stand up collar and down the front edges of a buttonless jacket, she looked different to Dominic. Businesslike in a feminine way. He hadn't seen her for two days, not since the extraordinary episode outside her apartment. He glanced away. Extraordinary and haunting. She'd felt so soft, so damn sweet. He'd wanted her. Unbelievable. He'd gone from finding the good chaplain a royal nuisance to dreaming about making her a willing bed-partner.

Dominic let his eyes run over her. Maybe he wasn't very noble. On the other hand, this lady, whose lovely, shapely legs were revealed by her short, straight skirt, had all the symptoms of turning out to be perfectly human. She was certainly eminently desirable. But there were certain mind-boggling obstacles to overcome. Undoubtedly he was wrong, but he'd gotten the notion that she might be completely inexperienced.

Finally her eyes met his. He smoothed his tie, tried for a friendly grin. Whatever those green eyes held, it wasn't disinterest. She was thirty, for crying out loud. No woman, regardless of how holy she was, could reach thirty and not have been with a man . . . could she? At moments like these he almost regretted that smoking wasn't an option. If he could, he'd willingly cling to some diversion.

At last Lambert finished shuffling papers. He was performing his famous "ignore-them-into-submission" routine.

Dominic quickly scribbled a note and passed it to Barney who read, cast Dominic a curious glance and smiled at Briar. "Glad you could make it in today, Miss. Lee. Reverend Lee?"

"Either is fine," Briar said.

Lambert cleared his throat and frowned darkly at Barney. "We are extremely busy on this committee. Our thrust will always be what it always has been—the furtherance of excellence in medical care."

"Commendable," Briar said.

She crossed and recrossed her legs—an exercise Dominic observed with fascination. Very slender ankles and nicely curved calves. Where the skirt hiked above her knee, a small but provocative expanse of smooth, silk-clad thigh was revealed.

Briar had trembled beneath his touch. But she hadn't disliked it, Dominic would stake his life on that.

"Perhaps you'd better present your material," Lambert said offhandedly. He checked his watch. "Please make this brief. We'll need to break for lunch shortly."

As far as Lambert was concerned, a double-martini lunch took precedence over any issue brought before the committee.

"I was here last in November," Briar said clearly. "Nothing has changed since then, but I'll be happy to reiterate what I said."

To Dominic's surprise, she produced a pair of horn-rimmed glasses and slipped them on. The effect was to make her already remarkable eyes more remarkable and to draw attention to her flawless skin and sweetly arched mouth. The hairstyle must have been concocted to make her appear more professional. He supposed it did in a way, but the curls that sprang around her face were purely beguiling. He concentrated on his notepad and began doodling.

"The Ocean Medical Center's chapel was not part of the original plan for the building. It is housed in what used to be a series of storerooms.

"The conversion was started in 1937 and the consecration as a place of worship took place two years later. Very little improvement has been undertaken since the installation of a stained glass window in 1960—over thirty years ago."

"Monstrosity," Dominic said, not quite under his breath.

"Did you have a comment, Dr. Kiser?" Lambert said. Whatever else might be failing, his hearing definitely wasn't.

"I said that window is a monstrosity."

Lambert gripped the edge of the table and drew himself up. "That window was a gift from a grateful patient," he said ominously. "Not that the thing matters one way or another in this discussion. What is it you're asking for, Miss Linn?"

"Lee. I'm asking for a significant financial commitment from the center to assist in the complete refurbishing of the chapel. My records—" she riffled through pages "—show that approximately fifty people a week go to the chapel. These are people seeking the peace of mind and comfort their faith affords. They deserve more pleasant surroundings. And respect for the function of the facility demands that improvements be made."

"Demands?" Lambert said, thrusting his chin forward. "Not a wise word when one is asking for something, Miss Linn."

"Lee."

"Mmm. Wouldn't you say that a man or woman ought to be able to pray wherever they are? Is faith likely to wobble because a window isn't aesthetically pleasing? Would a new kneeler make kneeling less onerous, do you think—or more efficacious, perhaps—to the soul, I mean?"

"I hardly think the direction of your argument is appropriate," Briar said. The glasses came off again and she absentmindedly polished the lenses on her skirt. "The carpets are a health hazard all on their own. They're so threadbare I'm amazed someone hasn't tripped and sustained an injury by now."

Particularly someone fleet-footed and full of rhythm and absorbed in abandoned dancing. Dominic chewed the inside of his cheek. His eyes met Briar's . . . again. August's collection, if he chose to make a donation of it, would do wonders for the unit expansion. It could also cover anything Briar wanted to do to her chapel—with a lot left over.

She kept right on looking back at him. He raised his jaw and felt his lips part a fraction. Was she thinking about the butterfly collection?

"Perhaps I could have a word or two," he said to Lambert.

"By all means. Time you started getting into the harness, Kiser." To Briar he said, "Dr. Kiser is our new chairman. He'll take over the reins next month."

The others might miss the alarm that passed over her features. Dominic certainly didn't. "Your, er… Aren't you in a position to expect matching funds, or whatever your church calls them?" he asked her.

"Funds to match what?"

A small wave of laughter went around the table.

Dominic allowed himself a smile. "Matching whatever you manage to raise elsewhere?"

"As in from the hospital, Dr. Kiser?" How easily she slipped back into formality.

"I'm not in a position to suggest that the hospital will be able to contribute anything. We're overextended at the moment and we have some extremely pressing improvements to make in crucial services."

She wrapped her arms around the open folder and held it to her chest.

She had held him against her—for an instant—a wonderful instant.

"The diocese is very large, Doctor, and spread very thin. We are heavily involved in mission work both here in the United States and overseas."

"Mission work here?" a surprised female member of the board said.

"Territorial boundaries don't dictate the absence of poverty and ignorance. The desperate people of the American inner city have no more hope than the downtrodden in underdeveloped countries." Briar looked suddenly weary. Her gentle mouth turned down. "I'm not here to discuss the world's troubles. I can't solve them. I can carry out my mission at the Ocean Medical Center to the best of my ability. I'm asking you to at least consider that people who feel lost and panicky and who can gain strength from their faith be given an opportunity to do so in a place that's welcoming and restful."

"I repeat," Dominic said after a moment had elapsed. "Can you expect assistance from your organization?"

The flare of her nostrils told him she found his cool rationality unsettling. "No. I don't think I can expect anything. I'm on my own in this. They have given me their blessing on attempting to raise the money."

"Generous of them," Dominic said. He wasn't making a friend here. In fact, he might be in the process of losing much more than a friend.

"I have copies of my proposal here." Even at a distance he noted the slight tremor in her hands as she pulled a sheaf of stapled papers from the folder. "May I leave them with you, please? I was going to raise another... Oh, it can wait. May I hope to hear some formal decision from you this time?"

The board members murmured unintelligibly.

"Could I answer any more questions that might help your deliberations?" Briar asked.

"Are you sure you may not be able to hope for substantial help from elsewhere?" Dominic heard his own voice with almost detached interest.

Her lips parted, and her brow puckered. Then the expression cleared to be replaced by hurt that quickly died into impassivity. "Would you perhaps have some information I don't have, Dr. Kiser?" she said. "Could I hope you've heard of some mystery benefactor headed in my direction?"

He almost told her that sarcasm didn't suit her. "No, Reverend. Not so far, anyway. But we never know, do we?"

"I don't suppose so. May I leave my proposals—since we can't count on angels?"

"Oh, you may leave them," he said.

"Good," Lambert boomed. "Lunch, thank God."

"I'm sure God appreciates your thanks," Briar said serenely. She rose from her chair and began arranging copies of her proposal on the table.

Members filed from the room, showing more animation than they had all morning.

"Will you join me, Dominic?" Barney asked. "It's pretty grim out, but I thought I'd head to Cutters. I like eating by the bay on a gray day."

"So do I. But I'll probably have to pass. If I can make it I will, but don't hold lunch for me."

Barney left, and Briar made to follow him out.

"Briar." Dominic skirted the table and cut her off from the door. "Don't run off."

"I need to change and get to work."

"Why not go to work the way you are? You look sensational." He wanted to move in, to touch her, but she was capable of bolting under the best of circumstances. These were probably the worst. "I think anyone looking at you today would be bound to feel a hundred percent better."

Color rose in her creamy cheeks. "What a nice thing to say. Thank you."

"Always polite, aren't you, Reverend?"

"I try."

"Why haven't you returned any of my calls for the last two days."

She frowned. "What calls?"

"The calls I made to your answering machine."

"Oh. I don't always get those."

He folded his arms. "Would you have called me if you had got my message?"

Briar tucked an errant curl behind her ear. "I don't know. Will you excuse me?"

"No."

"You don't have to. I'm leaving anyway."

"How come you've been making sure I didn't run into you on the unit?"

"You don't know I've done that."

Fencing with women was a new experience. Usually he called the shots. "Can you honestly say you haven't timed your visits with August or any of my other patients to coincide with my being in surgery?"

The fiery color swept into her face afresh. "No," she said very quietly. "No, I can't. Please excuse me."

"Damn it all." He stood aside. "I don't get any of this. If I had to guess, I'd say you were as affected as I was the other evening."

And he wasn't guessing when he thought he saw a brilliant sheen spring into her eyes. She said, "I was very affected."

"I'm sorry Briar." He went to touch her but she stepped away. "Look. Can we start this over?"

"There isn't anything to start over." Her voice broke.

This was killing him. "God," he said through gritted teeth. Then, "Sorry. Oh, I don't know what's happening here, but I do know I'd like to count you as a friend." He couldn't believe he was having this conversation. No one else would believe he was. A small thought flashed infuriatingly: *May would love every second.*

"I'm very happy to be your friend." Her next swallow was huge. Tears welled along her lids.

"Briar, I'm *sorry.* I've made you unhappy. I don't want to do that."

"It's not your problem."

It was, it most definitely was.

"What you said just now, about funds from somewhere—or someone," she said. "You meant August, didn't you?"

He narrowed his eyes.

"You were letting me know that as long as there's any question of August choosing to give some money to the chapel you won't recommend that the hospital underwrite anything."

"The thought about August did cross my mind."

"You're a very honest man. I love—I like that about you."

He worked the muscles in his jaw. "Ah, Briar, you really know how to make a man feel like a heel."

"You aren't a heel. You're very special—incredibly special." She smiled, and the tears came perilously close to overflowing.

"Don't cry," he murmured. "Please don't cry."

"I'm not going to." Her chin went up and she used the folder as a shield again.

"What you almost asked in there…the other thing. Was it about money for the children's Easter party?"

"Don't concern yourself—"

"I'll mention it to the committee for you, okay?"

She avoided his eyes. "Thank you."

Any toughness this lady pretended was pure fiction. Dominic never remembered feeling the way she made him feel—raw inside—and protective. "Would it help if I held you?"

Her small cry shocked him to his toes. "No!"

"I'm so sorry about the other evening. I overstepped the mark. I—"

"It was nothing," she said, sounding strained. "Forget it. I'm a little upset now. About the chapel. I'll be okay."

She ducked under his outstretched arm.

"Briar! Don't go!"

"Don't give the chapel another thought. I really do have some other ideas. I'll come back to the committee if I need to."

"Briar!"

She shot from sight.

Dominic hurried into the anteroom where the recording secretary pretended to be engrossed over a filing cabinet.

She raised her head as he drew level. "What time will you be reconvening, sir? Mr. Barron didn't say."

"Never would be too soon," he said through clenched teeth and strode into the corridor—in time to see a flash of yellow slip through closing elevator doors.

"A setback," he said grimly to himself. "Probably a terminal one." And probably a lucky break.

IF HE WAS FORTUNATE, he might get five hours rest before going back into surgery.

Dominic went into the on-call sleeping quarters to which he'd been assigned for the remainder of the night. Even in darkness he could make out a bundled shape in one of the two beds. Instead of flipping on a lamp, he went into the bathroom and turned on the dim fluorescent bar over a sink before returning to shut the door.

A distant rumble of thunder stopped him on the way to his own bed. The room's single window extended down from a flat skylight. Within seconds jagged streaks of lightning forked earthward followed quickly by more thunder.

He smiled. While he watched, rain began a splattering tattoo on the glass. Ever since he'd been a kid he'd reveled in a good thunderstorm. When they were little, he and Mike used to sit under a blanket in the corner of the attic room they shared and make up adventure stories to nature's angry sound effects.

And they'd felt so safe. . . .

Dominic averted his face and pulled his scrub shirt over his head. When his twin had really been threatened he hadn't turned to Dominic for help. And then it had been too late. The end. And that was enough time spent on useless reminiscence.

Rapidly shucking clothes down to his shorts, he returned to the bathroom to splash water over his face and use one of the toothbrush-kits provided. Within minutes he was sliding between cold sheets on the vacant narrow bed.

He settled on his back, his head cradled against his hands and watched the rain, heavier and heavier, as it slanted down the window.

Sleep ought to be automatic but he felt wide awake. He closed his eyes and tried to relax. Things had gone well in surgery today. They went well most days. This morning hadn't gone so well though, with Briar at the damned finance committee meeting.

The blaring of the phone on the table between the beds twisted his nerves. While he was in the act of reaching for the receiver, a hand emerged from the jumble of bedding piled on his roommate. Scrabbling fingers located the phone.

Dominic scooted down in his bed and pulled the covers over his head. The call wasn't likely to be for him.

Wild rattling preceded a jangling thud as the telephone was knocked to the floor.

Under the sheet, Dominic grinned. Poor wretch had probably only managed to pass out an hour or so ago. Now he was supposed to be ready to hop to attention and play the bright-eyed savior when he felt like hell.

"He—hello?"

Dominic's body leaped on alert. He lay very still.

"They need me where?" More clanking and banging followed before the sound came of the telephone being slid back onto the table. "Emergency room. Yes. A stab wound?"

He carefully arranged the covers to allow him a view of the person in the next bed. Getting out of this one might be tricky. He had a hunch that Briar Lee would be taken aback to find herself sharing sleeping quarters with the enemy.

"Oh, you've made a mistake. I'm not Dr. Willis. But…oh, dear, just a minute, I think there's someone else here now. That's probably who you want—" a rustling followed and the distinctive sound of smooth skin sliding over linen "—Excuse me." She tapped his shoulder very lightly. "Are you Dr. Willis? There's a call for you."

"No," Dominic said, muffling his voice in the sheet. "Wrong room."

"He says . . . the other person here says you've called the wrong room. Can I . . . Hello. Oh." After a short silence he heard her hang up.

Another silence followed, then the series of sounds were repeated, together with tugging, bumping noises that suggested she was settling in again. Then all became quiet.

Dominic's nose itched. He wrinkled it. She mustn't find out he was the man in the next bed. Not that a sneeze could possibly give away his identity. He did sneeze; loudly. Then he sneezed again and held his breath.

Briar didn't ask God to bless him.

These days he rarely decided he ought to crash at the hospital rather than go home. Only the decision that he simply couldn't get anywhere near enough sleep otherwise made him stay.

How often did Briar sleep here?

She hadn't seemed surprised that a man was in the room.

Neither had she sounded particularly uncomfortable.

He frowned and edged higher on his pillow until he had a clear view of the shadowy form separated from him by a scant foot or so.

Why wasn't she uncomfortable at the thought of sleeping in a room with a strange male?

She ought to be.

Lightning pierced the room, sending a shaft of brightness over Briar. She lay on her back, arms stretched upward beside her head. Her hair was spread in a wild tangle over the pillow and thin pale-colored shoulder straps disappeared under the sheet.

The light snuffed. Thunder rolled again, and rolled and rolled.

Idiot woman. This was one more example of her complete disregard for personal safety. Here she was, half-naked and sleeping in an unlocked room with any jerk who happened to wander in.

She probably thought a medical degree rendered men above weaknesses of the flesh. Hah!

He had no real means of knowing what she was wearing. His imagination was responsible for putting her in skimpy silk underwear...flesh-toned perhaps, and lace-trimmed. One of those bras that barely skimmed the nipples and panties apparently constructed of satin strings and lacy triangles.

Good lord, his mind must be reentering adolescence.

His mind was perfectly normal and healthy. He needed female companionship, and soon.

He turned over. And turned back. He wanted Briar Lee.

Dominic shoved the pillow against the head of the bed and sat up. A voyeur he wasn't. A saint, he also wasn't.

The miserable bathroom strip light he'd failed to turn off created a vaguely blue wash.

Her straps were probably white. Marvelous hair. Thick and soft. He knew it was soft from the other night when he'd slipped his fingers through it...and brushed his lips over her brow, her cheek...her mouth.

She muttered something.

Dominic inclined his head. She shifted restlessly on the pillow. "Out," she said clearly.

Carefully, he leaned to rest a forearm on the nightstand. Mumbling, she wriggled and settled on her side...facing him. If she opened her eyes she'd see him peering at her.

Although she was deeply asleep, her lashes moved against her cheek. Thick, dark lashes on a smoothly rounded cheek.

His gaze flicked lower, to where the sheet had been firmly anchored—before she turned over. His imagination had been pretty accurate. Lace. Very little lace that covered very little of the lady's full breasts. His smile fixed. The chaplain was all woman under those sweats, or the prissy white blouse, the yellow suit, or whatever else she chose to hide behind. *Not the kind of woman people take a second look at.* In a pig's eye unless every male she passed was legally blind.

"Hold on," she said suddenly. "No... No! Don't do it!"

Concerned, Dominic swung to sit on the edge of the bed. "Briar," he whispered. "Briar, honey, it's okay. Nobody's doing anything."

"Yes he is, the fool!" She shot to a sitting position, swayed and shook her head. "Men! They always have to push it."

He threw off the covers and crossed the space between them in one stride. "It's all right, honey. Shh. Shh." Gripping Briar's shoulders, he sat beside her.

Her scream jarred every tooth in his head, every bone in his body.

Small fists pummeling his chest brought his hands up to cover hers in self-defense. "Briar! Hey! What's with you? It's me, Dominic."

"I... Dominic?" Clearly disoriented, she tossed back her hair and stared at him. "What are you doing here?"

"Trying to sleep."

"Trying to sleep?" Her voice skated up to a squeak. She clamped her hands over her ears.

"Not very likely with you screaming at some mythical mad man."

She breathed in deeply with the predictable result that her breasts, already pressed together by her raised elbows, threatened to entirely escape the wisp of a bra.

He probably ought to hold her until she was fully awake...

"Safe on third," she said in a small, wistful voice.

Some people woke up slower than others. "Briar," he said softly. "It's all right. You're safe right here."

Looking at him, apparently lucid at last, she slowly let her arms fall and gave him a fey smile. "They all want to be Lou Brock, don't they?" Her eyes snapped wide open. "Oh, dear. Oh, my goodness. Oh, dear."

Dominic almost laughed. Instead, he smiled gently and gathered her unresisting body against him. "I get it," he said. "You were playing baseball in your sleep. I thought you were having a nightmare."

"I was," she said against his shoulder. Her fists were between them again but still he felt the erotic combination of silken breasts and fine lace pressed to his chest.

"What kind of nightmare?" He encouraged her, amazed she hadn't yet resumed fighting him off.

"Bases loaded. One out. Pop fly to left field. Caught. Two out." She sighed. "It was the Mariners. Bottom of the ninth and one run behind. And the player on third tried to steal home and didn't make it!"

Dominic began to laugh. "Oh, I see."

"We lost!"

"Terrible." And any second now something terrible would happen right here when Briar realized her mostly nude body was layered against his mostly nude body. "You'd better get some sleep."

"Mmm." Rather than lie down, she wrapped her arms around his neck and rested her head on his shoulder. "Mmm."

He stiffened. She was falling asleep again. Right where she was. Right in his arms!

For one crazed instant he considered slipping beneath her sheets and wrapping her pliant body into the curve of his own. The idea was quickly quelled.

Very gently he disentangled her hands from behind his neck, settled her back on the pillows and began to pull up her covers. He now had an unimpeded view of a slender ribcage, a small waist and softly flared hips. Her panties did barely skim her navel and rise high at the sides but they were otherwise demurely cut of simple cotton.

"What do you think you're doing, Dominic Kiser?"

He dropped the covers and stared into wide open, very awake eyes. "Hi."

Gathering the sheets and blankets up to her neck, Briar stared at him with undisguised horror.

"I was—" He pointed to the other bed, suddenly acutely aware that all he wore were very brief shorts. "I was, er, trying to sleep. You had a nightmare."

She tried to shrink farther away. "I don't know what you're talking about. I never have nightmares."

"About baseball." He spread his arms and saw her eyes shift quickly to the general area of his lower torso and speedily back to his face. "I swear it."

"Whatever you say."

Great. Now she thought he was Jack-the-Ripper. "Briar, listen to me. I came in here about an hour ago. It's too late for me to go home and get a good night's sleep before surgery, so I decided to stay. This is the room I was assigned. I had no idea you were the body in the other bed until you started yelling about people stealing bases, or whatever."

"I did that?"

"You did that."

"Oh, dear."

"You say that a lot."

"Oh, dear."

He smiled, sat on his bed and yanked the spread over strategic points. "Briar, how often do you crash in a resident's on-call room?"

"Now and then. Once a week max."

Disbelieving, he shook his head. "That means that once a week you sack out—pretty much naked—in a room with a variety of men you don't know."

"It does *not*."

"Oh, yes it does."

"For your information. They always give me a room of my own."

"Tonight they said I could sleep here."

"They made a mistake."

Patience was paramount. "It took you a long time to be surprised that there was someone else in the room."

"Well . . . It has happened before. Once or twice. The person has always slept and left without saying a word."

"You've been lucky. You probably didn't have nightmares or anything. Tonight you did and I could have been some other man. You were lucky it was me."

She laughed. "My, what a big ego you have."

"You know what I mean. I'm not someone you have to worry about."

For a few seconds she was quiet. Then she said. "Are you sure of that?"

Dominic got back into bed, punched his pillow and settled down once more.

"I asked if I can be sure I don't have to worry about you?"

"You can be sure, Reverend."

Her giggle was silver and not at all chaplain-like. "I only have your word for that. I woke up just now with you looming over me wearing nothing but part of your underwear, a very small part and . . . well . . . Oh, dear. I must be overtired. I don't usually say things like this."

"Go to sleep."

"Perhaps we shouldn't try to sleep in the same room." She sounded her old serious self again. "It really is inappropriate."

"Go to sleep." Even though he doubted he would.

"August's old-fashioned, you know."

"Yes, I know that."

"For all his shocking comments, he's quite straight-laced."

"Is there some significance to this line of conversation?"

More rustling. More snuggling sounds from a body made to be held.

"Briar? What are you implying?"

"Ohh, I just wondered what August would think of you sneaking up on me in the middle of the night. Particularly since I ended up being here so late because he needed a little company."

Dominic rolled toward Briar and propped his head on a fist. "Is this some sort of threat? Are you planning to see if you can use your own carelessness to make a point with August—one of those points he was talking about when he proposed his *Quest for the Butterfly Bounty?*"

"Never crossed my mind. Do you think the finance committee will give serious thought to my request for chapel funds?"

"This morning you said you had other possible sources to tap."

"I lied."

"Reverend!"

"Will you at least think about it, Dominic? I do believe it's very important."

He let out a long sigh. "I'll think about it."

"Oh, thank you!"

"Only think about it, Briar. I can't promise anything."

"You'll do your best. I know you will." Her smile was almost audible. "You said you wanted to be my friend. You are, Dominic. You're a very special friend. Promise me you'll let me know if there's something I can do for you?"

Squeezing his eyes tightly shut, he willed away the heavy heat in his body. "I'll do that."

"You probably don't think I could ever do anything worthwhile for you, but I'll just bet I'll be able to one day."

"I hope you're right." And he certainly intended to hope that day wasn't long in coming.

Chapter Nine

Blueberry pancakes. Briar could taste them, smell them. She deserved a splurge and A.Jays made the best blueberry corn pancakes she ever remembered tasting. Suggesting she and her sister-in-law meet there had been an inspiration.

Sprinting around the corner to 1st Avenue, she made a dash for the restaurant. She hated being late and in a minute or so she would be. Before she could reach for the handle, the door swung open and Sandra, petite, blond and smiling, walked out to wrap Briar in an enthusiastic hug.

"I'm sorry," Briar said, disentangling herself. "I didn't mean to keep you waiting."

"You haven't. I got here early." Sandra brandished a large paper sack. "A.Jays' world-famous cinnamon rolls and two large lattes. I thought we could walk down to Myrtle Edwards park and sit by the water. The fresh air would do both of us good."

Briar contrived to appear delighted. "Great idea." So much for blueberry pancakes.

Sandra, springy and fresh in a floral cotton dress and sensible sport shoes, set off at a brisk pace down Clay Street toward the bay. "John said I'd have to pin you down and he was right."

"John picks on me," Briar grumbled, enjoying the stiff warm wind that swept up the hill to meet them. "He was always a pushy kid and he hasn't changed."

"Your brother is the most wonderful man I know," Sandra said, her eyes screwed up against the sunlight. "And he cares about you. You said you'd be by to visit...the weekend before last was it?"

Briar scowled guiltily. "I'm sorry. The days get away from me."

"You're too much alone. But that's going to change, right?"

Briar raised her brows and said nothing. She had to run to keep up.

"I wish your folks were around. These are such exciting times and it would be wonderful if you and John could share them with your parents."

"Mom is still living, remember," Briar said noncommittally. "We talk every few months." Their mother had remarried ten years ago and relocated in New England. The threads of family were still there, but very tenuous.

They reached Western Avenue and paused for traffic. On both sides of the road, lines of men hoping for casual employment waited for prospective employers to check in with the Millionaire's Club located on a corner.

A chance came and Briar held Sandra's elbow while they crossed the street. "They always look healthy to me," Sandra whispered of the motley collection of men. "And strong. I can never understand why they don't already have jobs."

"Lots of reasons," Briar responded. "Deckhands from boats that have laid men off for a trip. People passing through town who need money to make the next leg of a journey. Some are just trying to get back on their feet after some sort of personal disaster. But they're all trying to do it the right way. They're prepared to work for it."

All the words sounded good and Briar spared a smile at several of the men as she and Sandra passed, but she still had an uncomfortable feeling that she should be able to do more.

After carefully crossing railroad tracks, they entered Myrtle Edwards Park. The grass was deep, emerald green, freshly mowed and sweet smelling. Here and there, the limbs of cherry trees shivered under their pretty burden of pink blossoms. Sandra promptly climbed up one side of a rise and thudded down out of sight toward the water. Briar followed, catching up on a narrow band of dark, drift-wood-strewn beach.

Sandra settled herself on a worm-eaten log and lifted her face to the sky. "Heavenly. Wouldn't it be great if we never had to work. We could come down here and sit all the time."

"And starve," Briar said pragmatically. "There's the little matter of needing to work to eat."

"You'd work anyway," Sandra said, grinning. "You wouldn't last five minutes as a lady of leisure."

"Maybe I'd like to try just once."

Sandra waggled her head. "Sit down. I've got some-thing to show you." From her voluminous shoulder bag she produced a small paper sack and carefully withdrew its contents. "You are still planning the Easter party for the children?"

She was doing her best with very little help. "I intend to find a way to do it, yes. What's that?" Briar sat down and leaned closer to Sandra.

"Do you think some of the children would like these?" She held aloft a papier-maché egg painted in brilliant, shiny colors and dotted with bright, glued-on beads. Gold rib-bon ran around its length and Sandra pulled the egg apart there. "See? I put a little chick and some jelly beans in this one. Some could have bunnies or little lambs. What do you think?"

"I think they're beautiful," Briar said, feeling a warm rush of happiness. "It looks like one of those glamorous Fabergé eggs. You made it?"

Sandra nodded, beaming. "Yes. I like doing it."

"I know the children would love them."

"Then I'll make a bunch." Sandra popped the egg away again. "Let's eat."

They sat companionably, shoulder to shoulder, their shoes making holes in the damp sand and ate huge cinnamon rolls that were still slightly warm. Gulls wheeled overhead, and made frequent passes hoping for handouts.

"So," Sandra said around a bite of sweet, tender roll. "Tell me all about him."

Briar choked.

"You all right?" For a small woman, her sister-in-law packed a mean thwack to the back. "Drink some coffee."

Briar did as she was told and her coughing subsided. Tears blurred her vision.

"He's the only reason I haven't bugged you earlier, you know." Sandra's gray eyes sparkled. Her oval face glowed with health. "John wanted me to call and make a fuss about you ignoring us but I told him it was a good sign because it must mean you're very busy."

Briar took another bite and chewed thoughtfully. "I'm not sure I follow you." But she was afraid she just might.

"Don't be coy with me. This is Sandra. Remember me? Your best friend and confidante, the one you helped through the dark days of convincing John he'd lose the best thing that ever happened to him if he lost me?"

"Oh, you do dramatize things. He didn't need convincing. A little nudge was all that was necessary."

"Well, anyway, you helped me and now I want you to know that I'm just waiting to help you. Tell me all about him, Briar."

This was John's fault. "Who?" she asked feeling contrary.

"Your new man, of course!"

"Who was the old one?"

Sandra laughed gaily and nudged Briar. "You can be so funny sometimes. You know perfectly well I'm talking about this handsome surgeon of yours. The one who's swept you off your feet so you forget all about the family that worries about you."

"John's lost his mind."

"Tell me about the man." Sandra bent to pick up a flat rock. She stood up and flipped it at the water. The rock skipped once, twice and sank in a spreading collar of rings.

"Come on, come on. Cut the shy bit. I want all the scuttlebutt."

Briar crossed her legs and hugged her knees. "I'll assume you're talking about Dr. Dominic Kiser." Of the unforgettable face and marvelous body who had stood over her the night before last wearing nothing but a virtual Band-Aid that did little to conceal his unquestionably considerable assets. She blushed.

"Uh huh." Sandra tossed a leg over the log and sat astride. "I see we both have the same man in mind. How far has this gone, Briar?"

"It hasn't," Briar protested hotly. "There isn't anything to go anywhere. I barely know the man." She'd known him barely, too—almost barely. Shifting, she looked away. Dominic had held her close and she'd been wearing only an abbreviated apology for a bra. He hadn't been wearing anything—not where their bodies touched.

"Aren't you protesting rather a lot?" Sandra asked evenly.

"If you knew Dominic Kiser you'd understand how ridiculous this is. John just seems to think that because I'm his sister, I'm good enough for anyone—"

"You are."

"Be quiet and listen. Dominic is a world-renowned cardiac surgeon. Men like that don't bother with mousy little chaplains."

"You aren't mousy."

Briar thought a moment. "He's really a very special man. Kind, although he seems to want to do anything rather than have too many people know it."

"Some people are like that. Humble, I suppose you'd call it."

"Hm. Scared is more like it. He'd shrivel up if he thought someone could get too far inside the shell he's built around him."

"Tough to deal with."

"Yes. Tough. He's got a reputation for being very hard on junior staff. They're terrified of him. That's not a nice way to be."

"Not nice at all."

"But people don't understand him." He'd stroked her shoulders so softly, and her hair. The hair on his chest had been thick but smooth against her cheek. And he'd smelled of that clean linen scent she associated with him. "He's really so gentle. So caring. That's why he's brusque with people, I just know it is."

"But he's not brusque with you."

"Not usually." She thought about him, the way his dark eyes looked black, warm black or deep, speculative black when he looked at her. "He's special, Sandra. Special people are often misunderstood."

"But you don't misunderstand him."

"I don't think so. I'd like to understand him very well." She hadn't slept last night trying to do just that, to understand Dominic better. "You should see him with August Hill. August is a very elderly cardiac patient. He's failing but he's in such good spirits most of the time. Actually he's a good-natured tyrant who likes to keep us all hopping. Dominic has more patience with that man than you could ever imagine."

"Oh, I could imagine."

"How?" Briar looked sharply at Sandra. "You don't know Dominic—or August."

"Listening to you I feel as if I do. You're interested in Dominic, aren't you?"

She remembered the cinnamon roll and halfheartedly nibbled at it, picking out raisins with her teeth. "Okay." There was no point pretending. "If things were different. If I was fascinating and highly intelligent and could make wonderfully magnetic conversation, I'd really enjoy being more than an acquaintance of Dominic's."

"But he's oblivious as far as you're concerned?"

Briar gave Sandra a sidelong glance. "Not exactly."

"What does that mean?"

"Oh, I don't know. He seems...concerned about me for some reason. I think he's decided I'm in need of someone to look after me."

"Oh, really." Sandra had finished her roll. She stuffed her empty cup into the sack and set it on the sand. "Why do you suppose he thinks you need looking after? And why would he appoint himself for the job?"

"I didn't say he had."

"Hasn't he?"

Briar wove her head from side to side. "In a way." Bending the truth was not something she approved of. "Yes, he has. And it's really charming of him because he doesn't have to bother with someone like me."

"*Don't* do that! Don't put yourself down. Oh, this is so exciting. I always knew it would just be a matter of time before someone who was wonderful and insightful enough realized what a prize you are."

Briar hooked a leg to the other side of the log and faced Sandra. "What on earth are you talking about? Dominic likes me. Yes, I think he does. And he worries a bit about my welfare. Don't try making a grand event out of it, please."

"You'll make a lovely wife and mother, Briar."

Her heart almost stopped. "Don't be ridiculous. Oh, I'm glad Dominic can't hear this conversation. He'd either run or die of laughter on the spot."

"I doubt it," Sandra said sagely. "How do you feel when he kisses you?"

"What?" Briar could scarcely breathe.

Sandra grimaced. "When he kisses you. How do you feel?"

"He's only..." She swallowed and shut her mouth firmly.

Sandra's grin held intense satisfaction. "He's only what, Briar?"

"Kissed me once," she said in a rush. "And that was just a sort of accidental thing."

"I see. Didn't you like it with him.?"

"With him? You make it sound as if I had lots of men's kisses to compare the event with."

"Did you like it?"

"I loved it." Briar buried her face in her hands. The wind swept her hair and fanned her burning ears.

"Briar—"

"Don't say anything. There are things you don't know about me. No one does. I loved it when Dominic kissed me. But then I ruined it, Sandy. And now I don't suppose he'll ever try it again." Even though he had held her so gently, and so close a couple of nights ago.

"How come you think you ruined it?" Sandy squeezed Briar's shoulder carefully and shook her a little. "Tell me about it."

"It embarrasses me."

"Try."

Briar raised her face. "It was the first time I've really been kissed by a man. There were boys when I was a teenager. But...well, I'm not exactly practiced in the fine art of kissing." Although she had been starting to get the hang of it quite nicely before she made an idiot of herself and bolted.

Muscles about Sandy's mouth slowly slackened. "Good grief. I hadn't really thought about it, but I guess I should have."

Briar wrinkled her nose. "So you see why this is all irrelevant anyway? Can you imagine a worldly thirty-six-year-old man trying to cope with a thirty-year-old *virgin*, for goodness sake?"

She didn't need insight to see that Sandy didn't know what to say.

"Oh, this is silly. I've got a busy career that takes up all my time. I never did intend to get involved with anyone. Not really. Don't give it another thought. I won't be wasting my time on it."

"No," Sandra said blankly.

"It's all moot anyway. Even if I was interested, he'd never seriously take a second look at a dowdy, unexciting thing like me." She couldn't read Sandra's expression. "I really should think about getting to the hospital, but this has been fun. You're a dear to think about the children's party."

"You can't go yet." Sandra smiled slowly. "Soon, but not yet. Here comes someone else to meet you."

Briar craned around in time to look up into John's face. "How did you know we'd be here?"

"Guess." He bent to kiss Sandra, dropped into a crouch and gathered her into a tight hug. "How're you doing, sweetheart?"

Briar studied her hands and smiled. She'd always be grateful her brother had found someone so special to love.

"We set you up," John said when he'd arranged himself behind Sandra on the log and wrapped his arms around her waist. "We decided we wanted somewhere private to talk to you."

"Oh." They'd evidently come up with a plan to try pursuing their Dominic Kiser myth into reality. "Sandra and I already talked."

"You did." He kissed his wife's ear and she snuggled closer to him.

"Not about us, John," Sandra said. "We've been talking about Briar and Dr. Kiser."

"And there isn't anything to talk about," Briar said, feeling like an old record.

"Obviously Briar is very interested in him and he's very interested in her. We're just going to have to be patient because she won't be hurried."

"Why wait if something's right?" John said.

Exasperated, Briar puffed up her cheeks. "Was there something else you wanted to talk to me about? Something interesting, I hope?"

"Yes." The answer came in unison. John added, "We're going to have a baby!"

"Oh, you two!" Briar did her best to hug them both. "It's lovely, lovely. Oh, I'm so excited. A baby!"

Sandra turned her face to John and he kissed her with enough tenderness to bring tears to Briar's eyes. Darn it. These days her tears never seemed too far from the surface.

Half an hour later she boarded a bus headed for the hospital. John and Sandra, arms around each other, waved her off. They looked so happy.

The bus gathered speed and she settled back in her seat. How perfect. Happily married and expecting a first baby they both wanted. Briar hugged her middle. There was, deep inside her, a teeny flickering of some yearning, a sad yearning.

Jealousy?

No. She wasn't jealous of the two people she loved most in the world, and would anticipate the birth of a little niece or nephew with incredible excitement. But she was, after all, human. Once she'd been sure marriage and parenthood weren't for her. The church, her work, were supposed to fill the place of a family.

And they did.

Rain began to fall lightly. People on the sidewalks hurried for shelter. Seattleites, famous for their optimism, invariably discarded their coats at the first hint of sunshine.

Dominic's children would probably be dark-haired and dark-eyed, like him. If he ever married and had a family... There was something so moving about the sight of a strong man holding his own helpless baby—about the love in the father's eyes and the unquestioning trust in those of the child.

A huge, suffocating lump formed in Briar's throat. She longed, so overwhelmingly strongly that her limbs felt weak, to see Dominic cradling his child. And she wanted that child to be hers... wanted Dominic to be hers, too.

"I'M GLAD YOU ENJOYED IT. If you like, I'll have one of the nurses bring you up again on Thursday—if you're still here."

"I'll still be here. Thank you."

Briar smiled as the young man, an accident victim on the road to recovery, was pushed from the chapel. She was still surprised when the young, particularly those of the Harley-Davidson and leather-all-over variety, attended services in the chapel and showed signs of wanting to at least explore spiritual growth.

"Hello. Is it all right if I come in?"

At the sound of Dominic's voice, Briar's legs did their now familiar flesh-to-jelly act. She held the end of a pew for support. "Hello yourself, Dominic. Of course you can come in. Anyone's welcome here."

"Ah, shucks. And I thought I might be more welcome than some."

"I didn't say you weren't," she said under her breath.

"I'll take that as encouragement," Dominic said heartily, giving her fair warning that he was possessed of very acute hearing.

Briar waited for him to continue, when he didn't she eyed him quizzically before returning to the pulpit and reassembling her sermon notes.

"I've got a couple of hours break and I feel like heading out of here," he said finally. "Do you suppose I could persuade you to go somewhere for a drink? If you drink, that is."

She hesitated. "No." But she wanted to be with him. She wanted to look at him, to listen to him . . . to touch him.

"Ahh." Dominic tilted back his head. "And you probably don't go with boys who do, huh?"

"I beg your pardon?"

"Nothing. Would you come anyway? It's still raining, but we could go someplace down by the water where we can see the bay. If you like looking at the bay in the rain, that is."

He couldn't possible guess how much she'd like looking at the bay in the rain . . . with him. "Yes, I do. I thought I was the only one. I do have to be back here at five, though, so maybe it won't work—"

"It'll work. I'll bring you back in plenty of time."

She could scarcely contain a great big grin. Her insides glowed . . . and her outsides. "It's a deal." In seconds she finished stacking her notes and placed her Bible on top.

Dominic waited until she picked up her purse, then looped an arm across her shoulders as comfortably as if their relationship to this point hadn't been a series of mini-disasters. Briar smiled to herself as he walked her from the chapel. She could really get to like this.

They drove to the waterfront and went to a small, second-floor café in a warehouse on one of the piers converted for shops and restaurants.

"This is great," Dominic said when they were seated by a window overlooking the steely, wind-whipped waters of Elliott Bay. "And you like it, too? We've got even more in common than I thought."

"*Even* more?" Briar eyed him quizzically. "Why don't you tell me what we already had. We'll compare your list with mine and see if we agree."

He put his hand on top of hers on the table and leaned closer. "I think we should wait. It'll be so much more fun to identify each item as it crops up."

Briar smiled and leaned away as the waiter set cups of coffee in front of them. She was incredibly aware of Dominic's hand pressing hers.

"I've tried not to think about you, but I expect you guessed that." His long strong fingers rubbed the tendons in her wrist.

Briar swallowed. "It never really crossed my mind that you thought about me at all." But in many quiet moments she'd hoped.

Dominic picked up his coffee and drank. He regarded her thoughtfully and set the cup down again. "Sometimes I think you're the most puzzling woman I ever met. All of the time, actually. You're very special."

"No, I'm not." Her heart thumped and thumped.

"I won't argue. Just take my word for it. Do you suppose we could try getting to know each other? Really know each other?"

She gulped coffee. Her eyes smarted from the steam.

"Briar, look at me. I don't play games with anyone, least of all someone like you."

"Like me."

"You know what I'm saying."

"Yes."

"Does that mean we can try to become friends? Good friends?"

"Perhaps." How could she be expected to know exactly how to behave with him, with this?

He turned her hand over, drew it to his lips and pressed a kiss into the palm. "That's a start." Folding her fingers over the place he'd kissed, he continued to hold on. "What made a lovely woman decide to become a minister?"

The question wasn't new, only new coming from a man like Dominic Kiser. And she wished, perhaps childishly, that he hadn't chosen now to ask.

"Briar?" He watched her face closely. "Why?"

She looked steadily back at him. "Why do you think?"

Dominic pushed his cup back and forth in its saucer. "I don't know." His mouth jerked suddenly downward. "This isn't meant to be...confrontational, I guess. But is it power? Does it make you feel powerful to tell people how to live their lives?"

From someone else the question might have been annoying. Dominic wasn't interested in annoying her. He really wanted to find an answer. "I don't feel powerful," she told him. "Most of the time I feel pretty helpless."

"Because there's really nothing you can do about any of it?"

"It?"

"Yes. *It.* The stuff that goes wrong in people's lives." He glanced at the window where rain beat against steamy panes. "You feel helpless because you can't change a thing for anyone."

Considering her response, Briar slowly drank some of her own rapidly cooling coffee. "No. That's not the reason. I feel helpless because I can't force people to be optimistic. I can't force them to give up their fears." Watching the rain herself, she told him: "Steps taken in faith—regardless of what you believe in—are big leaps. They're huge, Dominic. Great big tough steps taken by weak little people who are naturally afraid. I ask people to take those steps and they usually balk. That makes me feel helpless."

"You tell people everything will be okay if they can only believe in something they not only can't see, but that has never even shown them evidence of its existence. What gives you the right to ask anyone to do that?"

She drew in a breath, closed her eyes. "I've never said faith would make everything okay. I don't have the right to make statements like that."

"No," Dominic said softly. "You're a very bright lady, Briar. Perhaps the reason you feel insecure about what you do is because you don't really believe it either."

Her eyes snapped open. "Don't ever tell me what I believe!"

His sad smile hurt Briar. "We don't like that, do we—we strong people? Now you know how I feel when you try probing inside my head." There was no antagonism in his voice.

Briar stared at him. "It was your heart that interested me," she said very quietly. "I'm sorry if I intruded where I wasn't wanted. I'll try not to repeat the mistake."

"You'll try. But you won't promise. That's part of your job description, I suppose. Never give up on the sinners? Isn't that the way it goes."

Disillusionment. Why hadn't she realized before what was eating this man? "Did you ask me to come here just to say these things to me?" He wasn't ready to listen to her point of view and might never be.

Leaning back in his chair, Dominic checked his watch. "If there's one thing I never want to do with you, it's argue. What I said just now—about wanting to spend time with you—was for real." Looking up at Briar, he smiled his wonderful, lazy smile. "You do have green eyes."

Briar caught her bottom lip in her teeth. Only this man had ever caused the breathlessness, the sense of time suspension that she felt now. "Thank you."

He held her gaze. "You're more than welcome. I suppose I'd better get you back to the hospital. Not that I want to."

"I..." If she didn't hide her hands he'd know she was shaking. "You're right. We should get back."

They made the return trip almost in silence. Waves of confusion swept through Briar. He confused her. When they turned in at the hospital gates she was almost grateful, but not quite. More strongly she felt a longing not to have to leave him.

Dominic pulled up outside the lobby and got out of the car. He walked around to open her door. "Would you consider letting me pick you up later? We could go to a movie—"

"I can't." She let him help her out. "I've got so much to do and I may have to come back here this evening."

"I see." Muscles in his lean jaw flicked. "In other words, don't push?"

"No, I didn't mean that."

"It's okay." His smile was the old cool tilt of the lips. "Have a good rest of the day."

"Thank you," she said faintly.

Dominic turned and strode back toward the driver's side of the car.

He'd told her he liked her, that he wanted to spend time with her and get to know her better. And he'd asked her out—for the second time in one day.

And she'd blown it—again. And she'd never get another chance for sure this time.

His back was straight, his shoulders wide with a swing that suggested dismissal.

Briar ran one of her shaky hands over her hair. She was going to cry—again.

He reached the door.

"Dominic!"

At first he didn't seem to hear. When he straightened, it was slowly. "Yes?" Even at a distance she saw the set lines of his face.

"Would you like to come to dinner tomorrow night?" He'd be amused. He'd refuse. She'd be mortified.

"What time?"

Breath rushed back into her lungs. "Seven?"

"I'll be there."

Chapter Ten

"Thank you, Sandy. Yes, I understand perfectly. No, I haven't forgotten a thing. Goodbye, Sandy." Chuckling, Briar hung up the kitchen phone.

Yarrow walked in, frowning over a bunch of red tulips. "What did Sandy want?"

"She was making sure I haven't forgotten how to set a table." Or cook a salmon, or make sure the bathroom was clean, or to play "appropriate" music, or to have wine at the desired temperature and on and on. Allowing John and Sandy to find out that Dominic was coming to dinner had probably been a mistake.

"He's going to be here—" Yarrow consulted her watch "—in half an hour."

Briar checked her own wrist. "Forty minutes."

"He'll be early."

Briar took in a breath and blew it out slowly. "I doubt it." If she hadn't already been very nervous, her support group would certainly have made sure she became so. "He's a very busy man. He'll probably be late. He might even call and say he can't make it. He'll... Of course, he isn't a rude man, so he'd apologize and so on, but—"

"Whoa!" Yarrow held up a hand. "Hold it right there. You're losing it."

"I never lose it," Briar said crossly. "What are you doing here, anyway? You left."

"And I came back. These are for the table." Yarrow brandished the tulips somewhat awkwardly. "You didn't put flowers on the table, did you?"

Briar smiled. "No. And thank you."

"I'll put them in that Waterford vase, shall I?"

"That would be wonderful." She caught Yarrow's arm as she reached to open a cupboard. "Will you stop behaving like a worried mother. I can handle a simple dinner for a friend. I'm a big girl. A lot older than you."

"Not in some ways," Yarrow said, her mouth turning down.

The ways Yarrow meant were best left unmentioned. Briar doubted this disillusioned woman had any idea just how little personal experience her mentor had had with members of the opposite sex.

Briar took the vase Yarrow handed down and filled it with water. "They'll look great," she said of the red tulips, not at all sure how great they would look with or-an-y-peach colored table linen, the only good set she owned.

"Don't let him come into the kitchen."

"Why?" Alarmed, Briar stopped in the act of opening the oven.

"It doesn't look so good without the table."

The one table in the apartment had been moved from the kitchen to the usually empty dining alcove off the living room.

Briar bent to the stove once more. "Don't worry about it. He won't come out here anyway." Red tulips, pale orange linen and dingy avocado-green carpet... Well, he was coming to eat, not to do a pictorial layout for *House Beautiful*.

The salmon was baking perfectly. "Yarrow, you said you were meeting someone."

"I'm going, I'm going. Shouldn't you get changed?"

Briar shot upright and looked down on her sea-green silk blouse—that had cost far too much—and black slacks. "I already did change."

"*That's* what you're wearing?"

Dominic had said he preferred her hair down. Briar had deliberately drawn it up into a loose, curly pile at her crown. She didn't want to seem too eager to please. "I thought this was a nice outfit."

"It's not sexy."

"It's not *supposed* to be sexy," Briar said, outraged. "I'm having someone to dinner, not planning a seduction."

Yarrow smiled broadly. "The two don't have to remain separate. You know that silver dress—"

"No! No, thank you."

"It would look good on you. You've got nice breasts, if you'd ever show 'em, and—"

"*Yarrow,*" Briar said warningly.

"And a tiny waist and small hips—" she affected an aloof air "—and the legs are terrific, considering you're short."

"Gee, thanks."

"Try on the dress." Yarrow poked the tulips.

"I'm wearing what I've got on. Thanks anyway." The silver number might reach to within four inches above Briar's knees and the bodice was tight and low. "It's a quarter to seven, Yarrow," she added pointedly.

"Yes. I'll be on my way. Should I put some music on?"

"No, thank you." Briar took the vase from Yarrow and carried it to the table. The effect was awful. If Yarrow would leave, the flowers could be quickly removed.

"Briar!"

She shot around. "Yes?"

"You've forgotten your makeup."

"Oh, Yarrow, I thought something was burning." She touched her cheek. "I've got mascara on."

"You look washed out." A lipstick was whipped from the pocket of skin-tight leather jeans. "Put some of this on."

The doorbell saved her from an assault with one of Yarrow's brain-jarring lip colors.

"He's here!" Yarrow rose to the silver-tipped toes of her Western boots. "Let him in!"

Briar felt blood drain to her feet. "Please don't shout."
What a mistake this invitation had been. What *had* she
been thinking of?

"Open the door," Yarrow whispered loudly.

The bell rang again.

"Briar, *open the door.*"

"Yes. All right." Wishing Yarrow wasn't standing,
plastered with black leather, in the middle of the room,
Briar straightened her shoulders and went to sweep open
the front door.

Dominic, dressed in a dark suit, impeccable white shirt
and red tie, smiled down at her. "Hello. Am I too early?"

He was too much, too tall, too devastatingly good-
looking...too visibly strong and sure of himself...too
everything.

"Briar?" He ducked his head questioningly. She found
the mannerism irresistible. "It was tonight you asked me to
come? You *did* ask me to come, didn't you?" He held a
vast bouquet of spring flowers.

"Oh, yes, of course I did." She stood aside. "Please
come in. You look marvelous, Dominic."

Stepping into the apartment, he laughed. "You do have
a way of making a man feel good."

Great going. "You mean I have a way of speaking first
and thinking later—too much later usually."

"Oh—" he grinned and brushed the back of a finger
lightly over her cheek "—does that mean you're taking
back the compliment?"

"No. And that's the end of that subject."

"That blouse is wonderful on you, Briar."

"Thank you."

"Our own mutual admiration society, huh?"

"I guess." Though she still couldn't understand why he
seemed to want to spend time with her.

"I've been looking forward to this evening ever since you
asked me."

A small sound caused Dominic to swivel around and
stand beside Briar. Yarrow, her mouth slightly open, stared
at him with frank admiration.

Briar cleared her throat. "This is my, er, friend, Yarrow Stalk. Yarrow, this is Dr. Dominic Kiser."

Yarrow didn't reply.

"Yarrow lives here with me," Briar added.

Dominic rested a hand on her shoulder as naturally as if they'd known each other at least a lifetime. "Hi, Yarrow. Briar's mentioned you."

Yarrow pressed her hands together. "Oh, you're perfect together. Just right. The perfect couple."

Utter, awful embarrassment flooded Briar. She shot Yarrow a warning glare, which Yarrow showed no sign of noticing.

"Briar, he's gorgeous."

Predictably, her legs turned to water. "Yarrow's just on her way out. She's got an appointment. And she's already late, aren't you?"

The dreamy expression in Yarrow's eyes didn't fade. Absently, she pushed the lipstick she still held back into a pocket. "I always knew that any man Briar cared about would really be something. This is so romantic."

Head bowed to hide what had to be a terminal blush, Briar held the door open until Yarrow finally left.

Silence in the room lasted just long enough for the ringing sound of boots to fade on the outside steps before Dominic's laughter erupted.

Briar slowly closed the door. "I'm sorry," she said in as clear a voice as she could muster. "Yarrow isn't very mature in some ways."

"She's great," Dominic said, still grinning. "I brought you these. I couldn't be sure what you'd like so I bought a few of everything."

"So pretty," Briar said. She would forget Yarrow and enjoy this. "I'll find a vase."

He didn't follow her into the kitchen, not that she really cared. When she returned and placed the fragrant flowers in the middle of the glaringly ghastly triangular coffee table he was absorbed studying her books.

"You read everything," he said without turning around.

"I never throw a book away, you mean. I don't even know what half of those are anymore." The bookshelves were also ghastly, she thought, seeing them through his eyes. Usually she never thought about such things.

"Are you sheltering that girl?"

Briar hesitated in the act of rearranging flowers. "What are you asking me?"

"The bruises still show."

So he had seen Yarrow's face when he'd dropped Briar off near the market. "She needs a safe place to be. I choose to be that for her. Is that what you mean?"

"Are you sure that's such a good idea?"

"Yes, I'm sure. I'm no martyr, but helping people who need help is a great idea. It's what you do for a living, too."

"Yeah. But we're not talking about me. Be sure you don't get yourself into trouble you can't handle."

"I won't."

He didn't appear convinced.

The music. In a flurry, Briar hurried to sit on the floor before her very basic tapedeck. "What kind of music do you like?"

"What do you have?" He came to stand behind her.

This felt so strange. "Bits of all sorts. My brother gives me all the tapes he doesn't want anymore."

"You don't buy what you like?"

A date—she'd asked *him* on a date. "There's plenty to choose from." What did he think of a woman who asked him to her home—a woman who didn't know him very well really? "I expect you'd like something classical."

"Why do you expect that?"

Glancing up into his face, his eyes, she couldn't think of a response.

Dominic dropped to one knee beside her and took the pile of tapes she held. "Play this." He handed her one and waited while she slid it into the deck. The haunting theme from *Dances with Wolves*. "Is it okay?"

"I love it."

"I'm glad you invited me tonight," he said quietly.

Briar fiddled with the empty tape case. "Ever since I did, I've been feeling like a fool." Why, oh why, did she always say the first thing that came into her head?

"Can you explain that to me?"

"Nice women don't ask men out."

"Oh, Briar, Briar." He pulled her against him, used a knuckle to tilt her face up to his. "How can someone so bright be so backward?"

"I'm not backward." She didn't try to pull away.

"No, of course not. And you're not a nice woman because you invited a man to dinner—a man who'd just dragged you off for coffee and who was making a nuisance of himself trying to see you again last night. I didn't want to let you go yesterday, Briar."

Her stomach fell, and all her insides with it.

"Briar..." He paused, narrowing his eyes. "Sometimes I get the feeling... Forget it."

"Tell me." She did draw away then, carefully, taking his hand and squeezing it lightly before letting go.

Dominic stood and pulled her up. "I think I'm going to tell you several things, but not without some of whatever smells so good under my belt.

Automatically, Briar's eyes went to the point indicated. A very flat middle rested beneath that belt. His shirt stretched smoothly over the wide chest she remembered all too clearly—without the shirt.

When she glanced up he was watching her face intently.

"Do you like salmon?"

"Very much."

"Would you like something to drink first? I bought—I've got whiskey and gin and vodka." Thanks to John who'd delivered a bag of bottles on his way home.

"Whiskey would be nice." His gaze never wavered.

Briar swallowed. "What should I put in it?"

"I'll do it. Show me the way."

She was leading him into the kitchen before she remembered Yarrow's warning. "I'm afraid this looks pretty bare." She waved a hand and toed the step stool close to the counters. "I've only got the kitchen table. I had to put it in the dining room for tonight."

"I like the view." Dominic looked out over the roofs toward Seattle Center. "Gives a whole different perspective on this part of the city."

Absorbed in climbing to kneel on the counter, Briar only grunted. With typical brotherly oblivion, John had put the bottles in a cupboard over the refrigerator—far out of Briar's reach.

"Good God! What do you think you're doing?"

She stopped, wobbled, and braced her outstretched arm on the now open cupboard. "Getting down the whiskey. It's okay, short people get used to this sort of thing." Her hand closed on the neck of the bottle.

A much larger hand settled on top of hers. "Tall people don't. You could easily fall."

His chest was layered against her back. Through the thin silk blouse she felt his warmth. With his left hand, he removed the bottle and set it on top of the refrigerator. The fingers of his right hand slipped along her arm from wrist to shoulder.

Briar's heart thudded. He could move away now if he wanted to.

Dominic didn't move away.

All she could feel or think about was his warm, muscular body so close to hers, his hand slowly chafing back and forth on her shoulder. Suddenly, he gripped her waist and lowered her to stand on the floor.

"I don't get this," he said, twisting her to stand toe to toe with him. "This feeling I get with you."

The counter pressed into her back. "Do you want ice?" she asked in a small voice.

"No. I don't want anything." He framed her face and studied her closely. "I don't want anything to drink."

"You said—"

"I've changed my mind."

"I bought wine to go with the salmon. Chardonnay."

"You don't drink."

"I bought it for you."

"Briar..."

"Yes." She couldn't look away. The panicky little feeling in her chest grew, but so did an achy longing.

"I really like you. In fact... Yeah, I really like you a lot. On one level there's not a thing I understand about what you seem to be doing to me, but you're doing it anyway."

"What's the level you don't understand?" Maybe he could help her sort out the craziness in her head...and elsewhere.

His laugh, the flash of white, white teeth, the deepened groove in his cheek, turned her mouth dry. "I'm not going to discuss this quite yet," he said. "I'd rather kiss you."

She clutched at his jacket lapels. Her chest expanded, pressing her breasts against him. He glanced down and Briar tried to put space between them but Dominic snaked his arms around her.

There was no pulling away. He was too strong. And she didn't want to pull away anymore.

"I like the way you feel, Briar. Soft. All female. Very female. I like that very much. You have a beautiful body."

If he weren't holding her she'd probably fall. Nobody had ever said such things to her before.

"I've shocked you," he said as if he could read her mind. "Maybe that's not a bad idea."

He couldn't know how confused and inadequate she felt. "Say something."

Briar released one of his lapels and slowly raised her fingers to his mouth. A firm, wide, totally male mouth. With a sense of wonder, she stroked his bottom lip...and gasped when he gently caught the tip of her finger between his teeth. He sucked lightly, watching her eyes.

Slowly, he spread his hands on her back, urging her even closer. *The first time she'd ever felt the quickening in a man's body.* Briar felt his response with a kind of amazement. Even as her heart leaped, pounding in her throat—while her natural reserve and anxiety struggled to keep her aloof from him—the heavy, surging ache in her own body carried her on.

"We lie to ourselves, don't we?" With one arm firmly around her waist, Dominic caught her hand and kissed the palm.

Briar saw his eyes close, the fierce concentration that creased his brow. "How do we do that?" Her voice was tight and hoarse.

For a moment he raised his head and studied her hand, traced the lines on her palm with his thumbnail. "We...I guess I shouldn't include you. I told myself there were no hidden agendas tonight. Dinner with an intelligent, warm, lovely woman. That's all. You not expecting anything from me. Me not expecting anything from you."

"Isn't that the way it is?" Briar asked.

He guided her fingers to his neck, to the place where thick, dark hair curled to within a fraction of his white collar. "No. Not anymore."

Briar opened her mouth to breathe. Every second with him like this was a second on the edge of something she knew almost nothing about, something that yawned ready to suck her in.

"You mix me up. Nobody else does that." His gaze flickered between her eyes, her lips. "I'm not sure..."

"What?"

Rather than respond, Dominic kept watch on her face while he stroked circles at her waist. Dipping lower, he smoothed her bottom, cupped and held her, urged her ever more firmly against him.

Briar shuddered. He had no idea this was new to her. Dominic assumed what he could only be expected to assume, that a thirty-year-old woman had played this lust game many times. She shuddered again. *Lust?*

"What are you thinking?" He fingered her hair and it began slipping from its band. His firm but careful touch outlined her features.

"I'm not sure what I'm thinking," she told him honestly.

He smiled a little, inclining his face, testing her bottom lip with his thumb. "You're a puzzle, Briar Lee."

A puzzle and a challenge? She'd been warned more than once that some men found a woman like her—a woman of God—an incredibly intoxicating challenge.

Without warning, he swooped to kiss her neck. Briar tensed, but automatically wound her fingers into his hair and held his face against her.

He made a noise, a sort of rough groan, and leaned more heavily. Their bodies accommodated each other, his pelvis tipped into her belly, her hips fitting into the cradle his spread legs offered.

There was a leisureliness about the kisses he scattered along her jaw, down her neck, into the hollow above her collarbone.

Then the pacing changed. There was purpose in the nuzzling aside of her blouse to allow his lips and tongue to find the top of her breast.

No hidden agendas. ''Dominic—''

His mouth cut her off. Enfolding her in an embrace that was both gentle and unyielding, he brought his lips to hers, so lightly, so delicately, the heat within her turned molten. Back and forth, back and forth he brushed against her sensitive flesh.

For an instant he paused, looked into her eyes.

There was no suggestion of a smile, no humor.

''Kiss me,'' he murmured. ''Really kiss me.''

Briar gasped, and held on to his neck with both hands. There was a rhythm in his body, even though he didn't move she felt a pulsing rhythmic beat. This time she was the one who pushed at him with that part of her that answered his rhythm.

His dark eyes became black. ''Kiss me,'' he whispered.

Briar passed her tongue over her lips.

Dominic closed his eyes. His features tensed, the skin drawing tight over his high cheekbones, his straight nose.

Uncertainly, Briar drove her fingertips into his shoulders, drawing herself up to rest her lips on his.

He didn't respond. Only held very still.

She could taste him. Testing, she began to move her mouth as he had, grazing lightly, barely making contact,

from side to side. *Not enough.* Incredibly wonderful but
not enough. Experimenting, she touched her tongue to the
place where his lips weren't quite closed, drew a soft, moist
line to the dip at the corner.

His breathing became faster, shallower.

Still he didn't move.

She'd seen movies. Those nibbling, chewing kisses had
always vaguely embarrassed her.

Nothing seemed to embarrass her with Dominic, not in
this moment. Cautiously, Briar drew his bottom lip between her teeth. Her eyes closed and her body seemed
boneless. Reaching even farther up, she surrounded his
neck with her arms, locking her wrists behind his head,
arching her breasts urgently against his chest.

"Yes," he murmured. "Oh, yes."

Briar moved. She nipped, exploring with her lips, her
teeth, her tongue.

Dominic wasn't motionless anymore. He took com-
mand. Everywhere he touched her, the touch was a brand:
her bottom, her waist, her ribs—spanned by his broad,
strong, chafing hands. The only hesitation was in the instant before he settled his palms on the sides of her breasts
and began a slow massage that made her sag.

His kisses became an erotic assault: One instant soft,
tantalizingly tender, the next a harsh invasion that drove her
head back under the pressure of his reaching tongue.

He shifted his hands.

Briar clutched his hair and her eyes opened. Dominic's
eyes were closed. He lapped at the tender skin inside her
mouth, rocked her face to find her ear and dart his tongue
into the sensitive folds.

He covered her breasts, kneaded their softness, rotated
in tight little circles over her nipples.

Briar sank her teeth into her bottom lip. There had never
been any sensation like this. Her nipples hardened at his
touch. There was a raw, responsive surge from that eager
flesh beneath his hands and into the deepest parts of her.

This was not something that should be happening between a couple who could only feel lust for each other.

Briar squeezed her eyes tightly shut. She wanted this, whatever it was. She wanted him. And he wanted her.

But this was not love. This violated everything she professed to believe in about physical relationships between men and women.

Dominic breathed ever harder. He kissed her mouth again and again, delving deep inside. Between them, she felt him unbuttoning her blouse. Cool air smote her skin. Then Dominic's warm fingers closed out the air. Pulling the cups of her bra beneath her breasts, he looked down at her.

Hot blood rushed into her face.

"Wonderful," Dominic said quietly. "So beautiful." With each thumb he rubbed her nipples to turgid buds. Then his mouth took over, licking, suckling.

Shaken to the core, Briar struggled. "Please stop."

A beat passed, and another. Dominic gripped her shoulders and rested his cheek against hers. "What is it? What's wrong?"

"Please." She had no words to give him the right answer.

With visible effort he straightened, his face a rigid mask that could only be designed by frustration. "Oh, hell. Hell!"

She'd thwarted him. Something he hadn't expected. Now he was angry. She began to tremble. Even locking her knees didn't stop the steady shaking.

Before she could react, Dominic passed a fleeting touch over her breasts and eased her bra back into place. He fumbled with the buttons on her blouse but wouldn't let her help him.

"Dominic—"

"Don't say anything. Not yet."

She stared at him. He was trembling, too, but she didn't pretend she thought their reasons were the same. He must be angry. Everything she'd read about these situations warned of the anger men felt if a woman led them on and then backed away.

Had she led him on?

Yes, in a way, without meaning to. "I—I'm sorry, Dominic."

"You have nothing to be sorry about." With her blouse firmly buttoned again, he addressed her hair. "This will have to be undone and put up again." The band was pulled away.

"I can do it," she managed.

Dominic grasped her rising hand and placed it on his shoulder once more.

His attempts to smooth out her hair and gather it into a bundle again were suddenly amusing. Briar began to laugh and as she laughed the trembling became a convulsive shudder.

Dominic frowned and gave up on the hair. "Look, it's okay. I won't say I don't know what came over me, because I do. But I'm sorry."

She giggled—and shook.

"I've really upset you." He looked at her appraisingly. "Really shocked you."

Not knowing what else to do, not wanting him to see the confusion that threatened to drown her, and desperately needing to hold and be held, Briar pushed her hands beneath his suit jacket and rested her cheek on his chest.

She sensed his pause before he smoothed her hair. Again and again he ran his fingers over its length. "Men can be asses, but I expect you already knew that."

Turning her face to breathe in the scent of him, she smiled and nodded.

"You could try arguing with me."

Briar shook her head, no.

"Will you believe me if I say I had no intention of letting that happen?"

She nodded.

"When I lifted you down from the counter. When I felt you like that I had to kiss you." He paused. "And I wanted to do a whole lot more. I'd be lying to you if I didn't tell you."

She held him more tightly.

"That wasn't fair, Briar. I'm basing you on my...I've led a different life from you."

Now he would say that coming tonight had been a mistake and there'd never be another time in his arms. *Tell him you wanted it, too. Tell him you want more...*

"Okay." Gently disentangling her arms, he stepped back. "You don't have to hold on to me to make me behave now. I've got it all back together."

"Yes." But now she didn't want him to have it all back together.

"Can I help you with dinner?"

"Dinner?... *Dinner!*" The salmon would be dried out. She rushed to the oven and pulled out the fish. Fortunately the aluminum foil she'd placed over the top had stopped any charring.

"Let me do something."

"No, thank you." *Just don't let me have to look at you. Don't let me have to think.* "Go ahead and have... Have the drink you..."

"The drink I almost had before I found much better things to do?" he asked with a wry note in his voice. "I don't think I want that anymore. Shall I open the Chardonnay?"

"Oh, yes." She busied herself finishing the meal preparations. With every step she felt Dominic's eyes on her.

At last the meal was on the table and they sat facing each other. Dominic poured wine for himself, water for Briar.

"I just had a thought," he said when they'd been eating for a few minutes.

Briar waited.

"It's Lent, isn't it?"

"Yes," she said, her stomach falling away once more.

"What did you give up?"

She frowned, then bowed her head. "You mean what did I give up for Lent?"

"Yes. You don't have to tell me if you don't want to. But I've just decided what I'm going to sacrifice."

She had a sharp image of August telling Dominic to sacrifice himself for the benefit of her worldly education.

"I'm going to give up jumping to conclusions. How's that?"

"Good, I guess." He confused her too often.

Although he'd barely made a respectable dent in his meal he set his knife and fork aside. He looked at his watch. "Oh, would you look at the time?"

She did. A quarter to nine.

"I've got to be in surgery early."

"For a change?" she said, trying for a lightness she didn't feel.

"Yeah. The meal was great, Briar. Thank you."

"I'm glad you enjoyed it." She didn't bother to mention that they hadn't finished the main course and the dessert was still in the refrigerator. All he wanted was to get away from what must feel to him like a totally wasted evening.

"I did." He got up and started to lift dishes from the table.

"Leave it," Briar said. "I've got lots of time for that." All night. All night tonight and every night for the rest of her life.

"You didn't tell me what you gave up for Lent," Dominic said when they stood facing each other near the door.

"Nothing."

"Really. I'd have thought that went with the territory."

"You don't have any idea what goes with the territory." She closed her mouth firmly, detesting the snappish tone in her voice.

"No," he said slowly. "I'm sure I don't."

"Oh, I'm sorry—again. A long time ago I decided it was better to take something up for Lent—to *do* something rather than the other thing."

"Sounds good," he said, still without a smile. "Want to tell me what you took up?"

Briar considered. "I thought I might try taking a few more risks in life." She met his eyes unwaveringly.

"Sounds like a good idea." He took both of her hands in his. "I'm not going because I want to. You know that, don't you?"

"You don't have to explain."

"I think I do. Every time I get within feet of you I want to hold you . . . and that's not all I want to do. I believe in honesty and so do you, so I might as well tell the truth." His thumbs rubbed back and forth over her fingers. "I have the same thoughts when you're nowhere around. This isn't a minor event for me, Briar—this, whatever it is. But I'm having difficulty figuring out what *you* feel. If anything."

"I feel . . . Dominic, I feel a great deal." She stepped close and he slipped his arms around her. "I . . . I haven't had a great deal of . . ." She couldn't finish, couldn't bring herself to tell him what an innocent she was.

Dominic smoothed her back. He rested his cheek on top of her head. "I think I know what you're trying to tell me. If there's going to be anything ahead for the two of us, I'm going to have to learn a whole lot of patience. Am I right?"

"I guess so."

"Okay." He raised her chin and kissed her softly. "Thank you for being straight with me. And thank you for inviting me tonight. It was special."

With a brief touch to her cheek and an oddly serious glance, he left.

Briar trailed back to clear the table. A deep and powerful disappointment weighted her every move. He'd said nothing definite about seeing her again. He wanted her, but made no secret of expecting more, much more than friendly company. She wanted that, too, but not without deeper commitment.

Dominic Kiser wasn't looking for commitments.

When the dishes were stacked on the kitchen counter she opened the dishwasher—and closed it again. It didn't have to be all over with Dominic. She hadn't imagined the power of his passion while he'd held her. And she hadn't imagined that he'd told her how often he thought about her.

Leaving the mess behind, Briar went to her bedroom and undressed. He'd said her breasts were wonderful. She felt hot all over again.

No, it definitely didn't have to be the end of the story. He'd wanted her as much as she wanted him. That said it all. She wouldn't compromise what she believed. She *would* pray for opportunity and means to take some of those risks she'd invented for his benefit.

Chapter Eleven

August was quiet this morning.

"It's a beautiful day," Briar told him from her station by the window. "When I caught the bus I almost wondered if I should have left my jacket at home."

She was talking for the sake of filling up the silence. A check at the nurses' station on her way in had resulted in the progress report she'd known was coming: *"He can't go on much longer. He's worn out."* The nurse had smiled sadly. *"If he weren't such an ornery old man he'd have died days ago."* At Briar's sigh the nurse had added: *"We're all going to miss him."*

"Time you stopped hiding under those baggy whatever-they-ares that you wear."

August's raspy voice surprised Briar. She swung around. "And I thought you were snoozing. I'm so glad you could join me, August. I really like that snazzy outfit *you've* got on."

He smiled, but without the usual wicked edge. "Looks good on me, does it? Just as well. I'm practicing getting around in it for when I'm up there—" he raised his eyes to the ceiling. If I've already got the flowing white robes down, wings should be a cinch."

Briar faced the window again. "The first tulips are up. I've got a bunch of red ones from California. They're so cheerful." And every time she looked at them she thought about last night. "The daffodils are really wonderful this year." She was a long way from working through her feelings about Dominic.

"Have you given any more thought to what I talked to you about?"

Every time she saw August he mentioned his collection. "Not really."

"You'd best get on it. It's not a good idea to drop behind the opposition."

"I'll bear that in mind."

"How's it going between you and young Kiser?"

Briar shot around. "I beg your pardon?"

August smirked as only August could smirk. "I've got my sources, y'know. Better watch your reputation with a man like that. These buckos that look like movie stars always have a string of skirts trailing behind."

Crossing her arms, Briar frowned, at a loss for words. August might be meddling and joking but he'd hit a chord. She couldn't risk rumors about her conduct.

"You can play dumb if you want to, missy. I'll take what you don't say as positive."

"Positive for what?" she couldn't help asking.

"Positive that something's probably finally starting to spark between the two of you. Do you the world of good, missy." He paused, drawing a breath that cost him visible effort. "More than good for the doc. He's going to be one lucky man."

Touched, Briar grinned at him. "I think you're trying to get back at him for something. Why else would you wish a nuisance like me on him?"

August thought about that. "You'll never get me to say I believe a word of the garbage you dish out. But your heart's in the right place. And at least you believe in something and stick to it. You'll always stick with what you believe in, including people."

"I believe in you, August," Briar said.

He nodded slowly. "I know. Can't think why. You've helped Lottie and me more'n you'll ever know." Sniffing, he looked toward the sky outside. "Getting maudlin in my twilight hours. Hogwash. Never did believe in a lot of mush."

"Of course not."

"Daffodils, you said?"

"Yes. Masses of them. The crocuses are about gone. Down there in the woods—" she indicated the acreage behind the hospital "—there are bluebells. They look like bright blue fuzz waving in the breeze. And the cherry blossoms are out, of course."

"My kind of day," August said. "A butterfly day."

She eyed him thoughtfully. "Exactly."

"You'd probably call it an Easter kind of day, missy."

"Oh, yes."

The few quiet moments that followed were shattered by the sound of a sharp exchange in the corridor. Briar stirred. Even though she couldn't make out the words there was no doubt that one of the voices belonged to Dominic.

He strode into the room with barely a perfunctory hi-sign to August. "Where have you been?" His jaw jutted and he glowered at Briar.

"Good morning," she said.

"I've hunted all over this hospital for you, Briar."

"And now you've found me." For August's benefit, she kept her voice even.

"You're supposedly the chaplain around here." He showed no sign of having registered what she'd said. "When you're needed you should be in a place where you can be easily reached."

Briar met August's eyes. He raised his brows in sympathy but there was no mistaking his enjoyment of the situation.

"Good morning to you, too, doc," August said. "Nice day out, so I hear."

Dominic began to pace and Briar realized what was truly unusual about him: rather than scrubs or a white coat, he wore jeans and a sweatshirt. He hadn't shaved and didn't appear to have combed his hair.

Concern canceled out her irritation with him. "Dominic, what's the problem?"

"I'm not here because I think it's necessary." He stopped in front of her. "A patient is asking to talk to you."

Immediately, Briar gathered her appointment book and Bible. "You should have had me paged. Sometimes I forget to check in at the desk. I'm sorry about that."

"She's on Three. West. I don't get the big rush to talk to you but I couldn't persuade her out of it."

This was no time for anger. "I'll go right over." Later she would have a few words to say to Dr. Kiser about interfering with a patient's right to see a minister.

"Hurry, will you?"

Briar hesitated. "I didn't know there were cardiac patients outside the unit."

"She's not cardiac. Just get there."

Now, despite her best intentions, Briar seethed. "Certainly, sir. What's the patient's name?"

"I'm sorry," he muttered. "Forgive me, please. I'm not exactly... Her name's May Kiser. She's my mother."

THE WOMAN IN THE BED smiled at Briar. Mrs. Kiser's resemblance to Dominic was unmistakable. "Thank you for coming. My son's mentioned you. I'd hoped to meet you somewhere more pleasant than this."

Briar absorbed the surprising notion of Dominic talking about her to anyone, particularly his mother. "He said you wanted to see me. I checked at the station. You're here for some tests?"

"That's a polite way of saying I've got a bellyache and they don't know why. I'm afraid I was an awful nuisance in the night. I didn't want Dominic bothered but he's the only family I have so they insisted on calling him."

Which explained his disheveled appearance. "I'm sure he'd want to be with you. He's a very caring man." Arrogant, bossy, opinionated... And he was driving her mad. "Tell me what would make you feel good, Mrs. Kiser. Can I read something for you?"

"Later, possibly. Mostly I just wanted to meet you."

Briar pulled up a chair and sat down. "Dominic looks like you."

"Yes. But he looks more like his father."

Briar waited. She never asked questions unless prompted to do so.

"My husband died when the . . . He died when Dominic was a boy."

"And you still miss him." Briar smiled at the fond resignation on May Kiser's pretty face.

"This is almost a good thing—my being here," she said. "I knew yesterday there was something different about you, but I make it a rule never to push Dominic for information."

A wise woman, Briar decided.

"He stopped by to see me on his way to have dinner with you."

Briar traced the gold words on her Bible.

May Kiser chuckled. "He pretended it was just a casual visit. What he really wanted was my seal of approval on the flowers he'd bought for you."

The flush that crept up Briar's neck was inevitable. Everything about last night caused a devastating combination of embarrassment and longing.

"Dominic's been making his own decisions—about everything—for a very long time."

Briar understood what Mrs. Kiser was suggesting. "I'm sure Dominic likes to include you in things he thinks would interest you."

"He's thirty-six. And we don't have to talk about the fact that he's not exactly ugly. Dominic never asked my opinion about anything to do with a woman before."

"The flowers are beautiful."

"Yes, they are. And they're unusual, don't you think? Suggestive of his having seen you in a particular light? He told me you were unusual—fresh, unspoiled. Not an orchid type, he said. He seemed unsure of himself."

"Unsure?" Briar shook her head. "I think we both know that Dominic and the word unsure don't belong in the same language."

Mrs. Kiser rested her head back and closed her eyes. "Things didn't go entirely well between the two of you last night, did they?"

The blush became furious.

"I'm sorry." May looked sideways at Briar. "I'm taking advantage of the situation. But my son is very important to me and I worry about him. I'd like to see him happy—to know that he will be happy."

This sudden insight into Dominic's life felt strange. He managed to project a perfect image of confidence, almost of not being quite human. "I think he's happy," she said. "His work obviously gives him great satisfaction."

"It's the only thing that gives him satisfaction. He needs more than that. Briar... Dominic's angry."

"I noticed," she responded without thinking. "I mean, he was upset this morning. He's worried about you. That's natural." And endearing.

"You don't understand. I know he's worried about me today. My, he'd be furious if he knew I was saying any of this to you." She pushed herself higher on the pillows. "I'm going to say one or two things. Nothing more. You are the *last* kind of woman I would ever have expected Dominic to become involved with."

"We aren't *involved*," Briar said quickly.

Mrs. Kiser studied her. "Aren't you? I think that protest was a little fast. Perhaps you should be asking me what I mean when I say I'm surprised by Dominic's interest in you."

"I really don't think any of this is relevant."

"I'm surprised because I'd despaired of him ever risking involvement with a woman who had some depth," Mrs. Kiser continued, clearly undeterred by Briar's arguments. "I wanted to see if you might be what I've been hoping for... praying for. I think you could be."

Briar tugged at the neck of her sweats. "I know I should be flattered by this—and I am. But, really, all I seem able to do for Dominic is make him angry."

"Absolutely!"

The triumph in Mrs. Kiser's voice astounded Briar. "You'll have to explain this to me more clearly."

"Yes, yes. My son is an angry man, but he does a great job hiding that anger. I haven't seen him as angry as he is today since he was twenty and..." She worked her mouth, then shook her head slightly.

"Since he was what?"

"Let him tell you," Mrs. Kiser said.

"I doubt if he'll do that." Briar wished she didn't feel such regret. "Really, I think you're misreading him today. He obviously loves you very much and—given his occupation—he probably feels he should be able to wave a magic wand loaded with his own expertise and send you home immediately."

The woman nodded. Apart from some pallor and the evidence of too little sleep the night before, she appeared very fit. "I'm sure there's some of that involved. But you don't understand. I can *feel* that there's something else. I know there is. You threaten him."

Briar stared, uncomprehending.

"I don't blame you for being puzzled. All I can say to make this clearer is that Dominic has a lot of unfinished business to attend to. Heavy baggage. He *is* interested in you and because of who you are—what you are—you're forcing him to look at things he's managed to bury for a long time."

"You mean Dominic has—"

"No—" Mrs. Kiser shook a finger "don't ask me to explain. I always believe in allowing people to share their own demons. What I *am* asking you to do is be patient with Dominic. He's worth it."

"Oh, I *know* he is—"

For the second time that morning, with all the charm and sunshine of a tornado, Dominic marched into a room where Briar was.

"Well?" he demanded, looking from his mother to Briar.

"Well, what?" Mrs. Kiser said pleasantly.

"Have you two finished?"

"No, son."

"Oh, what the hell," he said, half under his breath. He cradled an elbow in one palm and scrubbed at his face.

Briar got up and went to him. "Are you okay?" She rubbed his arm, half-expecting to be pushed away.

He stared at her. "Frustrated. But okay. Yeah." He managed a faint smile and patted her hand. "Thanks. I'm sorry I've been such a pain in the ass this morning. I didn't get much sleep last night. Even less than usual. The less I get, the nastier I get. My mother will vouch for that."

"I certainly will."

"May," Dominic said with a very apparent effort to be pleasant. "Could I borrow Briar for a few minutes. I'd like a word with her about another patient."

Briar frowned. Her hand went to her throat. "August?"

"Er, no. I'll be right back, May."

"Take your time. I think I might be able to sleep now."

Once in the corridor, Dominic took Briar's elbow and propelled her to a small, deserted waiting area. Without asking her if she wanted any, he poured two cups of coffee and handed her one.

He began the pacing she was beginning to accept as a normal part of his thinking processes.

"How does she seem?" he asked abruptly.

"In good spirits." The coffee was bitter. "I think she's more worried about you than herself."

Dominic halted in front of Briar. "Damn. That's because I never learned to control..." He turned aside, slammed down his coffee and cursed as it sprayed in all directions. "I hate being out of control. Why is it I'm the rock for everyone else, but with my mother I... It makes me *mad*. Dammit, she's earned some peace. She's paid her dues a few thousand times over."

She wanted to gather him in her arms and console him. "Give yourself permission to be human."

"You don't understand. But I want you to. And then I want you to explain to me why things happen the way they do." He mopped, remarkably efficiently, at the spilled coffee and tossed the wet paper towels into a garbage can. "Why is it that good people, sweet, generous, hardworking people like my mother, get smacked down at every turn?"

A warning sounded loud and clear in Briar's brain. This was serious stuff. Dominic might actually be reaching out to her for help. "Are the test results back?" she asked gently.

"Preliminary," he said morosely.

"You're an optimist," Briar said, not needing to be told that the news wasn't good. "I've seen you with patients and you always inspire them to hope."

"This isn't a *patient,*" he said, his voice rising. "This is my *mother.* And they see something in the lower GI series that looks suspicious."

"That doesn't have to mean the worst."

He gave her a pitying look. "Don't forget who you're talking to."

"How could I?" she said, more sharply than she should. "Oh, Dominic. I know how you're feeling."

"Do you?"

"Yes. Your mother has faith, doesn't she?"

He turned his back.

"She does. I can feel it. And you should be grateful for that."

"I didn't say I wasn't. But I don't understand why she does."

Her skin turned cold. This man really was angry...with God?

"My father died when we... He died when my brother and I were ten. He left my mother with nothing." He raised his shoulders. "I mean *nothing.* And no marketable skills. I won't bore you with all the tear-jerking details, but we made it because she never believed we wouldn't."

Briar went quietly to stand behind him. She rubbed tensed muscles in his shoulder.

Dominic caught her hand and pulled her in front of him. "I had a twin brother. May managed to give us enough security and self-esteem to make sure we got through high school and into college." His eyes were seeing the past. "She does have faith, whatever you people mean by that."

"I think you know." He was holding her wrist. "And she's had her faith validated."

"Validated?" His eyes regained focus.

"Yes. Look at you. And I'm sure your brother—"

"My brother's dead," he said, his lips drawn back from his teeth. "He was the best of the two of us. He was the artist. He'd have created beautiful things that would have come to mean something to the world forever."

"But, you—"

"Let me finish. My brother made one little mistake. One lousy little mistake. He took one hit of cocaine. Sure, it was dumb, but it was human." Dominic narrowed his gaze. "My brother went into cardiac arrest and died."

The silence was absolute, except for the sound of Dominic's harsh breathing.

Revelation brought a gasp from Briar. "Is that why you became a heart surgeon? Did you decide to learn how to mend hearts because of your brother?"

"Why I do what I do is my business. I'm damn good at it. My skills are my own—I made them."

Reaching him in this mood would be impossible. "I'm glad your mother asked to see me. And I'm glad you told me about your brother. You probably won't ever want to, but you know you can always talk to me, don't you."

"I know," he said, sounding weary.

Briar closed her hand over his on her wrist. "Why don't you get some rest?"

Dominic nodded and let her hands drop. "Later. There was something I meant to give you last night. I forgot." His eyes met hers and she knew he was remembering what had happened between them. He took his wallet from a back pocket and pulled out a piece of paper. "This should cover what you need for the Easter party for the children."

A check. Briar glanced at it. "Thank you." Her throat closed.

"If it isn't enough, let me know."

The check was signed by Dominic—and drawn on his account. "You didn't have to do this. I don't know what to say."

"You don't have to say anything." Stuffing the wallet away again, he approached the door. "I ... The check's mine because it's easier that way. I'll get the hospital to reimburse me. See you later."

"Yes." She watched him go. It was easier for him to write a personal check, then get reimbursed by the hospital? No. They both knew he wouldn't be asking anyone to pay him back. Her smile felt a little wobbly—and very good.

Chapter Twelve

On any other night a warm bath would have relaxed her. Tonight it had warmed her: relaxation seemed a state vaguely remembered from another lifetime.

"Briar, you coming out?" Yarrow called from the living room.

Briar wrapped her terrycloth robe tightly around her body and tied the belt. She pushed her feet into slippers and scuffed out to join Yarrow.

"Geez, I thought you'd drowned or something."

Amused, Briar wound her hair in a towel. "I'm flattered you missed me."

"I've got to go out."

Briar fashioned a precarious turban and eyed Yarrow. "Out? It's after midnight. You're ready for... You were ready for bed."

"I've got to go out."

"So you've already said."

Yarrow glanced behind her. "Please... Look, I'll call you later, okay?"

"No, not okay." Pulling the towel from her head, she shook her hair, never taking her eyes from Yarrow's strained face. "What's happened?"

Dressed in an old black raincoat with a brown woolen scarf tied around her hair, Yarrow hovered near the door. "Nothing's happened. Please don't ask questions now."

Once more she looked around, behind her and toward the window.

Alarmed, Briar clutched her robe together. "*Tell me? Did someone call you? What?*"

"Lock this after me," Yarrow said, letting herself out. "And don't open it to anyone but me. Have you got that?"

"No!"

"It's okay. Nobody's going to come. I'm going to make sure of that. I just want you to be prepared."

"Yarrow!"

The door slammed and Briar heard footsteps running down the concrete stairs outside. Then silence.

"DOMINIC! HOLD UP!"

The shout accompanied the sound of running footsteps behind him in the parking lot. Without looking back, Dominic bent to unlock the door of the Jag.

"Hey, buddy." Norris Simpson arrived at his side. "I was just talking to Wally Frederickson."

"Yeah." Dominic slid behind the wheel.

Norris slammed the door and leaned down to look through the open window. "Rotten luck about your mother. I'm sorry."

Dominic stared grimly ahead at nothing in particular. "Yeah."

"They don't come any better than Wally."

"A first-class diagnostician," Dominic said of the center's leading gastroenterologist. "Which doesn't make me feel great right now."

"Tough." Norris drummed his fingers. "You need a little diversion. Get your mind off things."

Dominic pushed the key into the ignition. "Sleep is what I probably need."

"Maybe you could use a change of pace. Get back to spending time with the right kind of people."

The keys were cold under Dominic's fingers. He wrapped his arms over the wheel and gave Norris his full attention. "Does that mean I've been missed by someone, or that someone thinks I've been spending time with the *wrong* kind of people?''

Norris raised a palm. ''Just expressing concern, buddy. It's all probably rumor anyway.''

Dominic let a moment elapse before saying, ''Okay. I'll bite. *What's* probably rumor?''

''Forget it.''

''Come on, Norris. I'm not going to beg.''

''Okay. But you're the one insisting. Word has it you've got something going with the lady minister.''

Dominic let his hands slip from the wheel. *''Something going?* What the hell does that mean?''

''Aha! So it is true.''

''No, it damn well . . . Do you know Briar Lee?''

Norris snickered. ''Sounds like a good name for a stripper.''

Dominic clamped a hand around the other man's wrist. *''Do* you know her?''

''Hey, no offense.'' Norris tried to jerk away. ''I know who she is. But I don't actually *know* her. Why would I?''

Dominic held fast. ''She's a very special woman. Good, if you know what I mean. Good all the way through.''

''If you want me in surgery tomorrow, you'd better give me back my arm.''

''Sure.'' Dominic released him. An unpleasant curling attacked his stomach. He didn't like to think of anyone criticizing Briar.

''Look,'' Norris said. ''I certainly didn't mean to put the lady bible-puncher down, but—''

''That's enough. All of it. Do we understand each other?''

''Oh, we sure do. I must say I'm surprised, Dominic. Not exactly your type, is she?''

''Not exactly. Good night, Norris.''

The Jag's engine purred to life and he backed out before swinging a wide arc around Norris Simpson and driving from the hospital grounds.

He set his nose for Highway 405 and the floating bridge across Lake Washington to Mercer Island. He was only going home because May threatened to discharge herself from the hospital if he insisted on sleeping there.

Not exactly your type.

There was no greater truth than that it was impossible to keep secrets around a hospital. Briar wouldn't like it that there was gossip attached to her name.

Dominic didn't like it that there was gossip attached to her name—and that he was the cause.

He didn't roll up the window. Traffic was sparse and he heard the whine of the Jag's tires sweeping dry pavement. Once through the tunnel that led to the bridge, he settled into the slow lane. A warm day and evening had waned into a brisk night. A rim of moon rode a clear, gunmetal sky above the dark and shifting waters of the lake.

The drive home from Seattle, the familiar sight of Mercer Island's tree-covered slopes, usually filled him with a sense of peace.

Not tonight.

"Damn!" Tonight he needed something to hang on to...*someone.* Briar would know exactly what he needed to hear. And she'd know when he needed to hear nothing at all.

The first exit onto the island curved around above houses built along the shore. His own home was situated on the west side.

He needed to apologize to Briar for his behavior earlier today.

"Damn!"

Checking the deserted road in all directions, Dominic swung a U-turn and controlled an urge to floor the accelerator. He wanted to see Briar, to be with her...to talk to her.

The return drive to the outskirts of Seattle took only minutes. Through the deserted downtown streets he swept. White lights swayed on trees along 4th Avenue. Farther north, beyond the glass facade of Westlake Mall, the city felt asleep. Dominic kept his speed steady all the way to Clay Street. A left turn took him downhill to Western and Briar's apartment building.

No lights. Not a suggestion of life anywhere, except for the heap of blankets he knew belonged to Briar's vagrant friend . . . and the dog that raised her head when Dominic left his car and went into the courtyard.

He looked up at the third floor, at Briar's apartment, and felt a flicker of hope. A suggestion of a glow showed through the closed drapes. She must still be up. Although it could be that her flaky roommate was the one burning midnight oil.

Dominic peered at his watch. Early morning oil. In fifteen minutes it would be one o'clock.

Halfway up the second flight of stairs sanity kicked in. He had no right to bother Briar at this time of night—or morning. Tomorrow would be soon enough to say he knew he'd been way out of line that morning.

Slowly, he climbed two more steps to the balcony. He hadn't called. She'd think he was mad—and presumptuous—if he intruded now.

He couldn't do it.

A bang startled him. Good God! Her door had just slammed shut. She'd actually left the thing open. It would have remained open the rest of the night if the wind hadn't caught it.

Dominic started back down.

The light that suddenly flooded from behind him threw a bright shaft over the railings and across a tree in a tub. He turned again. That had to be a bedroom, Briar's or Yarrow's. The tree was a soft little cedrus. A soft, totally still little cedrus.

There was no wind in the lee of the building, no wind to shift tree limbs . . . or slam a door.

The next sound he heard was a heavy crash followed by the distinctive crackle of breaking glass—then a muffled yell.

Dominic didn't hesitate. Leaping up the top steps to the balcony, he launched himself at Briar's door. It gave immediately under his weight and he stumbled into the living room.

A towel lay in a heap on the rug, near a single backless white slipper. He walked across the room, careful to make no sound, and turned right into a narrow hallway that would lead to the bedrooms.

There he paused. The front door could have slammed in a draft and awakened her. Then she might have knocked over her lamp. Any moment she'd come into the hall and go into cardiac arrest at the sight of him.

"I don't know!" Briar's voice came, clear but too high. She screamed. "Let me go!"

Dominic's heart collided with his throat. A single stride sent him cannoning into the first room on the right.

It took only seconds to recognize the burly man who held Briar, face down, on the bed. A denim jacket covered the tattooed biceps, but this was the man who had approached Briar and Yarrow in Pike Place Market. In his free hand was a brass lamp, its glass shade shattered.

Dominic sprang and grabbed a handful of hair and collar.

"Son of a bitch!" The man came up swinging. Crazed rage twisted his features.

"Get out of here, Briar," Dominic shouted. "Now!"

"N-no."

"Briar—ah!" A fist connected with his gut.

Dominic doubled over, gasping. Through tearing eyes he saw a denim-clad knee aimed for his groin and side-stepped.

The man cursed. He cursed louder when Dominic drove the heel of one hand into his throat.

"Briar, will you get out?"

"N-no!" Her voice was a wobbly screech.

The man braced his feet apart like an animal ready to attack. "I asked you where Yarrow is?"

"I don't know. Dominic! Watch him!"

Another fist connected with Dominic's shoulder.

"Where's Yarrow?"

A blur of white entered Dominic's vision—Briar jumping from the bed. She landed on the man's back, gripped him around the neck and hung on. "Don't you hit him,

Dave.'' A red splotch stood out on each of her cheeks.
''Don't you dare touch him.''

She broke her assailant's concentration.

He flailed, tearing at her arms until he could fling her off.
''Bitch.''

Dominic clasped his hands together and swung. The blow
landed along the man's jaw with a sickening crack. Dominic ducked his head to charge.

Too late. This time the white thunderbolt came in his direction. Briar, her eyes like green fire, shot in front of him
and twisted to face Dave.

He bolted.

Running curses together, he half ran, half staggered from
the room.

''Get out of my way, Briar.''

Instead, she wrapped her arms around him and pushed,
using every ounce of her weight to stop him from following Dave.

''Don't you dare run after him,'' she panted.

Dominic worked her arms from his waist, but she slipped
down and clung with incredible force to his thigh. He
grasped the doorframe and made to pull himself free. Briar
held on while he dragged her into the hall.

''What the hell do you think you're doing?''

''You are not to fight anymore. It's wrong to fight.''

''He attacked you,'' he told her, totally disbelieving what
he'd heard.

''And now he's run away. Let him go.''

''He broke in here and assaulted you in your bedroom.''

''He assaulted me in the living room first. He knocked on
the front door and I let him in—I thought he was Yarrow
coming back. Then he dragged me back here.''

He spread his arms and looked down into her upturned
face. She knelt, her arms loosely around his leg now, and
stared up at him.

''He was going to—''

''No! No, he wasn't. I wouldn't tell him where Yarrow is
so he brought me back here because he wanted to be sure
she wasn't hiding out somewhere.''

"He did push you around. He must have hurt you."

She bit her lip. Her eyes shimmered anxiously. The terrycloth robe she wore gaped at the neck showing enough smooth, pale skin to tense every muscle in his body.

"We need to call the police."

"Not until I know where Yarrow is and whether or not she's safe."

"He could be miles away by then."

She released him and sat on the floor, wrapping the robe around her legs. "You don't understand this sort of thing, Dominic. There's a whole layer of society you've never had to deal with."

"And you have?" He stood over her, smoothed her damp hair. "You're a gentle woman who should never have to deal with this element."

"You're wrong," she said against his thigh. "This is the element I contracted to deal with. It doesn't frighten me."

"You weren't frightened when that thug was holding you down on the bed?"

She surprised him by rubbing his leg. "Yes, I was frightened." Slowly, she massaged his calf. "These people are caught in a trap they didn't make."

Her fingers were having an effect she undoubtedly had never considered. "If you mean they didn't get all the advantages some get I understand what you mean. But I don't understand why people have to be indulged because they choose to act out—particularly if they hurt others in the process."

"You're talking as if they thought the way you do. They don't."

"Briar, Briar, what am I going to do with you?" He dropped down and gathered her close. "You are upset. You're shaken, of course you are. Thank God I came when I did."

She nodded, leaned against him, rested a cool hand on his cheek. "Why did you come?"

Of course she would wonder about that. "I'm not sure." That was sort of true. Somehow he didn't feel like discussing his own problems now.

Briar sighed and curled against him. Dominic sat beside her and cradled her head in the hollow of his shoulder. "Do you have any idea how serious what happened here tonight was?"

"Not as serious as you think."

Her shoulder and the top of one pale breast held his gaze. He breathed in deeply. "I think you're far too vulnerable. There are always people willing to play on someone like you."

"Like me?" She tilted her face up to his. Her lips parted slightly—gentle, sensual lips.

Her skin was so soft, so beautiful. With each breath her full breast rose . . . tantalizing.

"Dominic?"

"Innocent people," he told her. "The worldly are very ready to prey on the innocent."

She twisted in his arms until she knelt beside him. Placing a hand on each of his shoulders, she studied him seriously. "You don't really have a clear picture of me. I'm no innocent, Dominic. I've been dealing with what you might consider the seamier side of life for a lot of years now."

And the miracle was that she'd evidently come through unscathed—to this point. "It's going to have to stop."

She frowned and got up . . . showing an expanse of beautifully shaped, naked leg. "You had a shock," she said matter-of-factly. "You'll get over it and so will I."

Dominic followed the lines of her from ankle all the way up to her eyes. "There are some moments we never get over." Like the feeling he had at this moment, a feeling that he'd like to strip off that white robe, toss her on the bed and make love to her until neither of them could or wanted to think anymore.

"I'm already over it," she said. "What would make me feel good would be the sight of Yarrow coming through the door—in one piece."

Dominic got to his feet. He put his hands in his pockets. They were safer there. "That man is obviously very involved with Yarrow."

"I'm afraid so. They go back a long way. Some habits aren't easy to break."

"You'll have to ask her to leave."

Her eyes narrowed. "I'm sure you don't mean to tell me what I ought to do."

"Yes, I do. If you won't take care of yourself, someone else is going to have to."

"And you're appointing yourself?"

He was aware of an uncomfortable tension climbing his spine. "I'm the one who's available."

"Dominic," she said with a calmness that didn't deceive him. "I make my own decisions. I've done that for a long time."

How easy it would be to sweep her up into his arms. Looking down on her, the thought held more appeal than almost any he'd had lately. Her damp hair tangled about her face in a way that made him think of how it would feel spread on his chest while he held her, length to length, with her on top of him in the comfortable-looking bed behind her.

Briar rested her fingertips lightly on his chest. "Let's not argue." He felt the subtle shift in her mood. She'd softened.

"I don't want to argue with you." Catching her behind the neck, he eased her head back and bowed slowly over her. "I want to taste you." He was going to anyway.

Her response was to pass the tip of her tongue over her lips. His arousal hit like a blow. He heard his own groan and her sigh before he settled his mouth gently on hers.

Briar's arms went around his neck. She used the tip of her pink tongue, played it along the inside of his lower lip.

His restraint fled. He crushed her mouth, opened it with the force of his own. She clutched his shirt, arched into him, pressed her firm breasts to his chest. Dominic's legs locked. He kissed her hard and deep—and hot—taking her with his tongue.

And he felt her tremble violently.

His heart hammered. Dominic raised his head. Her eyes had lost focus. "Briar, this isn't simple. And it's only going to get more complicated."

She nodded.

His body tightened. Bracketing her face with his hands, he struggled for control. As if she felt his fight, Briar slipped her hands around his neck and pulled his face down to hers. She kissed him passionately, matching the intrusion of his tongue with answering thrusts of her own. He enfolded her in a tight embrace and heard her moan into his mouth.

Not enough.

When he ran his hands down her neck and inside the robe to hold her silken shoulders she didn't draw back. His legs began to weaken. The jeans he wore were too damn tight.

"Briar." Abruptly, he stepped back and held her away. Now the robe covered less than it exposed. "I'm making love to you, do you know that? In everything but the real sense, I'm taking you. I can't hold back much longer."

She closed her eyes and he felt her tremble again.

"Do we go on or do we stop?"

The noise she made was half an anguished cry, half a sob.

Dominic's hands shook. Hooking a finger under her belt, he pulled it loose. "Answer me." The robe fell open. She made no move to cover herself.

"Answer me." Looking at her small but voluptuous body only sent his hunger over the edge. Calling up restraint he'd never known he had, he took one end of her belt and passed the rough fabric slowly over her nipples.

Her lips drew back from clenched teeth. She took a step toward him, her head dropping back.

Again he made a slow pass across her breasts. Their pink tips sprang to puckered awareness. Dominic dropped the belt and covered her urgent flesh with his hands while he kissed her again, assaulted her mouth again and again.

The phone rang.

Briar drove her fingers into his arms and reached to meet his tongue.

The phone rang again.

"I've got to get that," she gasped, pushing away.

"Let it go."

"It might be Yarrow."

"Damn Yarrow!"

"Oh, Dominic, you don't mean that." Briar dodged around him and picked up the phone. "Hello."

Dominic followed and nuzzled her neck, trailed tight little kisses all the way to a nipple.

She covered the receiver. "Don't. I can't think."

"I don't want you to," he whispered.

She angled her head at him and the desperate, gentle light in her eyes undid him. Cupping one breast, he lavished attention on the other with his lips and tongue—and heard her moan, saw the automatic jut of her slender hips.

"Where are you?" she asked the caller. How could anyone fail to hear the lambent tension in her voice?

Tentatively, Dominic explored her flat stomach, dropped his hand to her thigh.

Her body jerked and he glanced back to her face. She shook her head. In her eyes he saw alarm now.

"What is it?" He held her waist beneath the robe. "Who is it?"

"No, I don't want you to do that, Yarrow. I'm all right. Come home."

He gritted his teeth.

"He didn't break in. I thought he was you so I opened the door."

Dominic drew in a breath.

"He sounded desperate." She caught his hand and held it still. "No, he didn't hurt me. Okay...yes, okay. Okay. I'll see you later." She hung up.

"This is all wrong for you." Dominic pulled her back into his arms. "You were never meant to deal with these people."

"Yes, I was," she said quietly.

"No. You're a baby in a lion's den. Damn it, Briar. I want you out of this place tonight...*now.*"

Bending her head, she wrapped her robe around her and retied the belt. "I know you're concerned about me."

"Damn right I'm concerned. Someone's got to be. Pack your bags. I'm taking you to my place."

Briar stared at him. "No, you're not."

"Don't argue with me. One run in with your room-mate's muscle-bound friend is enough for me for one night."

"Dave's in police custody."

He frowned and stopped pacing. "How do you know? He only left . . . half an hour ago?"

She blushed brightly in the way he was coming to love. "A little more than that, I think. Evidently he called here earlier while I was in the shower. He told Yarrow that if she didn't bring him money he was coming for it."

"So she left you to face him?"

"She went to head him off and missed him."

"You're out of here."

"After Dave left us he was picked up for speeding. Evidently they've got enough on him to hold him. He won't be back for a while. He'll probably never come back here."

"Probably isn't good enough. Will you pack or shall I do it for you."

"Dominic, please don't do this."

"Do what?" He never remembered feeling more frustrated.

"Don't play the heavy with me. I make my own decisions."

"You obviously don't do that very well. I—"

"*You* have no say in what I do."

"No say?" He felt explosive. "I care what happens to you. And we're damn close to being lovers."

She sat on the bed and averted her face. "I'm no good at this sort of thing."

"And just what is this sort of thing?"

"This." She spread her arms. "This . . . Oh, please go home and leave me alone. I'm wrong for you."

"Wrong!" He laughed. "Wrong? Did what just happened feel wrong?"

"It *was* wrong." She covered her face and rocked forward. "Dominic, please go. Forget it happened."

"Nothing happened," he said, suddenly cold. What did she think he was—a high schooler who could be made to believe the hors d'oeuvres were an entire meal?

"Okay," she said from behind her hands.

"What's the matter with you?" In some ways the thoughts of walking away appealed, but he still wanted, more than anything, to make wild love to this woman.

"I've tried to make you understand. It's hard... What am I supposed to say? Think, Dominic. Use your very good head. Do you really believe I've been in a lot of deep relationships with men?"

The possible message behind what she said cooled his anger. Could she be a virgin? He put his fists on his hips and stared at the floor. Was that possible?

Briar dropped her hands. Her stricken face almost sent him rushing to hold her again.

"Briar—"

"It's all right. I know you're glad you were able to help me with Dave. But you're right about the rest of it. It would have been better if you'd never come if we can't... if we can't keep our hands off each other."

She was admitting she wanted him, but telling him she wasn't about to give in to anything so... *human.*

"So we'd better stay out of each other's way," she said, sounding miserable.

"If that's the way you want it."

"It's the way it's got to be. I'm sorry I couldn't be what you needed tonight."

He looked heavenward. "I didn't come here because I can't control what's in my pants." Instantly he regretted the comment. "I'm sorry. I tend to forget who... *what* you are."

"I'm not a child. Neither am I so fragile that a few gritty words break me into pieces."

"Oh, you think you're very worldly. But you are an innocent. Take it from me." If he asked her outright whether or not she'd ever been with a man she'd probably be furious or cry. He wasn't sure he could cope with either.

"Why did you come here tonight?"

"I needed to see you." He couldn't lie and there was no reason to do so.

"Why?" She got up and came toward him.

"Don't," Dominic said, turning away. "If you touch me sweetheart, it's going to be all over."

She followed him into the sitting room. The front door stood slightly open. "What happened was as much my fault as yours," she said.

"Oh, *please*. Don't start trying to take the blame for my sex drive."

"I wish... Do you know I want you, too?"

He looked at her and shook his head. "You sure send some mixed signals."

"You don't understand. How can you?"

"Will you come with me?"

"No."

"Then I'll stay here if you'll let me."

"No."

"Okay." He wouldn't beg. "Lock this door and don't open it to anyone. No one. Do you understand?"

"Yes. Are you sure there isn't something you want to tell me."

The earlier conversation he'd had with the radiologist flooded back. "This is going to sound crazy now. But I came here looking for some peace. I thought I could find peace just by having your peace spill over on me a bit."

"Tell me," she said gently.

He flexed his shoulders. "My mother's going to have a biopsy on Monday morning. It's probable... Things don't look too good."

Briar's face became blank. "Why wait three days? Why not do it now? Tonight?"

"We've decided to wait over the weekend. I want her properly prepped. And I want everything up and running in the lab and everywhere else before it's done."

"Why didn't you tell me before."

He laughed mirthlessly. "That's what I came to do. You were otherwise occupied."

"Oh, I'm sorry. Oh, Dominic." She went to touch him but he moved out of her reach. Briar dropped her hand. "I'll be there for you and your mother. I'll stay with her as much as you both want me to."

Of course she would. Back in her designated role she'd be comfortable. She'd feel *safe*. "Thank you."

"Don't thank me. It's what I do best."

What she did best was avoid that final giving of herself that would allow her—allow them—to be what they could be together. He could imagine what they could be together only too clearly. His pulse began to speed up again. "I'd better let you get some rest," he told her. He sure as hell wouldn't get any.

Briar opened the door. "Call if you need me. I'll be there on Monday."

"Thanks." He walked out and kept on walking. *Call if you need me.* If he didn't feel like yelling, he'd laugh.

Chapter Thirteen

She found him exactly where he'd said he would be—
standing at the corner of Western and Clay. Pacing at the
corner of Western and Clay would be more accurate.

Despite lingering embarrassment over what had passed
between them the previous night, Briar smiled at the sight
of Dominic doing what seemed to come most naturally to
him. He really did pace remarkably efficiently.

He saw her and stood still.

Briar waved.

Dominic thrust his hands into his pockets. Even at a distance she could see his scowl.

Darn him, anyway. Briar checked her stride. He'd called
her and asked her to have lunch. She'd told him she
wouldn't be free until three. He'd said he needed to talk and
didn't care how late he ate. So she'd finally agreed. Now he
was greeting her with about as much enthusiasm as a bear
greeting a trapper.

He began to walk slowly toward her.

"Hi," he said when he stood a few feet away. "You're
late."

"About a minute. I'd only just got back from the hospital when you called."

"That was an hour ago."

Briar stopped. "Yes, it was. And I've been busy ever
since and then I had to change." For him she'd put on a
dress—something she rarely did—and high heels.

"You saw May this morning."

Two men passed between them and cast interested glances at both Dominic and Briar.

"We did talk. She's very calm. She filled me in on exactly what the radiologist and the gastroenterologist said, but she's optimistic. So am I."

"Good. You made a point of getting there early enough to be pretty sure of missing me."

He was right. "Yes." And she was no liar.

"That's childish."

"I was feeling a little fragile and I wanted time to think before I saw you again."

"How do you think that makes me feel?" He raked back his hair. Another pretty spring day had graced the city but the afternoon breeze verged on a chilly wind.

"It wasn't supposed to make you feel anything. I wasn't aware you'd be monitoring my moves."

"You're monitoring mine."

She thought about that. "Yes, I suppose I am in a way."

"Are we going to stand here calling to each other or could we go and have lunch? I haven't eaten since breakfast." He looked meaningfully at his watch. "And we both know how long ago that must have been."

Briar opened her mouth to tell him he could go wherever he pleased—without her—if his mood wasn't going to improve. She thought better of it. "I'm starving." She walked to join him, hesitated, and slipped a hand through his crooked elbow.

He smiled, actually smiled and covered her hand with his. "Why wouldn't you let me come to your apartment to pick you up?"

"I just decided it wasn't a very good idea."

Casting her a quizzical glance, he started walking. "Why?"

"I think—" She might as well spit it out. "I don't think it's a great idea for you and me to be alone at the moment."

They reached his car. He didn't answer her until they were both locked and buckled inside and he'd swung into traffic. "We're alone now."

Briar slanted him a look. "In a moving vehicle with people all around."

"We're going to my place."

She sat bolt upright. "You invited me for lunch."

"You'll eat."

Eat and what else? "There are plenty of restaurants to choose from."

"With lots of people around as you pointed out. Anyway, not too many places are still serving lunch and it's too early for dinner."

"Dominic—"

"I want you to myself." A faint smile turned the corner of his mouth up. His dark eyes, when they came in her direction, signaled a warning: the man was very, very serious. "Are you expected back at the hospital today?"

"I don't keep regular..." She would never be good at playing games. "I may be called in at anytime. I'll have to let them know where to reach me." He wouldn't want them knowing she was with him.

"Great idea. I'll be calling in, too. I'll do it for both of us."

Any rumors of a liaison between her and a surgeon could be disastrous. "I'd prefer you not to do that." The story was bound to become distorted to her disadvantage.

"Worried about your reputation?"

They had already reached the bridge over Lake Washington. "My reputation is something I have to bear in mind. That and what my position demands of me."

"What does it demand?"

Mount Rainier rose, a perfect snow-covered peak on the horizon. Boaters zipped or meandered across the sun-tipped surface of the water.

"Briar—"

"It demands that I maintain high moral standards," she said, aware of sounding stuffy.

"Lady ministers don't sleep around?"

She turned cold, then burning hot. "I don't think I'm going to answer that."

"I shouldn't have asked. Sorry."

"Don't you think it would be better if we went to a restaurant."

"No. I was serious when I said I wanted you to myself. We need to spend some time alone, Briar, time expressly designed for us to be alone."

It sounded so cold—so calculated. "I'm not sure I agree with you."

Dominic drove from the freeway onto Mercer Island and set off along Mercer Way. "You responded to me last night."

She put a hand over her mouth.

"Don't be embarrassed." Dominic glanced at her. "There's nothing wrong with passion. You're a passionate woman. You're meant to use that passion with a man who can satisfy you. I'm that man."

Liquid heat pooled low inside her. The muscles in her thighs ached. No one had ever spoken to her like this.

"You didn't get much sleep last night," he said.

"Neither did you."

"No. Maybe we'll take a nap this afternoon."

Her heart stopped beating, then raced. "I think you should take me back to Seattle."

Dominic's laugh made her jump. "What do you think I'm going to do to you?"

She was now entirely convinced that she'd become a challenge to his male ego. "I think you're going to do your best to seduce me."

He sent her a wicked grin. "How very perceptive of you."

"It won't work. First of all . . . Dominic, I do not intend to— This is impossible."

For fifteen minutes neither of them spoke. The Jag hugged sharp bends that snaked around the island above houses scattered along the shore. Dominic's abrupt turn to the right caught Briar off-guard. She grabbed at the strap over the door. The car swept downhill on a narrow lane that led to a single flat-roofed stucco house. Circular towers faced the lane, their walls broken by panels of square glass blocks.

"Home, sweet home," Dominic said, parking on a gravel strip. Nearby, steps led up to double front doors flanked by more windows fashioned from glass blocks. He reached back to pull two paper sacks from the back seat. "Lunch. I hate to cook so I bought it."

"When you go to restaurants you don't have to cook," she said, deliberately obstinate.

"In restaurants you have to hold down the kissing and they probably frown on people stretching out for a nap."

She crossed her arms. "You sound strange. Not at all like yourself."

"I'm not myself. Not at all." He got out and came around to open her door. Leaning down he said, "It's all your fault. You've driven me to desperate measures."

"I'm not getting out of this car."

Dominic reached in and unhooked her seatbelt. "Come on. Can't you tell when I'm joking?"

Wondering if she was making a mistake, Briar swung her legs from the car.

Dominic backed away, but not enough for her to stand up. "You have beautiful legs."

"Thank you."

"I haven't seen them often but I've got to admit they have quite an effect on me."

"Am I still supposed to be assuming you're joking?"

"Naturally." He offered her a hand. She took it and let him help her from the car.

Immediately, he slipped an arm around her waist and walked her purposefully up the steps. The front door opened into a large square hall tiled with black and white marble. Healthy plants in shiny black tubs stood in groupings. A graceful staircase curved upward from the center of the hall.

"This is spectacular," Briar said, genuinely impressed.

"Nothing fancy, but it's home."

She definitely didn't like this flippant version of Dominic. Not that she didn't think he was deliberately behaving out of character.

He carried the bags of food into an almost glaringly white kitchen. White cupboards, white appliances, white-tiled counters and walls, white stone floors. Wonderfully stylish but too cold for Briar's taste.

"This won't take a minute." Even as he spoke he took out plates—white with black rims—and began dumping piles of cold pasta salad on each. The loaded plates were put on a tray, with silverware. He produced a bottle of cold wine from the refrigerator, snagged two glasses from a rack and led the way through French doors to a semicircular patio.

Briar trailed behind and reluctantly sat in the white wrought iron chair he indicated. Black and white striped cushions padded the back and seat. He set his tray on a glass-topped table and opened the wine.

"There." He smiled triumphantly while he filled the glasses. "Eat. You look as if you need feeding up. You're too thin."

Briar dragged her chair close to the table and lifted a fork. "I'm not thin. I never have been."

The inspection he gave her was thorough. "No, you certainly aren't thin. My mistake. Small, but just right in all the right places."

Briar studied a forkful of tortellini in pesto sauce. "I think you're completely strung out. You need a rest."

"I need exactly what I've got. A little private time with someone I can trust." He gave her a glass of wine which she set down without reminding him that she didn't drink alcohol.

Briar didn't dare ask the question that burned her brain: What did he really expect from her?

Sinking into a chair, he stretched out very long legs. There was no doubt that it was the man who made the jeans. The jeans he wore were mesmerizing.

He looked at Briar from beneath lowered lids. "You should wear dresses more often."

"Thank you." Briar ate some pasta. The bright orange full-skirted dress had been Sandy's idea. "I like silk."

"Mmm. So do I. Soft. Slippery."

With a sigh, she set down her fork. "You are in a very strange mood."

"I'm in an honest mood. I thought you appreciated honesty."

"I do." Below the patio, deep green lawns rolled smoothly to the edge of the water. Coral-colored azaleas bloomed in splendid banks.

"Why did you come with me today?"

"You invited me for lunch. I didn't expect this."

"You don't like this? You wish you'd refused?"

She looked at him directly. "I came because I wanted to be with you. There isn't anyone I'd rather be with." There, she might regret it, but she'd told him the truth.

Dominic rested his head against the back of his chair and closed his eyes.

When he didn't answer, Briar said, "Why did you want me to come?"

"Same reasons."

Her skin sprang into goosebumps.

"Surely you know where we're heading," he said, his voice distant.

"I'm not sure there's any point in pursuing any of this."

He pushed himself upright. "We're *going* to discuss it. Tell me why you wore that dress."

She swallowed. "I wore it for you."

"Why?"

"Because what you think matters to me. I wanted to look... I wanted to look nice for you."

"You couldn't play games if you wanted to." Leaning forward, he smiled—but only with his mouth. "You wanted to look sexy and you do. Everywhere the stuff touches you makes me want to touch you—in the same spot, in the same way. Slowly, Briar. I want to stroke your skin in the same soft, erotic way that the silk strokes you. I want to take off the dress, inch by inch, then take my time looking at you without it. I want to be where your bra is. I want to take it away and cover your breasts—with my hands and every other part of me.''

Briar caught her breath. Her breasts began to throb as if his touch were real rather than a promise.

''Yes,'' he said so very softly. ''You want that, too. Shall I go on? Are your panties silk? Or are they satin? Or lace, Briar? I remember the way you looked in the on-call room. I've only got to close my eyes and I can see you like that. And I can see you naked, like you were last night.''

She felt weak and pliable—and confused.

''Oh, hell!'' He stood up so forcefully the wine slopped over. ''What's the matter with me? What I'm saying is true, God help me. You're hearing exactly what's in my head but I shouldn't be saying a word of it to you. Not to you, of all people.''

''What does that mean?'' She felt drained and heady.

''It means that I know I'm being unfair. You're easily ruffled so I'm ruffling you. That's not what I want.''

Briar hesitated, then got up. She went purposefully to Dominic's side and linked her arm through his. ''Come with me.''

''Where?'' He frowned. ''I suppose you want me to take you home.''

''Just be led for once.''

He allowed her to guide him back into the kitchen and through the hallway. Briar peered into the first room she came to, sighted a soft-looking couch and maneuvered Dominic onto it.

''Sit,'' she ordered. ''Make yourself comfortable.''

He looked mutinous, but only for a second before he did as she asked.

Briar sat on the floor between his knees and draped her arms across one of his thighs. ''Comfortable?''

''Oh, very comfortable.''

''Good. Now I'm going to tell you what's going on here. Or part of it anyway. You are very upset, Dominic. About your mother. You are also—from what I can gather—pretty much alone, apart from her. All of this flaunting of... Well, you're not yourself and you're saying things you wouldn't normally say because it's a diversion from worrying."

"Quite the little psychologist."

"Psychology plays a part in a lot of people's occupations."

"So you've decided to analyze me?"

She picked at the seam on the inside of his jeans leg. "I've decided that I'm supposed to be here for you. And I want to be, Dominic."

He was quiet for so long that she ventured another glance at his face. Her stomach jumped, turned. He watched her with hooded eyes and every sharp, masculine line of his face was drawn tight with desire.

Briar continued to smooth denim. "Your mother is a wonderful woman. She's not afraid, Dominic."

"I can't talk about that now."

"She loves you so much."

"What's happening to her is driving me mad."

She rested her forehead on his leg. "I understand. It's because you can't put it right and you think you ought to be able to."

His hand, settling on her neck beneath her hair, sent a shiver all the way to her toes. "Being with you helps," he said. "Forgive me for letting my mouth run away with me."

She closed her eyes and absorbed the sensation of his long fingers massaging her skin. "I probably shouldn't have, but I liked what you said." She clamped her teeth together.

Dominic laughed. "Did you really?" He raised her chin. "What are we going to do about that?"

"No one else has ever made me feel the way you do." How could she explain that, with him, she wanted to be every bit as abandoned as he suggested?

"So?"

"Dominic, you aren't yourself. Whatever you actually say, I know that what you really want and need is comfort. Nothing more complicated than that."

He leaned back again. "I think you'd better not stay where you are any longer, sweetheart. Come and sit by me."

Frequently, she couldn't seem to fully understand what he meant. Briar used his leg to pull herself up...and promptly found herself tipped across his lap and firmly held in his arms. Her head fitted against his shoulder as if it had been made to go there. Her bottom settled neatly on top of his hips—and she was acutely aware that there was nothing soft about that area of Dominic.

"You look shocked," he said, smiling, concentrating on her mouth...when he wasn't using his eyes to caress the rest of her body.

"You're trying to shock me. I think you're just tired."

"To the bone, sweetheart."

She frowned. "You agreed you need comfort. I really want to be that for you."

"What do you think comfort means?"

This encounter was a live minefield. "You first. What does it mean to you." She felt his arm tighten. "Does it mean sex? Is that it?"

"Maybe. Sometimes, anyway. Your turn. What does sex mean to you?"

Briar became still. Slowly and carefully, she swung her legs over Dominic's until she sat beside him. What happened here today was in her hands. She knew that now. "Sex cannot be casual for me."

"And you think it can for me?"

"I think you'd have an easier time with that idea than I would. We don't have a thing in common."

"You're hedging." Resting an elbow on the back of the couch, he positioned himself to watch her face. "Tell me what sex means to you."

"It has no meaning except as an extension of something much bigger... For me, that is." Her life had been filled with moments when she'd had to say things that others didn't want to hear, things that set her apart or made people want to avoid her. This was likely to be one more such moment.

Dominic used a thumb to trace a lapel at her neckline. Where her bodice came together in a vee, then slid it beneath to follow the lacy edge of a low cut bra. His lips parted. "I'm seeing what I'm touching, Briar. Is it okay if I'm honest about that?"

"You will be anyway." He was deliberately testing her willpower.

"What is this bigger thing you're talking about?"

"Commitment." She shouldn't feel embarrassed to confess her convictions, but she did. "I don't think a man and a woman should share their bodies as a kind of pastime."

"You mean you disapprove of sex outside marriage," he said flatly.

"For me, yes."

"I see." He turned away and let his head fall back again. "I'd better warn you about something right now."

Briar tensed. She crossed her arms and waited. His breathing had become deep and regular and she looked at him suspiciously. "Are you asleep?" she asked incredulously.

"Oh, no, sweetheart. Just settling in for a long, quiet thinking session."

"Just like that?" She didn't know whether to laugh or be furious. "You're going to *think* and leave me waiting to hear some sort of dire warning."

"No. The warning comes first." One strong arm worked behind her and she was pulled close until her face nestled against his neck. "You can go right ahead with your plans to be virtuous. I intend to go right ahead with my plans to corrupt you."

Briar tried, unsuccessfully, to pull away.

"Even as we talk, I'm planning the ultimate, slow seduction of the lady minister."

"Dominic—"

"Slow, very slow. I may start at your toes and work up. Or I may start at your delectable mouth and work down. Makes no difference. Every inch is equally fascinating...almost."

"I just told you I don't intend—"

"Mmm. I know what you don't intend. I intend to change your mind. We're going to be lovers, Briar. I promise you that."

"Dominic, listen—" one of her arms was trapped behind him "—I need to leave. I forgot I've got another appointment."

"When?" His eyes snapped open. "Who with?"

"With John and Sandy," she said quickly. "My brother and his wife."

"When?"

"Seven. We're going to a jazz club in Pioneer Square."

"You meeting them there?"

"Yes. And I have to go home and change."

"You'd never make it if you did. You look great the way you are, anyway. We'll get there in plenty of time."

"We?"

He smiled lazily. "It's so nice of you to invite me. I think it's about time I met your family. Now let me think."

He settled himself comfortably, looped his arms around Briar and rested his cheek on her hair.

"Dominic?" she whispered fiercely.

His breathing was very deep, very steady.

"Dominic?"

"I'm thinking, Briar. And I don't have a whole lot of time before we'll have to leave."

Briar wiggled until she could see his face. "What are you thinking about? Really, I mean."

He settled a lazy, hooded gaze on her. "Really?" A faint smile tilted the corners of his mouth.

"Yes, really."

His smile widened a fraction. "I'm thinking that time is running out for you."

"What do you mean?" His tightened embrace stopped her from springing away.

"You're about out of excuses, sweetheart. And right now, at this very second, I'm kissing a spot midway between your navel and... Yeah, that's where I'm kissing you."

Briar tried to sit more upright. Her clothes felt too tight.

"Now I'm kissing your ribs, one by one, working up."
A deep breath expanded his chest. "I've reached that
smooth, soft skin under your breast—your right breast.
Still working up—to the other side. I'm using my tongue
and—"

"Dominic!"

"What's the matter. Am I getting to you?"

"No!" She could hardly bear to sit still. Every speck of
skin, every nerve, felt singed.

"'Course not." He sighed. "Ah, well. We'll be leaving
in a few minutes. But, every time you look at me and find
me looking at you, lovely lady, you can be sure I'm enjoying whatever I'm kissing...or touching...or feeling
touching me, or taking me."

Briar opened her mouth to drag in a breath.

"Not getting to you, huh? I'll shut up in that case. Keep
my thoughts to myself." His grin was completely wicked
now.

"Dominic?"

"Shh." He placed a finger on her mouth. "We have to
leave. But don't forget, will you?"

"What?" She was trembling, actually trembling.

He stood and pulled her to her feet. "That I'll be thinking and enjoying every second of it...every second of you."

Chapter Fourteen

"You don't want to do this."

Dominic heard Briar. He chose to pretend he didn't.

"It's very noisy. You can't hear yourself think in there."

"Great. I love places like that." He lied, but in a good cause. A car pulled out of an on-street parking spot and Dominic whipped the Jag beside the curb. "Fate, you see. We were meant to be here together at this moment."

"How do you figure that out?"

"I never find on-street parking convenient to where I want to go. This has to be a sign." One close look at the straggling line of humanity waiting outside the club Briar had indicated gave him grave doubts about just what kind of a sign he was getting.

"This dress is all wrong," Briar muttered.

He avoided looking at her. Regardless of her theories about tension and tiredness affecting his judgment—and his behavior—the truth was that every time he let himself dwell on Briar Lee he felt very much awake and more totally alive than he ever remembered feeling. She was scrambling his brains, laying waste to all the heavy decisions he thought he'd already made about his life—and he didn't have a single clear idea as to what he intended doing about it.

But he wouldn't be walking away from her, not until or unless he could do so and stop thinking about her, wanting her.

When they stood on the cobbled sidewalk she hung back. "You are *really* going to hate this."

"That's my problem." He hoped he didn't sound as grimly determined as he felt. "I've always loved Pioneer Square. I used to hang out there when I was an undergraduate."

"Somehow I find that hard to imagine."

He ignored the dig. Circular lights above the black wrought iron pergola in the middle of the square shone weakly on those of the area's itinerant dwellers who made their beds on wooden benches. University of Washington students sporting Washington Husky sweatshirts wandered between bands of long-haired, black-leather-clad teenagers. Couples bearing the stamp of solid, middle-class America strolled side-by-side with the eternal products of the land's granola cult. Lone guitar players with tin cups, a man with a tuba and a four-note repertoire fingered through cutoff ends of woolen gloves, a mime, a balloon artist, a clown: the melee ebbed and flowed before the lighted windows of a dozen rowdy clubs.

"Fester's, you said?" Dominic caught Briar's hand and held it firmly.

"Yes. It's our favorite."

He raised a brow. "There's a line waiting to get in." He had difficulty associating Briar with the gyrating life beyond Fester's grimy windows. Ministering to the folks on the benches near the pergola, perhaps, but . . .

"There's John!"

When she would have run ahead of him, Dominic fastened his hand more tightly about Briar's. "You really like your brother, don't you?"

"I love him," she said without hesitation. "And Sandy. Wait till you meet Sandy. She's lovely."

Briar's brother saw Briar and waved her toward him. When she was close enough he hugged her and kissed a proffered cheek. His smile, when he looked at Dominic, became slightly fixed.

Brotherly protectiveness. Dominic recognized the symptoms. A long time ago he'd felt them himself and not for such different reasons. He, too, had wanted to protect a sibling who was as dear to him as his own life.

"Hi," John said, thrusting a hand in Dominic's direction. "John Lee."

Briar started to mutter apologies for forgetting the introductions.

Dominic returned the hard handshake and accompanied it with his best attempt at a trustworthy-guy smile. "Dominic Kiser. Briar's talked about you. Everything she says is good."

"She's biased."

Dominic kept his smile firmly in place. "Briar's a great judge of character." In other words: she thinks I'm okay so you can take back the deposit on the shotgun. "If she thinks you're great, I believe her."

John eyed him just long enough to convince Dominic he'd laid it on too thick. What the hell, he hadn't had much practice at trying to impress overprotective brothers.

"We got here early," John said. "Sandy's holding the table."

The din inside the club was deafening. Dominic squinted through a pall of vaguely blue smoke at droopy-eyed patrons leaning over mugs of beer. Heads wagged in time to the noodly music of a piano player, a slumberous drummer and a base artist evidently removed to a higher plane.

"Isn't this great?" Beside him, Briar almost skipped. Her face glowed.

"Great," he said, with little thought for the music or surroundings.

A pretty blond woman awaited them at a table. She hugged Briar, made no attempt to hide her curiosity about Dominic, even though she smiled and welcomed him enthusiastically, but very quickly gave all her attention to her husband. Dominic sat down, eyeing the couple thoughtfully. Briar had never mentioned her parents. This was evidently her family. They must represent what she expected in man/woman relationships. The thought was vaguely intimidating.

"Briar told us about your mother," Sandy said, putting her hand on his as naturally as if they were old friends. "We're so sorry and we're praying for her...and you, of course."

"Thank you." He would behave—for Briar's sake. The arrival of a glassy-eyed waitress to take their drink order was a welcome diversion.

He noted gratefully that John drank beer and asked for the same. Sandy, like Briar, opted for orange juice and tonic water.

"So you like the group?" Briar asked, her grin openly sly.

Dominic lowered his eyelids and rhythmically jutted his chin. "Totally. What are they called?"

Briar sat close beside him. She leaned on his arm and giggled. "The Last Ditch."

"Appropriate," he said seriously. Her unconsciously intimate gesture pleased him more than it should.

"Did your sister talk to you about last night?" he asked John. Briar's shoe, connecting with his ankle, made him wince.

Briar needn't have worried. John showed no sign of being aware of anything or anyone but his wife.

Dominic tried again. "Have you met Yarrow?"

John gave him a preoccupied glance. "Yarrow? Oh, the girl Briar's got at her place?"

"Yes. Last night—"

"Dominic stopped by last night," Briar interjected in a loud voice. "I think he was a bit taken aback by Yarrow's, er, unorthodox appearance."

He wasn't about to be so easily silenced. "Her appearance doesn't bother—"

"John, did you go with Sandy for her appointment?"

Dominic frowned. This woman really was a maverick who didn't intend to listen to advice—from anyone.

"Sure did." John kept right on gazing at Sandy, who gazed right back. "The doctor says everything's going according to plan. Not a thing to worry about."

"Isn't that wonderful?" Briar said. Her slender hands wound tightly together on top of the rickety table.

"Our first," John told Dominic. "I don't suppose heart surgeons are too interested in obstetrics."

Realization dawned for Dominic. "You're expecting a baby?"

"Yes," Sandy said. "And we're all so excited."

Dominic observed and nodded and uttered pleased, approving noises in all the right places. But he felt himself move farther outside the little circle of this family.

John and Sandy were completely involved with each other. Their love bound them almost tangibly. Dominic studied Briar. She watched her brother and sister-in-law raptly. Her pleasure in them shone in her flushed face. He rested his chin on a fist. This woman didn't see herself as beautiful—she didn't even seem to care how she looked.

Briar's eyes flicked suddenly in Dominic's direction and she caught him looking at her. The smile faded slowly.

He couldn't look away; didn't want to. Marvelous green eyes. In this light they glistened with flecks of yellow and gold and the iris was circled with a black band.

Dominic pressed his teeth into his bottom lip.

Briar passed the tip of her tongue over her mouth.

Whatever was happening between them—and something was definitely happening—was in danger of passing beyond his control.

Dominic didn't like not being in control. He made a fist on the table.

"Hey!" Briar bounced to her feet. "This is my favorite piece. Let's dance."

Following her to the minuscule dance floor, Dominic was aware that they were at least as out of place as she'd said they would be. When she turned to face him, bumped this way and that by other dancers, he didn't care how they looked, he didn't care about anything but being with Briar.

She came softly into his arms, wound her hands behind his neck and leaned into him.

"What's it called?" he asked her.

Briar rose to her toes. "Hmm?"

"This," he said, bending to her ear. "Your favorite piece of music. What is it?"

She inclined her head, smiled and swung a half-circle, taking him with her. "I don't know. I've never heard it before."

Dominic laughed aloud. "Shame on you, Reverend. If you're not careful you'll find yourself unfrocked." He crossed his wrists at her waist and made little circles on smooth silk—and warm, firm flesh. "Which fits right in with my plan."

"Shh. Concentrate."

"I am. I've decided silk is my favorite fabric."

Briar rested her face on his chest and he closed his eyes. She felt so good there, so perfect.

He ordered his thoughts with difficulty. "Does your brother have any idea what happened at your apartment last night?"

She held him more tightly, pushed her fingers into his hair. "I don't involve John and Sandy in... Well, there's no point in worrying them about things they can't change."

He shook her gently until she looked up at him. "Do you always read concern as interference?"

"I do if concern means I'm going to be told not to do what I know is right."

"It isn't right to endanger yourself. And it isn't right to take on things you can't handle. Briar, you can't handle big angry men who have no respect for women."

Her face disappeared into the hollow of his shoulder. "I know that. Dave was released from custody this morning and he's left the state. We don't have to worry about him anymore."

"Unless he decides to come back."

"I'm not a fool. I realize all that."

"Good. Will you promise me you'll be more careful. Yarrow's probably a worthy cause but I'd feel a whole lot better if she wasn't living under your roof."

He felt her sigh. "You really don't understand a thing about me, do you?"

Dominic hesitated. "I think I understand more than you know." He wasn't prepared to blow his chances with Briar, not without a fight.

"Don't worry about Yarrow...not about her bringing me any trouble anyway. She's moved on. She came back and packed her things and she's gone."

"Good."

"I doubt if it is good, but I can't do any more for her."

The rush of relief he felt tightened his arms around her. "She'll be fine."

"Maybe. Maybe not. I can't carry all the people who need help all the way through their lives. All I can do is help for a little while. I did that for Yarrow."

"Absolutely right. Now it's time for you to help someone else who needs help."

"How true."

They turned, turned again, Dominic leading with the pressure of his hips and thighs against her supple body.

"I've got a new case for you," Dominic told her. He was growing hard again, dammit. Not that he could expect anything else when her breasts were an insistent presence against his chest with only thin layers of cotton and silk to separate them.

"I like a written referral when it's possible," Briar said. Almost absently, she ran her fingers along the rim of his collar, played them down his shirtfront. "I don't think I actually want to take anyone else in for a little while."

He sighed hugely, rested his chin atop her head to hide his smile. "That's too bad. I really had my hopes up."

Her movements were absentminded. They had to be. With her nails, she made scratchy little forays over his nipple. Dominic shuddered.

"Are you cold?" She glanced up anxiously.

"No. Maybe I can change your mind about taking someone else in. We could make it a kind of half-and-half arrangement: Part of the time at your place. Part at mine."

Briar frowned. "I'm not sure how that would work. It's very generous of you, of course. But we'd have to get the idea cleared."

"Of course we wouldn't. As long as *we* agree, no one else has to know."

"Oh, I believe in making sure everyone concerned is fully aware of what's going on."

Unable to bear the sensations her nails were creating, Dominic captured her fingers. He raised them to his mouth and kissed the tips, separated them and kissed the sensitive spot at the base of each one—and smiled into her darkening eyes.

"You . . ." she swallowed, blinking ". . . you do understand that we should do that?"

"Make sure everyone concerned knows what's going on? Oh, definitely. So there's no problem. When I'm at your place, you'll know and when you're at my place, I'll know. And we'll both know when we're together, which should be as often as possible."

She stopped dancing and stared, lips parted. Then her glorious pink blush swept over her face. "You don't know what you're saying."

"Yes, I do."

"Dominic, we have completely different lives."

"That's often a good thing for people who spend a lot of time together. They don't bore one another."

"We have different goals." Even as she spoke, she found the open neck of his shirt and smoothed her fingers into the hair there. "We'd never be compatible."

"I think we might be very compatible."

"You aren't looking at the big picture here."

He dropped a hand beneath her waist, to the gentle curve of her hip. What he felt with Briar was well beyond simple desire. He might be becoming obsessed. "Forget big pictures for now."

"I don't think you're suggesting we play gin rummy."

He laughed, but saw nothing humorous in what she said. "I want to sleep with you, Briar."

"Don't! Not here."

"Unless you want to make a big scene, you can't stop me from talking. I want to sleep with you in my arms. I want to undress you and hold you. I want to shower with you and bathe with you and wash you and have you wash me. And in every one of those places and a whole lot more and doing every imaginable thing that a man and woman can find to do together—" He paused for breath. "In all those ways I want to make love with you."

Briar's arms went around him. "What do you think of John and Sandy?" She clutched handfuls of his shirt.

"I like them." He watched her narrowly.

"They really love each other. This baby they're expecting is an extension of that love."

"I'm happy for them."

"That's how I think an intimate relationship between a man and a woman should be—total commitment."

He didn't need an explanation of where she was heading. "Total commitment is a good goal. I think you have to be prepared to work toward it."

"You've never been married?"

"No."

"How do you feel about having children?" Her words hit him like cold water. "Don't you think that sex should have some greater meaning than two bodies using one another for gratification."

He stiffened, but only slightly. She wasn't as clever as she thought she was. "I've never thought too deeply about having children," he said honestly. "But I know that if sex is right, it's a whole lot more than bodies using one another."

"Tell me what it is."

"It's caring," he said quietly against her ear. "And sharing and giving pleasure."

"And that's what you're saying you want from me? Mutual caring and sharing?"

The balance had become very fine. He wanted to admit that he might be in much deeper with her than he'd ever expected to find himself with any woman. But the risk of disaster was too great.

"Dominic?"

"Mutual sharing would be a great start. But I'd rather say I want it with you than from you."

So swiftly he flinched, Briar held his face in her hands. "Listen to me. Listen carefully because I'm only going to say this once and I'm going to say it fast before I lose my nerve."

He didn't move a muscle.

"I want everything you say you want—and a whole lot more. But I already told you I don't believe in casual intimacy."

"Neither do I."

She moistened her lips. "What would you say if I told you I'd like to try... Dominic, what would be your answer if I said yes to your suggestion?"

"I'd say you'd made the right decision." He ringed her neck loosely with his hands and kissed her temple. "Are you saying yes?"

"I might be... if we can come to an agreement. And I think you already know what that would have to be."

He did. He doubted she did. "Will you become my lover, Briar? Will you have an affair with me—no strings attached?"

Chapter Fifteen

With tiny patches of heaven thrown in, the past weekend would go down in his memory as the weekend from hell.

"What are you thinking, Dominic?"

He stirred and managed to smile at his mother. "I was thinking that this biopsy is probably a waste of time." All he'd learned, all the years of training and practice had done nothing to make him better at dealing with personal crisis. "But it's a good idea to be sure, of course," he added lamely.

"You're worried."

"No!" For strangers he could be a convincing optimist, with his own mother he was proving a negative force. "I resent you having to go through this, that's all."

May patted the bed beside her. "Sit by me." Despite hours of fasting she looked pretty and cheerful.

"Hospitalization agrees with you," he said, perching on the edge of the mattress. "You obviously aren't ill. I think you should be kicked out to make way for someone sick."

She found his hand and squeezed. "Stop worrying, Dominic. And stop putting on an act. The stage didn't lose a thing when you decided to go into medicine."

Continuing to pretend would be pointless. "Okay, I'm worried. But not because I think anything's wrong. Oh, certainly, there may be some small thing to be taken care of, but nothing—"

"Dominic." She interrupted him gently. "That's not what you think. But I do. Why don't *you* listen to *me* for a change? I feel that everything will turn out fine."

"Why... Good. That's terrific and you're right."

"You were going to ask me why I'm so sure we won't get bad news today." She smiled and met him eye to eye until he summoned a smile of his own. "That's better. Talk to Briar about the way I feel. She's so much better at putting it into words than I am."

He shifted impatiently. "Was Briar in again this morning?"

"Yes. Very early."

Avoiding him again. If she thought she could manage that very often—or for long—she was wrong. One thing was very clear between them now: Briar wanted him as much as he wanted her, but there would never be any question of a "no strings" arrangement with his beguiling little nemesis. No, sir.

"Dominic? Are you still with me?"

"Yes." He sandwiched his mother's hand between both of his.

"She told me you've paid for an Easter party for the children's unit. Her sister-in-law's helping her with some things. But Briar said it was only because of you that she could buy what she'd hoped to buy to make it really nice. That was sweet of you, Dominic."

Sweet! "I'm going to get the money back from the hospital."

May rested her head and smiled knowingly. "Of course you are, dear. Surely you aren't afraid of ruining your cynical image, are you?"

"I don't think we'll pursue that." But he had to smile. "You really like Briar, don't you?"

"Oh, yes. I certainly do. And so do you."

So much for his efforts to appear aloof. "She's interesting."

May's laugh shook the bed. "You always did have a way with understatement. She said you two went dancing on Saturday night."

"She's tying me in knots." He hadn't intended to say that aloud. "I mean—"

"I know what you mean. It's written all over you. You've met your Waterloo at last, my boy. Thank God! What are you going to do about it?"

"Do?"

"About Briar. By the way, I hope you're going to recommend to the finance committee that they fund improvements to the chapel."

"Holy hell." Exasperated, Dominic got up and walked to the window and back. "She's even working on you. I don't believe it."

"What do you mean? Working on me? We had a general conversation about the deplorable condition of the chapel and I asked what was likely to be done about it."

He set off on another trip to observe rooftops on a lower wing. "How would you know about the damn chapel if she hadn't brought the subject up? Wait till I tell her what I think about that."

"Dominic!"

"What?" He tromped back to her side.

"Stop pacing and listen to me. I know about the chapel because I went there yesterday."

"Oh." Clasping his hands behind his back, he regarded his shoes. "For a service, or something?"

"Yes. I went to one of Briar's services. It was beautiful. There's no way a single person could have left that hovel without feeling more hopeful than they did when they arrived."

Briar had refused to see him at all yesterday. "The chapel's shabby. It's not a hovel."

"Briar would really like to spruce it up. I think she's especially conscious of how it looks with Easter just around the corner. What are you doing about it?"

"Nothing at the moment! I've got more important things on my mind. Why would she be pushing this now, anyway? Nothing's any different this year than it was last year." He cast his mother an apologetic little grimace. "Sorry. I'm shouting. This isn't like me."

"Oh, yes it is. You always did get angry when you didn't get your own way. We won't talk about the chapel anymore—for now. But don't forget it was you who said it was in just as horrible condition last year as it still is." She waved away his attempt to answer. "Right now you're angry because you want to be able to spirit me out of this bed and make it not true that I need a biopsy."

"You always did understand me too well," he admitted sheepishly.

"Yes. And don't forget it. But that's okay. I'd want to do the same for you. What isn't okay is that you're fighting a very strong attraction to a woman who's one in a million."

"I'm not fighting it! I'm chasing her the way I've never chased another..."

May chuckled. "Is that a fact? Well, well. Maybe there's hope for you after all. How long is it going to take you to catch her?"

"You are impossible." And wonderful. This mother of his was also what he termed "a woman in a million" and she was right, he was mad as hell that she was going through this.

"I think you should snap Briar up, Dominic. I really do. It's amazing someone else hasn't done it already but it could happen at any minute and then—"

"*Mother.*"

She cleared her throat. "What's holding you back?"

"Did I say something was holding me back?"

"You didn't have to. I can feel it."

"I've only known her a matter of weeks."

"Quite long enough. She's wonderful and so are you." May settled her hands on her stomach. "Get on with it."

"She wants children."

May beamed. "Wonderful. I knew my prayers would be answered in time."

He couldn't believe they were actually talking about this. "She isn't interested in..." No, he *couldn't* be thinking of saying what he'd almost said.

"She won't sleep with you unless you're committed to each other?"

Dominic passed a hand over his eyes. "Other people have mothers who knit and bake cookies and don't even *think* about such things. What did I do to deserve you?"

"You must have done something right, I guess. And other people's mothers do think about 'such things.' Don't be so silly." Looking immensely self-satisfied, May sat up straighter. "You love her, don't you?"

"*Don't* say that word!"

"Good. I knew you did."

HE LOOKED, Briar decided, like a mutinous boy, a very handsome, mutinous boy.

"Hi, Dominic." Standing in the corridor with her head poked around the door to the doctors' lounge, she braced for rejection.

"Come in or go out," he said. The old cutting edge was missing. "I'd rather you came in."

Briar went to him quickly, pulled an ottoman close to his chair and sat by his knees. "How much longer will she be?"

"She wouldn't let me be there."

"While the colonoscopy's being done?"

"Yes. She said it was nothing and I should find something useful to do."

Briar had to smile. "It certainly isn't hard to figure out where you got your determination from."

He frowned. "My mother and I are nothing alike."

"Of course not. Not at all."

"We're not. How do you think I feel? How would you feel if your mother refused to allow you to be present during a procedure?"

"My mother would probably insist on having everyone—" That kind of slip was something she rarely made these days. "My mother has her own special qualities. A desire to save someone else's feelings isn't one of them. May only wanted to make things as easy as possible for you."

He leaned forward. "She talked to you about not wanting me there?"

"No." She shook her head, fighting for patience. "I'm only trying to interpret what's going on here."

"It's been over an hour."

"Is that unusual?"

"Not necessarily. Where do your folks live?"

"My father's dead. My mother's remarried. She moved away."

"You aren't close?"

"I'm very fond of my mother."

Dominic bowed his head.

"It'll be okay," she told him. "May thinks so and so do I."

"The gastroenterologist doesn't. He thinks they'll find cancer."

Cautiously, Briar settled a hand on his hair. He let his head hang farther forward and slipped his arms around her waist.

"Please trust." Beneath her fingers, the tendons in his neck felt like tightly strung steel chords. She kissed his hair, worked her fingers into the muscles beneath his collar, rested her cheek on the back of his head.

She felt him tremble.

"There's something about you that makes me feel strong," he said. He ran his hands up her back until he clasped her shoulders. "You and I need to have a long, long talk."

They'd already talked more than was good for her peace of mind. "We will." Anything she could do to ease his way, she would—for now.

Dominic's mouth found the vulnerable spot at the base of her throat. "I need you, Briar."

Need? Want? "I'm here for you." There was nowhere else she wanted to be.

"I can't... I don't have what you have." He spread his fingers through her hair and kissed the corner of her mouth. "You know that, don't you? You know there are some things we can't change?"

He was asking her to accept his lack of faith. Briar turned her head to capture his mouth. She grazed his lips lightly and felt the instant speeding of his pulse.

Dominic brushed slowly, so slowly back and forth, parting her lips just enough to admit the tip of his tongue. A heavy ache, hot and demanding, pulsed low inside Briar. Again and again he caused this feeling. Even when he wasn't with her she had only to think of him, to see him in her mind, to experience this surge of desire.

He brought his hands slowly down over her breasts.

All the things he'd said to her on Saturday flooded back. In the shower, while they bathed, everywhere and in every way he wanted to make love to her. And she wanted him to.

"Dominic!" The door swung open to admit a small, lean man with clear gray eyes. "There you are."

Grabbing Briar's hand, Dominic surged to his feet. "Wally. What did you find?"

The man wrinkled his prominent nose. "Not a damned thing. Can you believe it? That's what took so long."

"Nothing?" Dominic's grip on Briar's hand was painful. "But, the films—"

"I know. I know. All I can think is that the bowel wasn't completely empty."

"I saw those films."

"So did I. And what we thought we saw isn't there."

"Could it be something outside? Ovary, maybe? Something pressing in?"

"I thought of that. No. She's fine, Dominic. And she feels fine. Let her rest for an hour and she can go home."

Briar felt Dominic go limp. She glanced anxiously at him.

"Thanks, Wally," he said. "You'll never know how grateful I am."

"Sure I will," the man said, smiling broadly. "I do. So am I. Why don't you get up and see her. She'll be a bit shaky for a while but she asked to see you and—" He raised a brow at Briar. "That wonderful girl?"

Dominic sent her a wry smile. "We'll go right up."

"I'm so happy for you," Briar said when they stood together in the elevator.

He hooked an elbow around her neck and pulled her against him. "I'm so happy for me, too." Steadying her, he laughed down into her face, kissed the tip of her nose. "Could I have an answer to my question?"

Always a man to press an advantage. "What question would that be?"

"You know which one. The 'will you' question."

"I'm thinking about it," she told him and her heart stood still. "I actually said it. Good heavens, I'm not sure I intended to."

Dominic gathered her into a bear-like embrace and planted a hard kiss on her mouth. The kiss deepened and she melted into him, met his tongue, rubbed his back beneath his jacket.

"You did say it," he chortled when they came up for air. "And you're a woman of honor. You won't back out. But don't worry, I'll help you. I'll be there to advise you every step of the way."

She gave him a wry grin. "Gee, thanks."

He was lowering his mouth to hers again when the doors opened to reveal a band of medical students.

Briar tried to step away.

Dominic clamped her where she was and swept past the goggling group. "Carry on," he said to them serenely. "Best to keep your mouths shut around here. Pick up less germs that way."

He chortled all the way to his mother's room and entered with a wide beam in place. "May, you're a fraud," he boomed. "Didn't I tell you this was all a waste of time."

May, sitting up in bed with a food tray in front of her and looking anything but shaky, pursed her lips and eyed her son narrowly. "I'm very grateful. My prayers were answered."

Briar slipped from Dominic's arm and went to sit beside the bed. "The doctor said you could go home in an hour or so."

"Yes." May turned toward Briar. "Thank you, my dear. You gave me a lot of strength."

Briar avoided looking at Dominic. "The strength is always there, if we dare to ask for it."

"I know," May agreed. "I know."

"Any pain at all?" Dominic asked. Briar was relieved that he still sounded cheerful.

"None. I'm going to have to be a bit more careful about my diet. Living alone can make you careless. Could we say a prayer, Briar. Just a simple thank-you for such a blessing."

"Did you thank Wally?" Dominic said. There was no cheer in his harsh tone now.

"Of course," May said.

Briar's stomach made a slow revolution. Dominic's face had settled into hard, implacable lines. "If you have something else to do, Dominic, I'll be glad to spend some time with your mother."

"There's nothing else I want to do."

"I do believe you and I should have a little chat, son," May said with a touch of steel in her own voice. "A long overdue chat."

Dominic prowled about reading instructions on equipment as if he'd never seen any of them before.

"With Briar here I feel less intimidated by you."

"Less intimidated?" The words exploded from him. "What do you mean by that? Since when have I ever intimidated you?"

"You're intimidating me now."

His stricken face touched Briar, but she said nothing.

"Briar, has Dominic told you about Michael?"

"Yes, he—"

"Not now, May," Dominic said. "You need peace and quiet. Stress isn't good for you."

"Stress isn't good for *you,*" May said. "Talking about Michael makes me sad. Not talking about him—as you and I haven't talked about him in all the years since he died—makes me a whole lot more sad. It doesn't stress me."

"There's no point in hashing over what can't be changed," Dominic muttered.

Briar knew she couldn't say anything to help.

"When Michael died I thought the pain of it would kill me," May said evenly. "I loved him as much as I love you, Dominic. Part of me died with him."

"*Half* of me died with him," Dominic said venomously. "And for what? Why? Give me one reason to justify the death of a great kid with everything to live for."

"He chose to do what he did," May said. She dropped her head and looked up at Dominic. "He was responsible for his own actions."

"He was twenty!" Dominic shouted. "A kid. He made one mistake and died for it. Where was your God then?"

"It's doubtful that the dose that killed him was the first one." May spoke so quietly Briar had to lean closer.

"Damn it!" Dominic rammed a hand into his hair. "You had to say it, didn't you? You just had to say it. No one knows it wasn't the only hit."

"Dominic," Briar said, trying to keep the shakiness out of her voice. "God doesn't point the finger and say 'you die.' Surely you don't believe he does."

He let his hands fall. The anger drained slowly from his features. "He didn't stop what happened."

She felt a rush of triumph. He said he didn't believe in God, but he was admitting a higher power. "He gave us free will."

"It's all hogwash," Dominic said. "Let's drop it. I'm a surgeon, a scientist. I deal in what can be proved."

"But you believe there's something or someone that has the power to visit bad things on good people."

"I didn't say that. No, I don't believe it. And I don't believe this is something we'll ever be able to talk rationally about." He squared off with Briar. "But that doesn't mean you and I can't have something terrific together."

She glanced uncomfortably at Mrs. Kiser who appeared not troubled, but animated, happily interested.

"Does it?" Dominic prompted Briar.

"I don't know. That's going to depend a great deal on what exactly it is you want us to 'have' as you put it."

"Dominic wants you Briar."

"Mother!" He glared.

"Don't *Mother* me, my boy. You want to have something terrific with the best thing—woman—that ever happened to you? What *does* that mean?"

"We shouldn't be discussing this here."

"Seems like a fine place to me," Briar said, suddenly mutinous. "Your mother seems to have a very clear perspective on things."

"You probably want Briar to have an affair with you. Am I right?"

Briar was afforded the unique experience of seeing Dominic blush.

"I thought so," his mother said. "Do you honestly think this is a woman who will be happy to service you without some sort of involvement of the heart?"

Briar covered her mouth. Dominic silently formed the word "service" and his eyes grew almost black.

"Is it all right if I just spell out what I think may be going on here?" May asked.

Dominic swept wide an arm. "Aren't you going to anyway? You've already done enough damage. Why stop now?"

"I'd like to hear what you think," Briar said, struggling with the urge to laugh.

"Good." May settled herself more comfortably. "I think you, Dominic, are trying to decide whether or not you love Briar."

He closed his eyes and sat on the nearest chair.

"I think Briar is probably working her way through the same question. I think Dominic knows that if he wants you, Briar, he's going to have to consider marriage."

A strangled noise issued from somewhere deep in Dominic's throat.

"But I also think he knows that he doesn't have this one in the bag. You two aren't exactly Mr. and Mrs. Compatibility. Dominic knows you may not agree to have him, Briar. Men do hate to contemplate presenting the big 'M' question and getting turned down."

"That's it." Dominic held up a hand. "I can't take anymore of this."

"I'm going to finish. What on earth do you have to lose by asking Briar if she loves you? If she says she does, you can ask her to marry you. What could be more simple?"

Briar watched his face and her heart felt squeezed. His struggle was so clear. "And what could be more complicated?" she said, getting up. "Even if he does think he might love me and I might love him, he's afraid. He's afraid of becoming dependent on another human being. And he's afraid of losing some of the control he guards so jealously."

"Don't talk as if I'm not here, dammit." Dominic got to his feet and stalked to stand over Briar. "You don't know what I'm thinking. Neither of you do."

"Not for sure," Briar said. "But are we close at all?"

He seemed to hesitate, seemed unsure.

"Dominic?" Briar touched his arm.

"We don't have a thing in common," he said finally. "Nothing. Let's forget the whole thing."

Briar turned and hurried from the room and didn't slow down until she turned a corner in the corridor. She cast a surreptitious glance over her shoulder.

He wasn't following.

Curling her hands into fists, she stomped on. "Pompous ass," she said aloud. "I'm not through with you yet!"

Chapter Sixteen

At precisely six o'clock, Dominic drove along Western Avenue. *"An assignation,"* Briar had said on the phone the night before. *"That's what I have in mind."*

Friday evening traffic was predictably heavy. The city was emptying for the weekend. He'd probably have to drive around the block a few times to find somewhere to park. Then he'd be late. Briar's idea of an assignation was undoubtedly far different from the accepted one but he'd take whatever she was offering...for now. During the past week, despite his best efforts to fill up every hour, she'd crept into his brain repeatedly. *"Twenty-four hours alone"* was what she'd offered and he'd grab it, even if he'd probably be even more confused at the end of their *"little trip away"* than he already was.

He saw the bright pink and orange polka-dot shirt and black pants before he realized Briar was the woman wearing them. She stood in the middle of an empty parking space in front of her apartment building, blithely ignoring drivers who paused, honked and otherwise tried to get her to vacate the spot they wanted.

Dominic grinned and waited for the car in front of him to give up and move on. Briar saw him and vacated her post. Struggling with a blue nylon carryall and several string-handled paper bags, she reached the Jag and caught the door as he leaned to shove it open.

"What are you trying to do? Get lynched?"

"Nope. Just incite a riot," she said, handing over her burdens to be swung into the back seat. She slid in and slammed the door. "I can be a very determined woman."

"I believe you."

"Good. I was making sure we didn't waste time getting me into the car. We've got places to go and things to do."

He glanced at her. Briar sat, hands pressed between her knees, her eyes firmly trained ahead. *Okay.* This could prove to be a very interesting experience.

"Work your way to the freeway. Heading north."

"Yes, ma'am!"

She twisted to look at the back seat. "Where's your bag?"

"In the trunk. Toothbrush, you said."

"Yes. We'll be away overnight. Did you have any difficulty clearing your schedule?"

"No," he said, determined not to sound either amused or excited. "In my line of work one doesn't get to clear the schedule. I did arrange for someone to cover for me. Put your seatbelt on."

She slipped the buckles together. "You're a bit overbearing sometimes."

He wasn't about to touch that one. "May tells me you talked to her and she knows how to make contact if necessary."

"Yes."

"Where are we going?"

"North."

"That much I know. Where north?"

She switched on the radio and flipped between channels, settling for—surprise, surprise—some sort of modern jazz.

"Briar, where north are we heading? How far?"

"Not far. We'll take the Stanwood exit and head for Camano Island. It's not really an island in the real sense, but—"

"I know all about Camano. At high tide—for a river, that is—there may be four inches of water running under the bridge on the other side of Stanwood. That's what supposedly makes Camano an island."

"You've been there before." She sounded aggrieved.

"To the state park when I was a kid. We camped there."

"Oh."

When they were finally on the freeway heading north he relaxed as much as his curiosity would allow. "Why all the secrecy? We could have had a marathon haggling session at my place... or yours."

"I don't want a marathon haggling session. I hate arguing."

"Where exactly are we going?"

"To a little house someone lent me."

Every shred of information was going to have to be pulled from her. "Who owns the house?"

"A friend. A woman who runs one of the shelters in Seattle."

"Why do we have to go so far away?"

"So we won't be interrupted."

Dominic regarded her profile. Her nose tilted slightly. At the moment, her sharp little chin jutted, suggesting determination—determination to follow through on whatever quest she'd initiated.

"You wouldn't tell me a thing on the phone."

That chin moved even another fraction forward. "You could have refused to come."

"Refused?" He laughed. "What do you think I am? A woman who fascinates me says she wants to arrange a twenty-four hour assignation with me and I'm going to refuse?"

A faint smile touched her lips. "It was a test."

"Ah, I see. That explains everything." Or nothing, which was the case in this instance.

"You do know what an assignation is?"

"Um—" he cleared his throat "—there may be more than one connotation."

"I meant the tryst variety. An assignation. We're talking calculated opportunity to explore the possibilities of a mature relationship."

Dominic tightened his hands on the wheel. "Would you like to expand on that?"

"I thought that was expansive."

"I'm sure I misunderstood."

Briar kicked off her shoes and pulled her feet onto the seat. "You obviously didn't misunderstand. Dominic, do you want to find out if we're compatible?"

He swallowed and choked . . . then coughed.

Briar twisted in her seat. She pushed him forward and pounded between his shoulder blades. "You all right?"

"Fine," he sputtered.

"You did ask me to have an affair with you."

"Yes," he said weakly. His eyes were tearing.

"I can't do that. Not in the way you probably meant. Not on an ongoing basis."

Shaking his head, he searched for a response.

"I know. You don't understand what I'm getting at. I've made a decision, that's all. Times are changing and I have to change with them. That doesn't mean I could ever throw away my principles, but I do think I have to be prepared to bend them a bit if an issue seems to warrant that."

"Briar," he said, trying to sound patient. "Are we talking about . . . I don't want to make any false moves here, but could you possibly be discussing having a physical relationship with me?"

"You mean having sex?"

Nothing, *nothing* could have prepared him for this approach. "Do you have to be so blunt?"

"Like you, I've always believed in directness."

"Semantics," he muttered.

"If you'd rather not do this, I'll understand." Her voice was tight and small.

Dominic turned down the radio. "I wouldn't miss it for the world," he said, meaning every word. "Could you explain why you've had this apparent change of heart?"

"I suppose you think this is a pretty cold approach to the whole thing."

He faced her briefly. She appeared pinched, anxious. "No, Briar. Anything but cold. Look, I'm not going to get

you wherever it is you're taking me and then jump all over
you. Just the chance to be with you and talk quietly would
be great. I've missed you the past few days."

"That's your fault. You were an idiot the last time we
were together."

He let that comment hang between them before saying,
"Yes, I guess I was."

"All week I've been trying to decide what to do about it.
This is what I came up with. Can we be quiet for a while
now?"

"Sure." She really was the most unusual woman he'd
ever met. Perhaps . . . no, that *was* part of the allure. But it
wasn't all of it. He really had missed her this week, but
she'd steadfastly refused to have anything to do with him
until the telephone call and the bizarre invitation.

"Why don't we stop and get some dinner?" he asked
when they'd been on the road almost an hour.

"The turnoff for Stanwood's coming up. We'll be at the
house in half an hour. Are you really hungry?"

"Not really." Not at all if he were to be completely
truthful. Tense would describe his condition accurately. But
he was also growing aroused at some deep level he'd never
experienced before. He'd certainly been propositioned before, but not by a woman like Briar and not in a way that
suggested a clinical experiment. She'd made her pitch, her
offer of time together, like a small warrior issuing a challenge.

"I've brought food," she said, then announced, "This
is it. Take this exit."

The green and white sign for Stanwood loomed. He followed her directions through the small agricultural town,
across a bridge over the currently invisible trickle of is-
land-making water and onto roads bordered by heavy for-
estland.

At last they arrived at a tiny A-frame house enclosed on
three sides by its own towering forest. The third side faced
dusk-silvered water.

Briar was immediately a bundle of furious activity.
Reading to herself from a sheet of instructions, she rushed

back and forth, unlocking doors, throwing electrical switches, turning on water, flushing toilets. Dominic had to stop her from insisting on carrying in the bags from the car.

Inside, the house appeared to consist of one large room with a sleeping loft and a small kitchen. A black wood stove stood in the center of the building, its chimney rising straight to the apex of the roof.

Briar avoided meeting Dominic's eyes. With the groceries she'd brought stowed in a small refrigerator, she dropped to her knees before the stove and began stuffing newspaper inside. "It's not really cold," she remarked. "But it will cool off later and there's no real heating in this place. Anyway, I always think a fire's rather romantic, don't you? In the movies, they always—"

"Whoa," Dominic said, pulling his hands from his jeans pockets. "I don't want to interfere here, but you'll be missing a bet if you don't let me light that fire for you. I'm an expert."

Her glazed expression suggested she only half-heard him, but she got up and let him take over. By the time flames roared steadily up the chimney, the smell of something spicy emanated from the kitchen.

"There's no table," Briar commented, carrying in a tray and setting it on the floor near the fire. She sat cross-legged on the shaggy, wool rug. "Do you mind sitting here to eat?"

Dominic looked down on the top of her bowed head. Firelight shimmered on russet waves. He felt a rush of tenderness. "I don't mind." She was complex and he liked her that way.

"It's just toasted sandwiches," she said. "And celery and carrots and apples."

He joined her. "Sounds great."

"That's beer," she said, pointing to a glass. "You like that, don't you?"

Dominic nodded. He made no attempt to drink.

"I thought you did. You had some when we went out with John and Sandy. John told me to get this kind."

He paused in the act of picking up a carrot stick. "John? You asked your brother what kind of beer to buy for me?"

"Yes."

"Did you tell him why?"

"Because I was bringing you up here for the night, yes."

"Ah." And what, Dominic wondered, did John Lee think about that?

The sandwiches were smoked turkey and cheese. Once he began to eat, Dominic found he was hungry after all.

"I do have fantasies, you know."

He almost dropped his sandwich.

"I knew that would surprise you." Briar sounded almost smug. "You probably thought I was some iceberg of a woman who'd never had a sexy thought in her life, didn't you?"

"Er..."

"It's all right. I'm not offended. I know I could never be considered the, um, sensual type. That is, outwardly I don't seem to be, but I think I am really."

Dominic regarded her serious, wide-open, beautifully green eyes and forced the mouthful of sandwich he'd taken down his throat.

Briar hadn't touched her food.

"Did you mean what you said?"

"Said?" He wished he could say the right things now.

"At Fester's. You know. About wanting... You said you wanted to..." She puffed up her cheeks and leaned forward until her hair obscured her face.

"I know what I said," Dominic said, remembering all too clearly. "And I meant it, Briar. Surely you know that."

"On Monday—in your mother's room—you said you wanted to forget everything about me."

"That's not exactly what I said." He'd been scared to death by the direction the conversation had taken, but he wasn't about to confess as much. "I'd had a difficult day and was on edge. I needed time to think."

"Do you think what I'm doing is disgraceful?"

"You couldn't do anything disgraceful if you tried."

She raised her face. The sheen in her eyes needed no explanation. "I don't want any food. Have you had enough to eat?"

Rather than answer, he got up and carried the tray back to the kitchen. When he returned, Briar stood at the foot of the loft stairs with the blue nylon bag in her hand.

"Are you tired?" she said.

He covered the space between them quickly and took the bag from her. "I'm not tired. Are you?"

She shook her head.

"Briar, I'm not interested in some sort of sex by numbers with you." The instant flare of hurt in her eyes turned his stomach. "But I do want to make love with you," he added and touched her cheek gently.

"That's what I want." She leaned toward him until he dropped the bag and gathered her into his arms. "It's all right to want that, isn't it?"

She was asking *him?* "As far as I'm concerned it's absolutely all right."

Briar put her hands on his shoulders. "Good. I think so, too."

He kept on watching her and waiting. What he had to remind himself was that this woman was different, with a different set of values and rules. But she was also passionate. That was something he could feel so strongly it shook him.

She'd let him know what she wanted and she would set the pace.

"It's nice by the fire, isn't it?"

"Yes," he said. This would not be like anything else— like being with anyone else.

After Briar, after tonight, he would never be the same. His mouth dried out. This was what had made him draw back from her, this powerful sense that she could change him.

"Come up to the loft."

She'd made up her mind. Briar would lead and he would follow. His body quickened, turned hot and heavy. She took his hand and pulled him behind her up the open staircase.

"Where's the light?"

She urged him across the loft to a doorway. "The bathroom's here. There's a shower. And a bath. I can see well enough by the light of the fire, can't you?"

He looked over his shoulder at the flickering glow that leaped over weathered rough cedar paneling and beams. "Yes, I can see."

Stepping away from him, she began unbuttoning her shirt. He saw her faint, seductive smile and the quickening became a pulsing hardness that made him long to throw off his clothes and fall with her on the low, wide, quilt-covered bed.

Her terms. Her game plan. He had to wait, to be patient.

Patience was out. "Come here," he told her.

She dropped her hands. The shirt hung open. He saw the sweet curves of her breasts, the deep shadow between.

"Come here, Briar," he repeated—more softly.

She came.

He reached for her but she held his wrists, placed his hands on her slender hips. "Wait." Her fingers trembled, but she managed to unbutton his shirt and pull it free of his jeans. Stroking his skin, she passed her palms over his naked chest, murmuring words he couldn't make out, tangling with hair, pushing the shirt from his shoulders and pulling it down his arms. She let it fall.

When she pressed against him, he felt the erotic graze of the lace that didn't disguise the springing pressure of her budding nipples. "I love kissing you," she said, her breath whispering across his mouth. "I've never told you that. I should have."

"Yes, you should." And he'd wondered if she was inexperienced! Yes, she was sweet. Yes, there was a newness to her giving, but she was playing him like a master musician who gave only rare performances with a unique touch.

Standing on tiptoe, Briar held his face and set about a very thorough sampling of the kisses she loved. And while she tested the contours of his lips with her tongue, and teased his into her mouth, and reared back to bring him foraging for her, it was the satin of her bare breasts above the bra that drove him wild.

"Briar," he said into her hair. "Briar, I can't . . . I need you, sweetheart."

The shudder that racked her only drove his desire higher. He found some little lace flower thing between her breasts. "I love kissing you, too. I want to kiss all of you—I need to kiss all of you." The merest tug made room for his fingers to slip inside the bra. He passed his knuckles gently back and forth. Her nipples were twin straining pebbles.

She said nothing, but he heard her moan.

Dominic took off her shirt, unhooked her bra and stripped it away. Desperation drove him now. When he reached for her waistband, she stopped him and unfastened it herself.

Hurrying. She was hurrying, too.

His heart surged, his whole body. This was right for them both. No more thought. His jeans scraped down his legs, giving him blessed freedom. He felt the spring of his flesh and gasped aloud.

"Now," Briar said in a voice he barely recognized. She pulled him with her. In the rise and fall of the firelight, he dimly saw the beauty of her. Small, perfectly proportioned and voluptuous in the promise she offered him.

The bed met the backs of her legs and she lost her balance. She buckled onto the mattress and he slipped to kneel on the floor between her thighs.

"Oh, love," he said. Leaning over her, he kissed her flat belly, ran a moist line upward over her ribs to capture a nipple and suckle until she cried out and caught at his hair. "Love, oh, my love."

"Dominic?"

He smiled into her smooth skin. She was asking him to join her. The quest was a joint one now, no longer only her own. Pushing her breasts together, he worshiped them with his mouth before darting up to capture her lips in a long dominant kiss that left them both gasping.

She would get no rest, not yet. No, not yet. And she wouldn't want rest until they were both sated. He heard her mindless sounds, saw a moving glow through his closed eyelids and felt only the helpless jutting of Briar's hips. Sliding down, branding every inch he passed with his lips and teeth, he found the slick center of her.

"Dominic!"

Grinning, nuzzling, crazy for more of the taste of her, his answer was to push her thighs farther apart to accomplish what he would soon accomplish again—in the final way he yearned for. But first this. Even as she convulsed under his driving touch he smiled anew, knowing that before the waves of pleasure faded, and because of them, she would be more for him and he for her.

Her flailing hands thrashed at his shoulders. Her cries became a beseeching whimper. The waiting was done. Dominic rose over her, drawing her higher on the bed and settling himself between her legs. "Now, sweet," he murmured.

She moved almost restlessly, silent now. When he positioned himself at the opening to her body, he felt as much as saw the way she turned her face aside. He thought she bit down on her own hand.

Control whirled, spun away. He thrust into her. *Small and tight.* The contraction he met inflamed him. He drew back and thrust again, and then the rhythm of his body took over.

Only dimly he heard her cry out. Only dimly did some warning sound in his brain.

Again and again the automatic pumping of his hips took him into her. *So very tight.*

At his release, his own shout rang in his ears. For seconds his body kept moving of its own volition. Briar's arms wound around his sweat-slick neck in a crushing embrace. She held him as if she'd break if they moved apart.

And she cried against his throat.

Dominic became still. He buried his face in the pillow and stroked her hair. "Sweetheart," he said. "Oh, my sweetheart." Exhaustion weighted his limbs. "Don't cry."

"I'm happy," she said brokenly. "Really happy."

That contraction around him? His eyes opened. Keeping her head firmly cradled in his hand, he rolled away just far enough to look down on her face. Briar reached for him blindly. She trembled steadily.

"Briar?" He shook her gently. "You were a virgin?" Damn it. He'd guessed as much weeks ago, but then she seemed to change, to send different signals.

"Just hold me."

He did as she asked, carefully gathering her to him. "Why didn't you tell me?"

"I tried." She kissed his neck and burrowed her head beneath his chin. "It just made me feel stupid."

He couldn't hold her close enough to make him happy. "How can a lovely, totally feminine woman be thirty and still untouched? And why did you decide to change that...with me?"

"Don't you know?"

Dominic covered her with his body. If he could, he'd keep her here, covered and safe, forever. Yes, he knew the answer to his own question. "Tell me." He needed to hear the words.

"There was never anyone else who made me want what I want with you. I love you."

"Oh, Briar, Briar."

Never letting her go, he wrenched at the quilt until he could pull it over them. He'd asked his question and she'd given her answer.

They didn't speak again. Finally she slept. Dominic felt the gentle slipping away but he continued to hold her close. She had made a gift of herself to him.

Turning onto his back, he eased her to lie on top of him. He'd been right: he would never be the same.

Chapter Seventeen

"August died," Dominic said.

Briar rested her ear heavily on the phone and closed her eyes.

"Briar?"

She blinked against tears. "Yes. Oh, Dominic... Oh, no. I knew it had to be soon, but I'm not ready."

Several seconds passed before he said: "Neither am I. He was some guy, wasn't he?"

"Yes." Her throat hurt. "When did it happen?"

"Early Friday evening."

"Oh." On Friday evening while she and Dominic had been...

"When did you find out?"

"Not until I made rounds this morning." His voice, even and flat, held resignation. "There was nothing on my service when we got back last night. I asked why I wasn't informed. Apparently Mrs. Hill saw no reason to bother me."

"Or me," Briar said. She felt numb. "I'd better find out when the services are."

"There won't be any," Dominic said. "Evidently he was a very organized man. I don't have to tell you he had definite ideas about what he did and didn't want. All the arrangements had been made. He was cremated yesterday afternoon."

"Poor Mrs. Hill."

"Yes," he said. "It's always seemed useful to me to have some sort of official parting for the living after someone dies. A little interim mourning before the real thing."

Briar could no longer pretend that Dominic was un-emotional, but he did seem very good at presenting his matter-of-fact side.

"Briar? Are you still there?"

"Yes."

"We couldn't have done anything for August even if we had been here."

He was certainly becoming adept at reading her thoughts. "Medically perhaps not. But I might have been able to give him some comfort."

She heard him expel a short breath. "August was hardly turning into one of your converts."

"No," she said, becoming irritated. "But he liked me in his thorny way. And I think he trusted me. Anyway, maybe I needed to be there for myself."

"I think you needed to be exactly where you were. *I* needed you, Briar."

"I'd better get in touch with Mrs. Hill."

"Don't turn your back on me."

He felt so free to say what he wanted from her. "This is going to be a busy week. And next weekend." The Easter weekend. Usually she went into this week feeling sad but optimistic, knowing that in the end there would be the sense of starting afresh.

"Briar, our twenty-four hours were so special to me."

She fastened her eyes on the bright blue sky beyond her kitchen window. "To me, too." But there had been no commitments, no response when she'd said she loved him.

"I understand how busy you'll be this week." He sounded strained. "Is everything ready for the big party?"

He hadn't forgotten. The thought shouldn't bring her quite so much pleasure. "Pretty much ready. Thanks to you."

"I didn't—"

"Yes, you did. Don't argue. You did something really nice and I'm grateful. Okay?"

"Okay. I bet you'll look cute in a bunny suit."

She frowned. "Why... Oh, the Easter Bunny. Sorry to disappoint you but I don't think that would be at all cute under the circumstances."

"If you say so." He laughed. "No, I suppose not."

Briar had a brief vision of herself with big, white floppy ears and coming face to face with one of her superiors. Not a pretty sight, but she smiled anyway.

"If nothing unexpected comes up I should be through here by noon today," Dominic said. "Where will you be then?"

"I'll be at the hospital all day. Then I've got a counseling session downtown. Sundays aren't days of rest for me."

She could almost hear him considering and discarding retorts. "When will the counseling session be over?"

"By six-thirty."

"Give me the address. I'll pick you up."

Briar leaned against the counter and frowned. "I can't." He didn't understand that she had no intention of simply sleeping with him whenever he felt like it, which, if their brief sojourn at Camano was a measure, would be most of the time.

"Why not?" Dominic sounded genuinely surprised.

"I've got to get to the hospital. I'm already late."

He was saying something as she hung up. The phone rang again but she ignored it, pushed her keys and wallet into a pocket and ran from the apartment.

Why couldn't she be there whenever he wanted her to be? That was the message Dominic was sending.

Morning sunshine warmed her face. Her hair blew behind her. Spring was alive with the promise of summer to come. Warm days and nights. Dark and heated hours in the arms of a man who knew all about things she'd only guessed at before she met him. His hands on her skin, the deliberately slow, slow arousal he accomplished with every clever sensual touch; the memory made her ache. She paused on the steps. How could it be right that thinking of him, of the things he had done to her and taught her to do to him could make parts of her swell and throb when she wasn't even with him? His mouth was so beautiful, so talented. And his fingers . . . his slim, agile hips . . .

She loved Dominic.

Running once more, shutting out the images, she flew down the rest of the staircase.

"Morning," Fred called as she left the courtyard. He sat on his blankets, legs stretched out, his back resting against the wall. Tinkerbel, sporting what looked like a new pink kerchief around her neck, twitched her nose and closed her eyes against the light.

"Good day for new beginnings," Briar told Fred as she passed. "I heard they're looking for roadside cleanup crews—down at the Millionaire's Club."

"That a fact?"

Briar stopped and looked down into Fred's leathery face. "How old are you?"

"That's a new question." He sniggered, showing surprisingly strong teeth. "Far as I can remember I'm probably close on sixty or thereabouts."

She frowned. "You don't look anywhere near that old."

He laughed aloud. "Take note of that, my girl. Close on sixty and don't look a day over forty-five. Why d'you suppose that might be?"

Briar pursed her lips suspiciously. Tinkerbel had insinuated herself strategically to allow Briar to scratch her head.

"Don't know, eh? Well, because I like you I'll tell you my secrets. Never worry about where the next meal's coming from or where you'll sleep or where you're going to be tomorrow." He worked a greaseproof paper sack from the pack beside him and extracted a flattened peanut butter and jelly sandwich. "And above all, avoid organized labor handed out by do-gooders."

"And what if the next meal doesn't come and there's nowhere to sleep?" Briar said.

"I've got my permanent bedroom." Fred indicated the sidewalk and the sky and laughed again. "And it was you who told me God looks after the poor and needy. What do I have to worry about with Him taking care of me—and you?"

Shaking her head, Briar took off in the direction of the bus stop. Nobody had ever said her job would be easy but it might be nice if it weren't so darn frustrating so often.

By the time she arrived at the hospital, she'd made plans to contact Mrs. Hill and offer whatever support the woman might need. The thought of not seeing August again made a solid knot of unhappiness in Briar's heart. She'd said goodbye to a lot of people she cared about, but it never became easier.

"There you are."

She heard Dominic's voice and then saw him. Leaving a group of doctors clustered in discussion, he closed purposefully on her.

"Hi, Dominic." She kept right on walking until she reached the reception desk. He was at her heel. She told the receptionist, "Good morning" and signed in.

"We need to talk," Dominic said, putting his hand under her arm. "We can use my consulting room."

Briar faced him. "Not now. I'm sorry, but I want to get in touch with Mrs. Hill. And I have to get ready for a service and visit patients before I'm due downtown."

"And you have to take care of your own life," he said, leaning closer. "And mine. We have to take care of us, Briar."

"We'll talk about it." The attempt at lightness was a miserable failure. "Later."

A feathery tap on her shoulder finally broke her eye contact with him. She turned to find Mrs. Hill standing behind her—smiling.

"Hello, Briar," the woman said. "I'm very glad I found you without having to search this place." She brought her shoulders up. "I find this such a big, intimidating building."

"I'm sorry I wasn't here on Friday night," Briar told her.

"How are you, Mrs. Hill?" Dominic put in. "We're all going to miss August but I know these next months will be especially hard on you. If there's anything I can do to help you, please call. You can always reach me through my service—here or at home."

Briar glanced at him in surprise. He sounded as if he meant every word. Did he throw out offers like that to every bereaved relative? Or, like her, was he feeling guilty that he hadn't been here at the end when August needed him most.

"August slipped away in his sleep," Mrs. Hill said. She held a worn black leather handbag before her. "I wasn't there. August would have been pleased it was like that...no one standing around crying. He was ready to go. I'm happy for him. If he regretted anything he didn't say much about it."

Briar met Dominic's eyes. He raised his brows. "What can I do to help you?" he asked the woman.

She opened her purse and took out an envelope from which she extracted a single sheet of paper. "Nothing, thank you. We really do have things in good order," she told them both. "There are just a few special things to deal with for August. Then I'll be off to Minnesota to live with my sister. She never did marry. She'll be glad of the company and so will I."

This woman had made her preparations, Briar realized. Mrs. Hill would miss her husband, but she was at peace with carrying on.

"August wanted me to read you this, Briar. He said the words would mean more if they were said aloud. They'd make you think of the way he'd say them was what he said."

There, in the middle of the hospital lobby, Mrs. Hill began to read:

"You've got a good heart, Briar. But I already told you that. Don't forget you're a woman—as well as a woman of God, whatever that means. It's a waste when good and special people let the works they do take the place of really living their lives. I once heard it said that some people become human doings when they ought to be human beings. Don't let that happen to you—not all the time anyway."

Mrs. Hill looked up dreamily. "August always did have a way with words. He was deeper than people thought."

"I knew how deep he was," Briar said. She touched Dominic's arm. "We both did, didn't we?"

"Yep." His dark eyes were unreadable.

Mrs. Hill continued from the note.

"I made a decision about you, missy. What I think about that God of yours is between Him and me. But I'm thinking He might not be too approving of my butterflies under glass, so I'd best not give them to Him."

Briar laced her fingers together. Without dwelling on the subject, she had allowed some hope that August might relent and decide to help the chapel. But she'd manage anyway. She smiled at Dominic and inclined her head. The unit expansion was a worthy cause and she was glad for him that he'd get a boost for the project.

Mrs. Hill rattled the paper as she read again.

"No, can't quite do that. So what I decided is that I'd leave the collection to you personally, Briar. What you do with it is up to you, but it makes me happy to know you'll get to decide. Thank you for not giving up on me. Maybe I'll see you up there. You'll find me. I'll be the one arguing with Him!"

Briar pulled out her keys and jiggled them. She blinked tears away. "Um. Oh, dear. I can't take it, of course."

"Of course you *can,*" Mrs. Hill said. "That's what August wanted."

"The collection should be yours, Mrs. Hill." She looked at Dominic. He stared ahead. "I wouldn't dream of—"

"No, no. I've got more than enough of everything." Mrs. Hill snapped her purse shut. "Anyway, I've got to get on. Our lawyer will be in touch. You do know it's a very valuable collection?"

"Oh, yes." Valuable in more than monetary ways as far as Briar was concerned. It represented a man's passion and his generosity of spirit.

"I'll be on my way then," Mrs. Hill said. "When I get to my sister's I'll drop a line. And to you, Dr. Kiser. Thank you for everything you did for August. He trusted you. He said that getting to know you was one of the only two good things that came from his illness. Meeting Briar was the other."

Standing beside Dominic, at a loss for words, Briar watched the old woman leave.

"Congratulations to the winner," Dominic said softly.

"Winner?" Briar cocked her head at him.

"August's contest," he said, but with a smile. "You won the prize. I'm sure you'll put it to good use. That chapel should end up a showpiece."

"Yes." Briar fingered the letter Mrs. Hill had pressed into her hands before leaving. "I suppose so."

"Although he did leave the money to you personally. You could buy yourself a round-the-world cruise, or a Countache. Maybe a few diamonds or whatever else takes your fancy."

She grinned. "Those are some very good ideas, doctor. All exactly my style." Suddenly there didn't seem to be anything she absolutely had to do at this moment. "Do you still want to have that talk?"

Rocking back on his heels, Dominic raised his chin. "Maybe a little later. Even tough people like me sometimes need time to think things through. August's letter certainly makes me want to think a while."

"Okay," she said, disappointed. "Later then?"

"Later."

"Yes." Reluctantly, Briar turned away.

"Briar!"

"Yes?" She walked back to him. "Yes, Dominic?"

"Being with you was wonderful." He held her shoulder. "All of it. The night, the morning . . . all of it."

"Yes."

"Thank you. I guess that's what I wanted to tell you. Thank you for everything."

"You're welcome."

"All right then." Holding his bottom lip in his teeth he stepped back. "Talk to you later."

"Later."

"Yeah."

And that was all he'd wanted to say? Thank you for everything? For that he'd needed the privacy of his consulting room?

Briar walked past him and into an open elevator. Without looking back, she punched a button and heard the door close behind her.

It wasn't until the door opened again—in the basement—that she realized she didn't know where she was going. "Men!"

THIS HAD TURNED into a truly stinking day.

"Something wrong with your soup?"

Dominic started. He scowled into his bowl of clam chowder, then at May. "What do you mean, is something wrong with my soup? Why would there be anything wrong with my soup?" What Seattleite didn't know Duke's chowder was great?

"Well, you haven't—"

"Just because I like to take my time when I eat you have to make a big deal out of it. Some things never change. When I was a kid you were always trying to hurry me up. Some people take longer to eat than others. It's healthier to eat slowly. I . . ." He swung his spoon between finger and thumb. A woman at an adjoining table realized she was staring into his eyes and returned to her own meal. "Good grief, would you listen to me? I'm sorry. That little outburst had nothing to do with you."

"I know."

Dominic scrutinized his mother. She gave him a smile that looked suspiciously pleased and ate the last of her own chowder.

"Do you want to explain that?" he asked her.

"I wouldn't think I'd need to. We both know what's on your mind. Why are you dragging your feet over this?"

He set the spoon down. "Will you stop speaking in riddles?"

"Don't you think I'm looking well?"

"I . . . Very well. You look marvelous."

"God's good, Dominic."

He closed his teeth, snapping the muscles in his jaw.

"Anyway, that little tantrum had nothing to do with being told to eat your soup, my son. It had everything to do with someone by the name of Briar."

Hooking his toes behind the legs of his chair, Dominic took a long, thoughtful swallow of water. "We're going to miss August Hill."

"Yes. From what you and Briar have told me, I'm sure you will."

Condensation sent icy rivulets down the outside of the water glass. "He left his butterfly collection to Briar."

"So she told me."

"When?"

"An hour or so ago. Not long before you called and invited me to lunch."

"Oh." He used a forefinger to make a crooked B on the frosty glass.

"Did you talk to her after this morning?" his mother asked.

"She told you we'd talked?"

"Evidently. Do you know what she's decided to do with the collection?"

Dominic shook his head. "Build a bloody cathedral?"

"Dominic!"

He smiled. "Sorry, again . . . No, I don't, not really."

"Briar called the University of Washington. She's donating the collection to the appropriate department in August's name."

Very slowly, Dominic put the glass down. "She's what?"

"You heard me. Briar said August told her to do whatever she thought was best with the butterflies. She said what will give her most pleasure will be to see his name on a plaque and know that other people who appreciate that sort of thing will see it. Isn't she special?''

"Yes," he muttered. "Very special."

"She said the chapel will just take longer to get fixed, but she'll find a way in the end."

"You bet she will."

"And you love her, don't you."

"Yes." Startled, he rested his hands flat on the table. "You feel very free to ask any question you please."

"Of my son, yes, I do. What's stopping you from getting on with it?''

"Getting on with it?"

"Don't pretend to be obtuse. That was never one of your problems. How was your trip to Camano?"

He concentrated hard on the blue-and-white checked tablecloth. *"Fine."*

"Only fine?"

"May, it was wonderful. She's wonderful. And if I don't figure out a way to be with her on a permanent basis— soon—I'm going to lose my mind. What's left of it."

"Good. When's the wedding?"

Dominic caught the neighboring diner's eye again. He gave her a narrow-eyed smile and she blushed. "I doubt if she'll marry me if I don't ask her," he said through his teeth.

"Why haven't you?"

"She intimidates me." He slapped the heel of a hand to his brow. "Hell!"

"Briar?" May leaned across the table. "Briar intimidates you? She's gentle, Dominic. Totally kind and gentle. The sweetest woman I've ever met."

"Yes, I know."

"So?"

"So the problem's obviously with me. I was going to ask her this morning. I waited for her at the hospital and asked her to come to my office."

May reached farther across the table. "And?"

"And she said she didn't have time."

"Well!" She settled back into her chair. "That's all right then. You'll get to it later today, I'm sure."

He rubbed his eyes miserably. "Then she said she had time after all."

May was silent and he didn't look at her.

"And I said all I'd wanted was to thank her for the trip. I don't expect you to understand, but there's something weird going on. Every time I get near her I feel . . . I feel as if there's a third party present. Yeah, that's it. And it's as if he's going to punch me out for having the nerve to lay a finger on her." He coughed.

"Who would this third party be?" his mother asked softly.

"No one! I know it's just a feeling."

"Mmm. Just a feeling. Some people would say God is just a feeling, Dominic."

"*Don't* lay that God stuff on me."

She held up a hand. "Wouldn't dream of it. Consider it unsaid. What would you like me to do? Propose for you?"

He felt himself redden. "Of course not."

"Good. Thanks for lunch. Let me know if you figure out a way to separate Briar from part of herself."

Dominic watched his mother put her napkin on the table. "What exactly does that mean?"

"Work it out," May said. "She'll take you without trying to make you change. I know that. The question is, can you accept Briar as she is?"

Dominic signaled for the check. He tossed down a credit card and waited for the waiter to leave.

"Thanks, May. I think you just simplified things for me."

Chapter Eighteen

Pushing a grocery cart borrowed from the hospital volunteers, Briar made her way down the wide corridor in the pediatric unit.

"Hello, Ms. Lee." A student nurse whose face was as pretty and fresh as her pink uniform paused to smile and raise her brows at Briar's heap of treasures. "The children are getting excited. They know something's up." She continued taping crayon drawings of flowers and eggs and bunnies and unlikely-looking suns along the walls.

Briar breathed in and felt filled with pure happiness. At the nurses' station she stopped to admire a row of potted miniature trees decorated with painted eggs on bright yarn.

"This is so nice." Eileen Donelly, pediatric charge nurse, bustled from a nearby storeroom. "We all appreciate you giving us part of your Saturday evening like this."

"This is the *highlight* of my Saturday evening," Briar said. "I'm taking a whole lot more than I'm giving."

The nurse smiled. "Do you enjoy children?"

"Oh, yes." She caught her bottom lip between her teeth. Perhaps she'd rather not think too deeply about just how much she enjoyed them.

"You don't have any of your own?"

"No," Briar said. "I'm not married." And might never be. One thing that was completely certain was that there could never be another man for her other than Dominic and in the past week he'd done nothing more than call a couple of times to wish her a happy Easter week. Strange, but probably the result of wanting to disengage from her without being too cruel.

Eileen finished stacking an armload of supplies on a shelf. "We've gathered all the patients into three rooms. It might be best if you went to the babies first. It'll be lights-out time for them soon. Or maybe you didn't plan anything for the babies?"

"Oh, yes I did." No way was she going to miss out on the littlest people. "Don't worry, no candy."

"Oh, I'm not worried. Wait here a minute while I check to see if they're ready."

Leaving her cart, Briar followed just far enough to see into the big room lined with cribs. In the center, several preoccupied toddlers in brilliant plaid pajamas played on the floor. No anticipation of greater things here. This part was strictly selfish for Briar.

She grinned and turned back to get her cart. And almost walked into what had to be the strangest creation ever to appear in the corridors of the Ocean Medical Center.

She clapped her hands over her mouth and giggled. But while she giggled, her eyes filled with tears.

"If you're not very good," Dominic said in a high-pitched voice. "You will *not* get to share my cawwots."

Briar shook her head. "I don't believe this. You'll never live it down around here."

One side of a yellow shirt was tucked into amazingly pink pants. The other side of the shirt hung out. Carrots, very long carrots, stuck from the breast pocket. More sprouted from the pockets of the ugliest multicolored checked sports coat Briar had ever seen. A huge blue bow tie, polka-dotted with red, obscured Dominic's neck.

"You like it, huh?" He revolved slowly. "May helped me out. Got all this marvelous gear from a thrift shop. How about the ears?"

"Not so good." Struggling not to laugh aloud and attract the children's attention, she pressed her lips tightly together.

"Whadaya mean, not so good?" Wriggling his nose—
and its layer of penciled-on dots—he flipped the furry flaps
attached to a headband. "May did this, too. And I know
you don't want to hurt her feelings."

"No." Clutching the neck of her blouse, Briar went to
him and wrapped her arms around his slightly lumpy middle. "Most of all I don't want to hurt you. You are really
something, Dominic Kiser. You knock me out. You never
stop surprising me."

"Aw, you're just sayin' that to get my cawwots."

She smiled up at him. "Maybe I am."

"They're ready, Briar. Oh..."

Briar turned in time to see Eileen Donelly correct her
stunned expression. "The Great Bunny managed to fit us
into his schedule this year, Eileen. Aren't we lucky?"

"That's the Great Pumpkin," Dominic whispered loudly
behind her. "He comes at Halloween. I'm the *Easter
Bunny!* Forgive her, nurse, she's a very new trainee helper.
You just can't get good help these days."

Eileen's mouth twitched. "I'm sure she's doing her best,
Doctor.... Yes, anyway, they're as ready as they're going
to be."

Feeling as close to complete joy as she ever remembered, Briar pushed the cart, only to have Dominic take it
from her and lead the way into the babies' room.

An immediate wail rose from the toddler section.
"Speaking of lousy help," Dominic muttered and whipped
off his ears. "Nothing like scaring babies to death with
good intentions."

Grabbing a box lid packed with woolly white lambs, he
tiptoed slowly to the middle of the room and sank to sit
cross-legged and surrounded by the little ones.

He held up a black-faced, black-legged animal, looked
closely into its eyes, patted its back and hugged it to his
awful bow tie. "This little lamb is sleepy. He's so sleepy
from getting ready for Easter."

A dark-haired boy to his right pushed his diaper-padded
bottom off the floor and moved tentatively closer.

Dominic examined the lamb again. "Maybe this little lamb needs someone to cuddle him." He smiled at the child. "Do you want to cuddle this Easter lamb?"

Nodding very seriously, the boy held out plump fists and received his gift. And Dominic lifted him into his lap.

"Oh, my," Eileen Donelly said softly. "Is there anything more special than watching a strong man with a young child?"

Briar shook her head. Perhaps watching this strong man with his own young child would be even more special. She didn't trust herself to speak. While she watched, Dominic made room for a growing crowd of animal lovers, in his lap and in his arms, and Briar saw him forget himself and what he did or didn't believe.

And he thought he'd done this only for her.

THE PALE YELLOW SHIRT she wore under her gray suit jacket lessened the severity of the starched white band at her throat, but not enough for Briar's taste. The collar was something she avoided whenever possible. It wasn't possible on Easter Sunday morning.

She was ready early, very early. As a child, in the days of egg hunts and chocolate bunnies, she and John used to leap from bed before the sun came up. Briar still awoke on this day with a bursting sense of anticipation.

A day for new beginnings.

A day that celebrated life and hope.

The doorbell rang. John and Sandy had mentioned that they might come to the service if they got up in time. Smiling, Briar cradled her coffee mug in both hands and went to open the door.

"Good morning," Dominic said.

Her heart expanded. The previous evening, after he'd made himself a hero on the pediatric unit—and with Briar—he'd had to leave for an emergency consultation. Seeing him now, she wanted so badly to throw her arms around him that she almost dropped the mug. "Happy Easter!"

"Yes." Grave described his expression perfectly. He wore a dark gray suit, white shirt and perfectly knotted blue silk tie.

He looked marvelous...and heartbreakingly handsome...and daunting. "Would you like to come in, Dominic?"

"Yes." He was staring.

Briar stepped aside to let him pass. He went only as far as the middle of the sitting room before turning to face her, his hands clasped behind his back.

And he was still staring at her.

"You were wonderful with the children last night," she said. "Absolutely wonderful. Just try to make anyone believe you're a stone-hearted cynic after that. It won't work. Thank you, Dominic—for me as well as the kids."

"Yes."

Her heart missed a beat. "Is something wrong?"

"No."

"Would you like some coffee?"

"I've had coffee."

Briar's stomach flip-flopped. Whatever was on his mind was definitely important—to both of them if she guessed correctly. "I'll be leading an Easter service at ten."

"Mmm."

Perhaps that was it. Perhaps he'd decided he wanted to come and was feeling awkward. "It's always such a lovely celebration. So full of hope. Look at the day." She nodded toward the blue skies. "New sunshine. Flowers in bloom. It makes me feel as if everything will be all right if we just trust in..."

His brows had drawn closer together.

"What is it, Dominic? What's wrong?"

"I've never seen you in one of those things before."

She didn't need further explanation of what he meant. Her hand went to her collar. "I don't often wear one. Sometimes I think if I were more dedicated I would all the time, but I find it restricting."

"I find it terrifying."

"Oh." Briar let out a long, slow breath. "It's just trapping, Dominic. It's really nothing more than your mask or rubber gloves are to you when you're operating."

"It's different. The mask and gloves have a specific function."

"So does my collar. It says who I am. It says *what* I am."

"That you belong ... You belong to your God."

"He isn't *my* God. Not mine exclusively."

"I don't want to talk about it."

She smiled. "We don't have to." Today she would not be beaten by anything. Today she would take the strength she'd been given and use it as it should be used, not for herself, but for others. Dominic qualified in the category of others, even if he might never admit as much.

"Could we sit down?" he asked.

Wordlessly, Briar led him to the couch, sat down and patted the seat beside her. She set her mug on the coffee table.

Dominic lowered his tall body to the sagging cushion and faced her. "You are very beautiful."

She flushed with pleasure. "So are you."

He laughed and spread his hand over her cheek and ear. "There can't be another woman like you anywhere. It wouldn't be possible for anyone else to say the things you do."

"I mean them. Is there anything wrong with my telling you the truth. I could never get tired of looking at you."

"Stop." His fingers closed on her neck and he pulled her toward him until he could kiss her brow. "You're stealing all my lines."

She hunched her shoulders, slipped her arms around his neck and kissed him soundly. As he would have grabbed her, Briar pushed firmly on his chest.

"I want to hold you."

"And I want to hold you. But I've got to leave for the chapel in a few minutes and it wouldn't do for me to go looking as if I just got out of ... As if ... It just wouldn't do."

He smiled and eased her against the back of the couch. "All right." With his forefinger, he traced her lower lip. "I came because I wanted to talk to you about something."

Now her heart seemed to stop beating entirely. Capturing his hand, on its way down her neck now, she held it in her lap. "Tell," she ordered him.

His chest expanded and he smoothed his tie. "I've thought about what you said when we went out with John and Sandy—about having children."

Suffocation seemed imminent. "You did?"

"Yes. I think we'd make quite good parents. I did okay last night, didn't I?"

The desire to laugh almost undid her. Rolling in her lips, she nodded.

"So that shouldn't be a problem." He nodded slowly. "And you're a very intelligent woman. With my increasing responsibilities in the administration of the center I'm going to need someone I can trust with things like handling social engagements. It's time I entertained more. I know you probably haven't had a lot of experience with that sort of thing but you'll manage very well."

Dominic put his hands in his pants pockets. What was happening to his face gave frowning a whole new meaning.

"You'd like me to become a sort of social hostess and manager for you?"

"That would be part of it. You're going to be a hit, Briar. I know you are."

She blinked rapidly. A little nerve flickered in her eyelid. "A hit as a hostess and . . . You did mention children?"

"You said you wanted children, didn't you?"

"Do you?"

"I think so. I'm sure you'd be very—"

"Very good at bringing up children?"

"Well—yes. I think we could be happy together."

The urge to cry was becoming stronger than the urge to laugh. "I take it this is a proposal of marriage."

Sudden animation overtook him. He shot to his feet and fumbled in his pants pockets, then his jacket pockets—and finally his inside breast pocket. "Wow, I thought I'd lost it." In his hand he held a small, blue velvet box. This he gave to her. "I had to guess at the size. The jeweler said we can take care of that later."

"*Dominic!*"

He jumped and took a step backward. Briar surged up from the couch. "That is the most awful proposal of marriage I've ever heard."

His eyes darkened. "How many proposals of marriage have you had?"

"This is the first one. I meant it's the worst one I can imagine."

"Maybe that's because it's the first one I've given. I could get a few days off at the end of the month."

Now she was getting mad. "I hope you have a nice time."

"We could go somewhere really warm. Where would you like to go?"

"Do they have camps for hostesses?"

He crossed his arms. "This isn't going well, is it?"

"No. Let me see if I understand you clearly. You're asking me to marry you, have your children and be a good social secretary."

"You're being unreasonable." He tried to reach for her but she moved away. "I'm really excited at the thought of having you as my wife. My mother's excited, too."

"Dominic," Briar said carefully. "Would you excuse me, please. I have to get to the chapel."

"I'll drive you."

The temptation to turn the offer down was quickly quelled. She refused to be childish, even in the face of the disappointment he seemed unaware of piling upon her.

"Thank you."

By the time they reached the hospital, the silence between them had strung Briar's nerves to skinny strings.

Dominic parked and walked with her into the building. In the flower-filled lobby he hung back. "Could we have lunch?"

The tears that prickled at Briar's eyes infuriated her. "No, thank you."

"I expect you've got a family thing on, huh?"

Why didn't he have the sense to know that, as pitifully awkward as his attempt at a proposal had been, she could find it endearing and turn it into something wonderful if he'd only try to meet her part way with what mattered so much to her—her work? What would be so terrible about coming to the service?

"Briar?" He leaned closer. "Are you all right, sweetheart?"

"Yes," she said, straightening her back. "Everything's absolutely wonderful. Perfect."

"Briar. Oh, my darling, you're going to cry. Tell me how I can help. Have I done something wrong? I know I've made a bit of a mess of things this morning, but I can try again if—"

"Oh, please go away. And take this with you." She still held the jeweler's box. He hadn't even opened it and offered her what was inside.

"Briar—"

She left him there and didn't look back.

LILIES, BRIAR THOUGHT, lilies banked in every corner could make any room, even her tacky little chapel, look as if it were garbed for a wedding.

Wedding.

"Doesn't it look lovely?"

It was Sandy who spoke in Briar's ear. John stood, a determinedly cheerful smile in place, at his wife's elbow.

"Yes. I can't look at lilies without thinking of Easter and of how God dressed the flowers so beautifully."

Sandy darted a worried glance in John's direction. It was one of those "we mustn't make him feel uncomfortable" glances. Briar patted Sandy's arm. Everyone must make the effort not to push their beliefs on others—including those who made faith a career.

The chapel filled quickly. There was no organ or piano but the sound system was behaving this morning and Briar's favorite tapes filled the room with cheerful sounds.

When the time came for her sermon, the old nervousness swept in. She supposed it always would. Her, "God tells me He's the only one who knows how fast my heart beats every time I give a sermon," brought the expected ripple of polite laughter. And then the anxiety was gone.

Sun transformed the ugly window to beams of amber and gold that rubbed a warm glow over the uplifted faces of the congregation.

Briar told them what it meant to her to be an Easter woman, what it meant to her to be among Easter people. And they smiled. And the breeze through the open doors moved the lilies and fluttered the pastel satin ribbons tied around their pots.

And she felt peace—almost perfect peace.

John was there, his smile relaxed now. Sandy, her sweet mouth serious, sat slightly forward as she concentrated. And back there, on the end of a pew, a bright sprout of bleached hair caught Briar's eye. She grinned. Yarrow gave a thumbs-up sign and crossed one long, red silk-clad leg over the other. To the right, almost at the front of the chapel, May Kiser, her hands curled over the pew in front of her, listened with rapt attention.

Briar's eyes filled with tears all over again. Just one more person would have made it so perfect. Or maybe two.

With August sitting right there, refusing to believe a word, but there anyway, she'd have been full to bursting with happiness.

And Dominic.

"That's most of it, really," she told her listeners. "Walk with the people, side by side, shoulder to shoulder and heart to heart. Be of the world, not against the world. Find the good." She paused, glancing from face to face, from pew to pew. "Let's always be Easter people. And let's always love one another."

The last eyes she met—dark, dark eyes—belonged to Dominic.

She held those eyes until her vision blurred. Bowing her head, she offered a blessing, folded her sermon and gathered it together with her Bible.

He'd come.

"Briar, that was lovely." May Kiser reached her first and took her hand in a firm grip. "So lovely."

Others crowded around. She nodded and smiled and worked her way down from the altar.

"Yo, Briar!"

She bit her lip and sought Yarrow's face. "Yo, Yarrow."

"You do good, kid."

"Thank you. You okay?"

"Okay," Yarrow said. "I'll call you soon."

"Make sure you do."

John took her arm, with Sandy on his other side. "Let's take you for brunch somewhere."

"Um—" She searched toward the back of the chapel. "Maybe we could ask . . ."

Dominic had left.

Briar patted John's shoulder. "You take Sandy to brunch. I'll clean up here, then I've got something to sort out."

HE'D SOUNDED LIKE a stuffed shirt. A calculating, self-centered stuffed shirt.

Leaning against a wall with his back to the crowd leaving the chapel, he waited. Unlike men, women were romantics. Any fool knew that. So, he'd do a knight-in-shining-armor routine and sweep her off her feet.

The crowd thinned to a straggle with several patients being pushed in wheelchairs bringing up the rear.

Of course, if her brother and sister-in-law were with her it might be harder . . . but not impossible.

"Good to see you, Dominic."

A slap on the back followed John Lee's greeting.

"Hello." Dominic shook the hand proffered and smiled at Sandy before the two strolled on. He expected them to look back. They didn't.

Neither did the next person to pass. His mother.

"Make a good job of it, son," she said under her breath as she walked by, looking straight ahead.

He couldn't help smiling. May was something. He thanked ... Yeah, well, he was damned grateful the scare over her health had been nothing more than that.

Walking swiftly and silently, he returned to the chapel. Only Briar remained. She moved along the pews straightening the books.

Dominic flattened himself against the wall outside the doors and almost held his breath. If someone came he'd look and feel a fool. That was a chance he could take.

The lady chaplain's approach was heralded by an off-key rendition of something to do with yellow submarines. Dominic gritted his teeth to hold back a laugh.

She took only two steps into the corridor before he swept her up into his arms.

"Oh!" The need to keep a grip on her Bible stopped her from completing the swing she took at him. "Oh, Dominic. You scared me to death!"

"No, I didn't." Luckily she didn't weigh much. "You're still talking." Trying not to jostle her too much, he strode toward the elevator.

"Put me down."

"Nope." And the elevator was a bad idea. People were the last things he wanted to see.

"Dominic!"

He backed through a door to the stairwell and started up the steps.

"Dominic, put me down!"

"Dominic, put me down," he mimicked. "No way, lady. You're coming with me."

She began to giggle. "You've been drinking."

"I almost wish I had." Starting to puff, he made it to the top of the second flight and started on the third. Fortunately, they were in the right wing for what he had in mind. He could probably get exactly where he wanted to be without seeing a soul.

"Dominic!" Briar wailed as he emerged onto the sixth floor.

"You're beginning to sound like a very scratched record." One of the blessings of Sundays as far as he was concerned—particularly this Sunday—was that they'd probably have this part of the hospital to themselves.

His consulting room was blessedly close. Hiking Briar higher, Dominic unlocked the door, went in, and locked the door on the inside. He carried her across the blue-carpeted floor to the patch of sunshine that puddled across his desk from a French door leading to a tiny balcony.

"What are you doing? Have you lost your mind?"

"You told me my marriage proposal was the worst you could have imagined, didn't you?"

"Yes." Her face was very close, so close that only inches separated him from her wonderful mouth. She frowned. "It was."

"So you say. What you really meant was that a man is supposed to sweep the woman he loves off her feet and carry her to his tent."

The sunshine lighted gold flecks in her eyes. "Tent?"

He'd managed to mix up his white knights with sheiks. "You wanted me to carry you away to my tent and make wildly passionate love to you."

"You can't... *We* can't."

"We certainly can. We must, in fact." He raised his brows. "It is the way of the desert."

"You are truly, wonderfully nutty." Briar passed her tongue over her lips. "Did you say...the woman you love?"

Dominic swallowed. "I love you." Very carefully, he lowered her until her feet touched the ground. "That's what I should have said first this morning. I love you. And you've got to marry me."

Briar put her papers on the seat of a nearby chair. "I'd be very happy to marry you...and have your children." She fiddled with his tie. Downcast, her lashes were thick and dark. "I'll enjoy looking after all of you. I'm quite a good cook, you know."

"That's great." This was one woman who would never say the conventional things.

"I can even sew a bit." She wrinkled her nose. "If I have to."

"As far as I'm concerned you're very good at a lot of things, sweetheart." Not the least being what he had in mind for her to do right now.

"I'm not an ornamental type, though." She sounded so serious. With absentminded concentration, she undid his tie and let it hang. Her touch was light but it seared, even through his shirt.

Dominic framed her face. "You are the most ornamental woman in the world." And the sweetest, the most special.

"I'm not sure about the hostess thing. I'd never be any good at fluffy chitchat."

"You don't have to be." He could never get tired of looking at her.

"Dominic, I'm not going to become something different. What you see is what you're going to get."

"Good." He slipped his hands around her waist.

Briar stood on tiptoe. She brushed the back of a finger along his jaw and back over his cheek. "I'll try to be the things you need."

She already was the things he needed. Spanning her slender waist beneath the austere suit jacket he picked her up effortlessly and set her on the desk. "Love one another. When you said that this morning they all knew... I knew you were talking with your heart. Watching you there, seeing the way your eyes shone when you spoke... I don't want to change you, Briar."

"Even if I take in stray people you don't approve of?"

He bowed his forehead to hers. "I'll do my damnedest to keep my mouth shut—within reason. You're a dreamer, y'know, sweetheart. Such a dreamer."

"I don't want to be anything else. If I didn't believe in what is supposedly impossible there wouldn't be any point in anything for me."

"Teach me to dream," he said.

"You mean to dream again?"

He looked into her eyes. "I guess. I'm counting on you to keep on changing my heart."

"Done!" Smiling up at him, she focused on his mouth. "Would you kiss me, please?"

Wordlessly, he tasted her lips, closed his eyes and brushed them with his own. The clamping down in his belly jarred him. His fingertips grazed her throat... and met the stiff, alien-looking collar. He gripped her shoulders.

"It unbuttons," she said, her voice filled with laughter. She reached back and fiddled, taking off the band and setting it aside.

Dominic shrugged out of his jacket and threw it on the nearest chair.

"It's warm," Briar said, sending her own jacket after his. Her simple short-sleeved blouse buttoned down the front. The intense green of her eyes glittered while she slowly undid those buttons.

He trailed his fingers along the hollow above her delicate collarbone. Her bra was another of the wispy lacy things she favored, this one palest yellow and sexy as hell.

Shaking her hair back, she rested her hands behind her on the desk and slid forward until she sat on the very edge. Her slim skirt hiked high up her thighs. Lace-topped stockings and garters, the same pale shade as her bra, weren't what he'd expected.

A fresh jolt, part pain, all fierce pleasure, drove him over her. The force of his kiss buckled her arms. Dominic parted her legs and stood, his body pressing hers through too many layers of clothing.

"Oh, lady," he murmured. "My sweet lady." Somehow he shed his shirt. "I've got to feel you."

It was Briar who undid his belt, her sure fingers that helped him be where he had to be. Her body arched and he saw in her face the glow of triumph at their joining.

He cupped her bottom and held her still, held his length buried within her. Glancing down, drawing short breaths through his mouth, he gasped. With one hand, he smoothed the fullness of a breast, slipped inside her bra to work the nipple to a straining nub.

"Please, Dominic."

His attention returned to her parted lips. He kissed her again and bent to her breast while he stroked the soft white skin on her thigh. Looking at his tanned hand on the paleness of her leg between the teasing little garters, at the bonding of their bodies, such different bodies, broke him. Taking her yet again with his lips and tongue, Dominic withdrew to thrust into her, and thrust and thrust until she threw her arms around his shoulders and cried out.

Briar's waves of fulfillment broke over him, drawing him with her. He felt her sudden helplessness and the rise of his own savage drive to possess.

She made no more sound and when he was spent, Dominic carried her to the one comfortable chair in the room.

Still holding on, he sank down, settling her head in the hollow of his shoulder, cradling her, smoothing her heated skin, murmuring meaningless little sounds that meant so much.

"I DIDN'T KNOW you had a view like this up here." Briar slipped an arm around Dominic's waist and hugged him.

"Neither did I," he said and laughed. "I don't think I ever thought about it until today—until now."

They stood before the open door to the balcony outside his consulting room. Tall evergreen trees rose close to the stone wall around the balcony. A pot in one corner held a cluster of hyacinths, their delicate heads bobbing. The early afternoon sun shone bright and warm, gilding the dark hair on Dominic's arms and chest. Somewhere in the whispering, clinging hours he had slipped on the beautiful emerald ring she wore.

"D'you suppose August would approve of all this?" Briar asked.

"I think so. I do know what you did with the collection."

"Mmm."

"You'll get your chapel renovation."

"Oh, yes, I know I will in time."

He rocked her. "You'll have help."

She smiled. "There's something magical about today. Do you feel it?"

Dominic turned her in his arms and tilted up her face. "I feel something magical in you."

Her happiness swelled until she wanted to shout and sing. "It *is* a magic day, Dominic—an unforgettable day." She received his kiss and drew back to smile at him.

Dominic kissed her lightly. "I forgot to ask if there's anything you'd particularly like for Easter."

Briar framed his face with her hands. "I've already got what I wanted for Easter."

HARLEQUIN
American Romance®

ABOUT THE AUTHOR

Spring is a special time for Stella Cameron. It was during the Easter holiday, twenty-five years ago, that she and her husband, Jerry, took their wedding vows. They started a tradition that has lasted through the years: each year they embark on a romantic vacation for their wedding anniversary. This year, like many others, they journeyed to the paradise island for all lovers—Hawaii.

Stella has written nine books for American Romance, and also writes for Harlequin Intrigue and Superromance. Before turning to writing full-time several years ago, she was an editor of medical texts. Her dream then, and even as a child, was to become a writer.

Stella, her husband and their three children live in Washington State.

SCCOR

Following the success of **WITH THIS RING,**
Harlequin cordially invites you to enjoy the
romance of the wedding season with

BARBARA BRETTON
RITA CLAY ESTRADA
SANDRA JAMES
DEBBIE MACOMBER

A collection of romantic stories that celebrate the joy,
excitement, and mishaps of planning that special day
by these four award-winning Harlequin authors.

**Available in April at your favorite Harlequin
retail outlets.**

THTH

HARLEQUIN

A Calendar of Romance

Be a part of American Romance's year-long celebration of love and the holidays of 1992. Celebrate those special times each month with your favorite authors.

Next month, we salute moms everywhere—with a tender Mother's Day romance.

**#437
CINDERELLA
MOM
by Anne Henry**

Read all the books in *A Calendar of Romance*, coming to you one per month, all year, only in American Romance.

"GET AWAY FROM IT ALL" SWEEPSTAKES

HERE'S HOW THE SWEEPSTAKES WORKS

NO PURCHASE NECESSARY

To enter each drawing, complete the appropriate Official Entry Form or a 3" by 5" index card by hand-printing your name, address and phone number and the trip destination that the entry is being submitted for (i.e., Caneel Bay, Canyon Ranch or London and the English Countryside) and mailing it to: Get Away From It All Sweepstakes, P.O. Box 1397, Buffalo, New York 14269-1397.

No responsibility is assumed for lost, late or misdirected mail. Entries must be sent separately with first class postage affixed, and be received by: 4/15/92 for the Caneel Bay Vacation Drawing, 5/15/92 for the Canyon Ranch Vacation Drawing and 6/15/92 for the London and the English Countryside Vacation Drawing. Sweepstakes is open to residents of the U.S. (except Puerto Rico) and Canada, 21 years of age or older as of 5/31/92.

For complete rules send a self-addressed, stamped (WA residents need not affix return postage) envelope to: Get Away From It All Sweepstakes, P.O. Box 4892, Blair, NE 68009.

© 1992 HARLEQUIN ENTERPRISES LTD.   SWP-RLS

"GET AWAY FROM IT ALL" SWEEPSTAKES

HERE'S HOW THE SWEEPSTAKES WORKS

NO PURCHASE NECESSARY

To enter each drawing, complete the appropriate Official Entry Form or a 3" by 5" index card by hand-printing your name, address and phone number and the trip destination that the entry is being submitted for (i.e., Caneel Bay, Canyon Ranch or London and the English Countryside) and mailing it to: Get Away From It All Sweepstakes, P.O. Box 1397, Buffalo, New York 14269-1397.

No responsibility is assumed for lost, late or misdirected mail. Entries must be sent separately with first class postage affixed, and be received by: 4/15/92 for the Caneel Bay Vacation Drawing, 5/15/92 for the Canyon Ranch Vacation Drawing and 6/15/92 for the London and the English Countryside Vacation Drawing. Sweepstakes is open to residents of the U.S. (except Puerto Rico) and Canada, 21 years of age or older as of 5/31/92.

For complete rules send a self-addressed, stamped (WA residents need not affix return postage) envelope to: Get Away From It All Sweepstakes, P.O. Box 4892, Blair, NE 68009.

© 1992 HARLEQUIN ENTERPRISES LTD.   SWP-RLS

"GET AWAY FROM IT ALL"

Brand-new Subscribers-Only Sweepstakes

OFFICIAL ENTRY FORM

This entry must be received by: April 15, 1992
This month's winner will be notified by: April 30, 1992
Trip must be taken between: May 31, 1992—May 31, 1993

YES, I want to win the Caneel Bay Plantation vacation for two. I understand the prize includes round-trip airfare and the two additional prizes revealed in the BONUS PRIZES insert.

Name _____

Address _____

City _____

State/Prov._____ Zip/Postal Code_____

Daytime phone number _____
(Area Code)

Return entries with invoice in envelope provided. Each book in this shipment has two entry coupons — and the more coupons you enter, the better your chances of winning!

© 1992 HARLEQUIN ENTERPRISES LTD.   1M-CPN

"GET AWAY FROM IT ALL"

Brand-new Subscribers-Only Sweepstakes

OFFICIAL ENTRY FORM

This entry must be received by: April 15, 1992
This month's winner will be notified by: April 30, 1992
Trip must be taken between: May 31, 1992—May 31, 1993

YES, I want to win the Caneel Bay Plantation vacation for two. I understand the prize includes round-trip airfare and the two additional prizes revealed in the BONUS PRIZES insert.

Name _____

Address _____

City _____

State/Prov._____ Zip/Postal Code_____

Daytime phone number _____
(Area Code)

Return entries with invoice in envelope provided. Each book in this shipment has two entry coupons — and the more coupons you enter, the better your chances of winning!

© 1992 HARLEQUIN ENTERPRISES LTD.   1M-CPN